PRISON NOIR

PRISON NOIR

EDITED BY JOYCE CAROL OATES

$26.95

Published by Akashic Books
©2014 The Ontario Review Inc.
Series concept by Tim McLoughlin and Johnny Temple
Map by Aaron Petrovich

Hardcover ISBN-13: 978-1-61775-238-4
Paperback ISBN-13: 978-1-61775-239-1
Library of Congress Control Number: 2014938699

First printing

Akashic Books
Twitter: @AkashicBooks
Facebook: AkashicBooks
E-mail: info@akashicbooks.com
Website: www.akashicbooks.com

ALSO IN THE AKASHIC NOIR SERIES

BALTIMORE NOIR, edited by LAURA LIPPMAN
BARCELONA NOIR (SPAIN), edited by ADRIANA V. LÓPEZ & CARMEN OSPINA
BOSTON NOIR, edited by DENNIS LEHANE
BOSTON NOIR 2: THE CLASSICS, edited by DENNIS LEHANE, JAIME CLARKE & MARY COTTON
BRONX NOIR, edited by S.J. ROZAN
BROOKLYN NOIR, edited by TIM McLOUGHLIN
BROOKLYN NOIR 2: THE CLASSICS, edited by TIM McLOUGHLIN
BROOKLYN NOIR 3: NOTHING BUT THE TRUTH, edited by TIM McLOUGHLIN & THOMAS ADCOCK
CAPE COD NOIR, edited by DAVID L. ULIN
CHICAGO NOIR, edited by NEAL POLLACK
COPENHAGEN NOIR (DENMARK), edited by BO TAO MICHAËLIS
DALLAS NOIR, edited by DAVID HALE SMITH
D.C. NOIR, edited by GEORGE PELECANOS
D.C. NOIR 2: THE CLASSICS, edited by GEORGE PELECANOS
DELHI NOIR (INDIA), edited by HIRSH SAWHNEY
DETROIT NOIR, edited by E.J. OLSEN & JOHN C. HOCKING
DUBLIN NOIR (IRELAND), edited by KEN BRUEN
HAITI NOIR, edited by EDWIDGE DANTICAT
HAITI NOIR 2: THE CLASSICS, edited by EDWIDGE DANTICAT
HAVANA NOIR (CUBA), edited by ACHY OBEJAS
INDIAN COUNTRY NOIR, edited by SARAH CORTEZ & LIZ MARTÍNEZ
ISTANBUL NOIR (TURKEY), edited by MUSTAFA ZIYALAN & AMY SPANGLER
KANSAS CITY NOIR, edited by STEVE PAUL
KINGSTON NOIR (JAMAICA), edited by COLIN CHANNER
LAS VEGAS NOIR, edited by JARRET KEENE & TODD JAMES PIERCE
LONDON NOIR (ENGLAND), edited by CATHI UNSWORTH
LONE STAR NOIR, edited by BOBBY BYRD & JOHNNY BYRD
LONG ISLAND NOIR, edited by KAYLIE JONES
LOS ANGELES NOIR, edited by DENISE HAMILTON
LOS ANGELES NOIR 2: THE CLASSICS, edited by DENISE HAMILTON
MANHATTAN NOIR, edited by LAWRENCE BLOCK
MANHATTAN NOIR 2: THE CLASSICS, edited by LAWRENCE BLOCK
MANILA NOIR (PHILIPPINES), edited by JESSICA HAGEDORN
MEXICO CITY NOIR (MEXICO), edited by PACO I. TAIBO II
MIAMI NOIR, edited by LES STANDIFORD
MOSCOW NOIR (RUSSIA), edited by NATALIA SMIRNOVA & JULIA GOUMEN
MUMBAI NOIR (INDIA), edited by ALTAF TYREWALA
NEW JERSEY NOIR, edited by JOYCE CAROL OATES
NEW ORLEANS NOIR, edited by JULIE SMITH
ORANGE COUNTY NOIR, edited by GARY PHILLIPS
PARIS NOIR (FRANCE), edited by AURÉLIEN MASSON
PHILADELPHIA NOIR, edited by CARLIN ROMANO

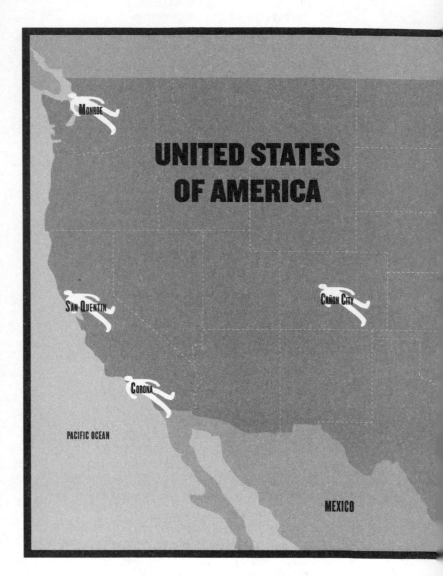

CANADA

MARQUETTE

PORT

OXFORD

IONIA

DETROIT

COLDWATER

YPSILANTI

JACKSON

PITTSBURGH

McALESTER

ATLANTIC OCEAN

RAIFORD

GULF OF MEXICO

TABLE OF CONTENTS

13   *Introduction by Joyce Carol Oates*

PART I: GHOSTS IN THE MACHINE

25   **CHRISTOPHER M. STEPHEN**   Federal Correctional Institution,
     Shuffle   Oxford (*Oxford, Wisconsin*)

44   **SIN SORACCO**   California Institution for Women
     I Saw an Angel   (*Corona, California*)

56   **SCOTT GUTCHES**   Fremont Correctional Facility
     Bardos   (*Cañon City, Colorado*)

69   **ERIC BOYD**   Allegheny County Jail
     Trap   (*Pittsburgh, Pennsylvania*)

80   **ALI F. SAREINI**   Coldwater Correctional Facility
     A Message in the Breath of Allah   (*Coldwater, Michigan*)

PART II: CAGED BIRDS SING

101 **STEPHEN GEEZ**   Ryan Correctional Facility
     Tune-Up   (*Detroit, Michigan*)

116 **B.M. DOLARMAN**   Oklahoma State Penitentiary
     Foxhole   (*McAlester, Oklahoma*)

133 **ZEKE CALIGIURI**   Minnesota Correctional Facility, Stillwater
     There Will Be Seeds for Next Year   (*Bayport, Minnesota*)

155 **MARCO VERDONI**   Marquette Branch Prison
     Immigrant Song   (*Marquette, Michigan*)

170 **KENNETH R. BRYDON**   San Quentin State Prison
     Rat's Ass   (*San Quentin, California*)

PART III: I SAW THE WHOLE THING, IT WAS HORRIBLE

187 **LINDA MICHELLE MARQUARDT**   Women's Huron Valley
   Milk and Tea   Correctional Facility *(Ypsilanti, Michigan)*

201 **ANDRE WHITE**   Ionia Correctional Facility
   Angel Eyes   *(Ionia, Michigan)*

221 **TIMOTHY PAULEY**   Monroe Correctional Complex
   How eBay Nearly Killed Gary Bridgway   *(Monroe, Washington)*

229 **BRYAN K. PALMER**   Jackson State Prison
   3 Block from Hell   *(Jackson, Michigan)*

243 **WILLIAM VAN POYCK**   Florida State Prison
   The Investigation   *(Raiford, Florida)*

256 **About the Contributors**

INTRODUCTION

T he blood jet is poetry"—these words of Sylvia Plath have reverberated through my experience of reading and rereading the fifteen stories of *Prison Noir*.

In this case the blood jet is prose, though sometimes poetic prose; if we go a little deeper, in some chilling instances, the blood jet is exactly that: *blood*.

For these stories are not "literary" exercises—though some are exceptionally well-written by any formalist standards, and artfully structured as narratives; with a single exception the stories are stark, somber, emotionally driven *cris de coeur*. (The exception is the collection's only fully comic/satiric story, "How eBay Nearly Killed Gary Bridgway" by Timothy Pauley.) We may feel revulsion for some of the acts described in these stories, but we are likely to feel a startled, even stunned sympathy for the perpetrators. And in several stories, including even murderers' confessions, we are likely to feel a profound and unsettling identification. As the protagonist of "The Investigation" says, at the end of the story that fittingly concludes this volume, "I saw the whole thing. It was horrible."

These fifteen stories, highly diversified in language, setting, point of view, subject matter, and "voice," have been chosen from a wealth of material—nearly one hundred story submissions—solicited by Akashic Books publisher/editor Johnny

Temple, with whom I assembled the anthology *New Jersey Noir* several years ago. Over a period of months we encountered much writing that was extremely promising—distinctive voices demanding and deserving to be heard; virtually all of the submissions were serious and sustained efforts at writing fiction, and a number of the authors submitted multiple stories. Perhaps it shouldn't be a surprise that so much well-crafted writing comes from the incarcerated when we consider that, hardly to our credit, the United States locks up nearly 25 percent of the world's prison population, while having only 5 percent of the world's overall population. Or, in other terms, the United States incarcerates more than 2.2 million individuals, a far higher rate per capita than any other nation. (According to the International Centre for Prison Studies, the US is number one, with St. Kitts and Nevis just below at two; Rwanda at six; South Africa at thirty-seven; Iran at thirty-nine; Israel at sixty-four; the UK at 104; China at 127; and Canada at 135.)

And why, we wondered, were so many good stories being written in Michigan prisons? It must be that prison writing programs are particularly strong in that state, but there are long-standing writing programs in New York, California, and elsewhere as well. So strange, we did not receive a single publishable story from any New York State facility. Undoubtedly, this is a reflection, in part, of the difficulty we had spreading our call for submissions far and wide to a population intentionally cut off from mainstream society . . . We discovered along the way, for example, that some institutions don't allow prisoners to write, while in others they are allowed to write but not, perversely, about crime or prisons!

It wasn't always a "pleasure" to read this frequently raw, crude, and disturbing material, but it was definitely an engaging and illuminating experience; there are a number of stories here which I've reread several times, as if mesmerized, and one or two which I still don't quite fully fathom, in the way that we are drawn to meditate upon highly subjective, introspective works of prose and poetry that don't yield their meanings easily. Indeed, there is beautifully rendered prose in this volume—in "Bardos," "Tune-Up," "There Will Be Seeds for Next Year," and "Angel Eyes," among others—but writerly prose is probably not the primary reason one might be drawn to read stories by prison inmates. More likely it is the wish to see life from a perspective only imagined by most of us, and to speculate how, in the writers' places, we might manage to survive, or fail to survive.

So suffused is prison fiction with seemingly autobiographical material, so steeped in the intensity of private anguish, it is tempting to describe most of it as "memoirist fiction"—at least, virtually all of the stories in this volume have the disconcerting ring of authenticity, and not invention. The author is compelled to write about him- or herself and to bear witness to what has been seen, heard, and experienced inside prison, no matter how painful, humiliating, or appalling. Not one of the stories I read evoked a fictitious world other than the claustrophobic prison-world, except in memory (and sometimes, as in the deceptively titled "Milk and Tea" by Linda Michelle Marquardt, the past is more nightmarish than the present); still less did any writer explore such popular genres as fantasy, mystery, or science fiction. Though the prisoners' lives as recorded here often touch upon the surreal, the hallucinatory, and the frankly horrific, no one chose to write in the "horror" genre. How revealing this is, and how appropriate, the reader of *Prison Noir* will soon discover.

There is no need for fantasy-horror in a place in which matter-of-fact horror is the norm, and mental illness is epidemic. Vividly rendered realism is the predominant literary strategy, as in a riveting documentary film: "'Meatloaf,' grumbled Al. To him, it smelled as if someone had taken a dog and boiled it in its own offal" (from "Shuffle" by Christopher M. Stephen). "On days that they planned to kill [a condemned man], you could hear the men on H-South singing some kind of sound . . . the most mournful sound my ears have ever heard" (from "Foxhole" by pseudonymous B.M. Dolarman). The tensely lyric "Tune-Up" by (also pseudonymous) Stephen Geez brings together prisoner-musicians in a touching and (to a degree) triumphant affirmation of the power of music to bind individuals together—"It's play music or fight a lot," as one of them says. The surreal, minimalist "Trap" by Eric Boyd moves in a quick, skidding jump to its stark conclusion: "I stared at my shirt, the word *INMATE* printed on the breast-pocket, thumping with the rapid beat of my heart."

In one of the most bizarre and original stories in this collection, "A Message in the Breath of Allah" by Ali F. Sareini, a strange sort of vernacular poetry is spoken by a psychotic killer—unless this devout Muslim is a religious mystic: "Only the fading light of day was visible through the barred window as I entered the cells at Coldwater. The shadows were silent."

The very antithesis of a psychotic, compulsive killer is the naive young Mexican illegal immigrant of Marco Verdoni's "Immigrant Song," who finds himself imprisoned in freezing Michigan without ever quite comprehending what is happening to him, or why:

> *It was spring when [Celso] came to the States; summer when they arrested him. The jail didn't have any windows, so when the van came to take him to prison, he didn't*

> *know what the brown slush was on the floor. He thought it was vomit.*
>
> *"It's a blizzard," the driver said, pulling out of the jail. "Total whiteout."*

Poor Celso, knowing no English, finds himself convicted of felony murder in a drug dispute; he thinks he will be released at the age of twenty-two, and learns belatedly that he must serve a *minimum* of twenty-two years. Interesting to note that the most bloody, barbaric killings in *Prison Noir* take place in this story, in a turkey slaughterhouse in which the young Celso works until he is fired and forced to support himself by selling drugs.

Most of the inmates in these stories are mature in their acceptance of "guilt," and resigned to their fates; most, in fact, are older prisoners, and several are old enough to be grandfathers. (As the self-admitted murderer of "Angel Eyes" acknowledges at the age of seventy-eight, he has outlived his own children.) In the volume's most sensational story, "3 Block from Hell" by Bryan K. Palmer, a serial killer boasts of having killed 198 men—"Each one of them deserved it. You don't believe me? I'll let you be the judge"—and his identity, revealed only at the story's end, is a shocker. In Andre White's "Angel Eyes," an intensely narrated story with a stunning ending, it is noted:

> *Fish! Every day they come in younger and younger. Pretty soon they'll be babies, and I'll end up having a work detail changing diapers . . . I was once like the one or two young bucks of a batch that ain't a cur. Oh, I 'member wings in my stomach flapping 'bout when I done my first stretch, was eighteen years old and ready for whatever. I'd seen*

some wild ones come through that bit hard, like a piranha in a fishbowl.

The entertaining "How eBay Nearly Killed Gary Bridgway" by Timothy Pauley provides a most unusual perspective on the infamous Green River Killer (Washington State, 1980s and 1990s, convicted in 2003), as an enterprising fellow inmate and his mercenary wife drum up business selling the serial killer's autograph online. As P.T. Barnum once observed, no one ever went broke underestimating the taste of the American public.

The blunt opening of "Milk and Tea" by Linda Michelle Marquardt takes us immediately into the spiritual paralysis of Women's Huron Valley (Michigan), or "Death Valley":

Her feet must have been only two feet from the ground as her body dangled like a rag doll from the door hinge. There was chaos: screams, officers running, hands shaking, fellow inmates praying, everyone watching with morbid curiosity as her limp body crashed on the cement floor, cracking her skull. Not that it mattered: she was already dead. Damn! I was jealous . . .

In flashback scenes of unrelieved tension we learn how the depressed and suicidal protagonist has been sexually abused and threatened with death by her late, psychotic husband—ironically, "a licensed attorney in three states [with] a master's degree in medical anthropology. Still, he'd never had a job—he died at the age of thirty-two and had never worked a day in his life."

In "I Saw an Angel" by Sin Soracco, a story with an unexpectedly upbeat ending, we are privy to the intimate lives of women prisoners in a facility in Corona, California, where time passes with stultifying boredom "built on broken trivialities . . . thinking, but to no real purpose, just mind beeps puddling up in the swamp." In both "I Saw an Angel" and "Milk and Tea"—the only stories by women writers in the volume—the sympathetic and intelligent protagonists are seen as victims of crimes perpetrated against them by men, rather than as criminals themselves. But the stories have radically different endings. (Please note: we tried very hard to locate more stories by women prisoners. But since less than 10 percent of inmates in US prisons are female, two contributions out of fourteen isn't so very disproportionate.[1])

In the cleverly constructed "Shuffle" by Christopher M. Stephen, a veteran of decades of incarceration in the segregation unit of an Illinois prison is agitated by having to share his cell with another man who, by degrees, comes to dominate him as his old, long-repressed crimes are invoked; until at last, the older prisoner's final defense is taken from him and he is left utterly bereft—"You can't gamble what you've already lost." Another feat of sustained suspense, the almost entirely conversational "Rat's Ass" by Kenneth R. Brydon, limns the exposure of a criminal con man/sociopath in staccato dialogue reminiscent of David Mamet.[2]

The most ambitious of *Prison Noir* stories is the poetically composed "Bardos" by Scott Gutches, divided into four quarters in mimicry of the four cyclical seasons; partly a eulogy for an older inmate who has died unexpectedly, and partly a eu-

---

1. For readers interested in exemplary writing by women prisoners, there is no better anthology than Wally Lamb's much-acclaimed volumes *Couldn't Keep It to Myself: Testimonies from Our Imprisoned Sisters* (2003) and *I'll Fly Away: Further Testimonies from the Women of York Prison* (2007).

2. Disclosure: Kenneth R. Brydon was one of a dozen or so writing students in a course at San Quentin State Prison which I visited several times in spring 2011, though this was not a story taken up in the workshop at that time.

logy for the protagonist whose sensitivity and intelligence suggest a tragic disparity between character and fate. He is living a suspended, bardo-like existence between life and death, the "bardo" state being, according to the ancient revered *Tibetan Book of the Dead*, "a progression of moments before, during, and after life leaves the body." The protagonist is transfixed in his bardo-state, unable to break free of the cyclical existence of things. The great sin of his life seems to have been his betrayal of his father, who had originally betrayed him by having led a secret homosexual life; the prisoner allowed his father to die when the man's life might have been prolonged, and is consumed with guilt: "Sometimes remorse and guilt come first, then the act which justifies it."

Another ambitious, introspective story is Zeke Caligiuri's "There Will Be Seeds for Next Year," narrated by an inmate who has tried, and failed, to commit suicide by slashing his wrists: "They were strange times at Stillwater, the walled-in fortress of buildings sitting on the Minnesota side of the St. Croix River." An eerie malaise seems to have fallen over the facility, infecting prisoners and guards alike, and provoking younger inmates to set fires in their own quarters, out of frustration and despair. In this place, each day resembles the next: "We basically lived in a hallway that attached to everything: cellblocks, chapel, gym, yard, school, chow"—a place of "sleepwalking zombies." (Many of the inmates, mentally ill, are heavily sedated.) The story ends with a fiery apocalypse that brings with it a kind of redemption:

> It burned for every soul this place ever held captive . . .
> It told us that for all the things we knew this place to be,
> even the oldest of institutions can burn, break down into
> ash. I was proud to watch its destruction. Sirens blared,

and the ship sank . . . To see the animals burn down the zoo. I swear I could see the faces of all those trapped souls escaping . . . Let the motherfucker burn. There would be seeds for next year.

In the sparely written "The Investigation," a veteran inmate is summoned to the office of a prison official who is investigating a brutal murder, with the hope that the man will identify the killer or killers. The setting could be a generic prison in Michigan, California, or Connecticut; it happens to be Florida. The inmate is a man named Cotton who has been a witness to innumerable murders over the years, who has never informed on any fellow prisoner. Now, as if for the first time, Cotton takes particular note of "a dusty, moth-eaten county fair keepsake" in a corner of the investigator's office: "a large stuffed rattlesnake, fangs bared, ready to strike, coiled around a stuffed, ratty, furred mongoose, snarling in response, the two forever frozen in locked mortal combat . . ." Cotton stares at this display of what might be a "metaphorical message"— or what might have no meaning at all. The reader is struck by the pathos of the situation: the inmate's wasted life and the tawdriness of the combat-to-the-death between stuffed rattlesnake and stuffed mongoose, as between prison administrators and inmates, inmates and inmates, and inmates divided against their own selves. This is the material of comedy or farce, yet also the material of tragedy. Keenly we feel the inmate's yearning for meaning in a moral void, but we are not at all certain that meaning is within his reach. Like most of the protagonists of the stories collected in *Prison Noir*, Cotton faces an unresolved, uncertain future.

And what pathos, too, to consider that this powerfully understated story is being published posthumously. Its talented author, William Van Poyck, was executed in June 2013, just as we began editing this volume, in the Florida State Prison at Raiford on a charge of felony murder.

Joyce Carol Oates
June 2014

PART I

GHOSTS IN THE MACHINE

SHUFFLE

BY CHRISTOPHER M. STEPHEN

Federal Correctional Institution, Oxford (Oxford, Wisconsin)

Al Webber stood just inside his segregated cell, his pale, doughy skin still beaded with water from his trip to the shower. He was naked but for his boxers and shower shoes, his hands cuffed behind his back.

He stared partially in disbelief, but mostly in anger, at the man in his cell—an invader of what had been his private domain just fifteen minutes prior.

"Who the fuck are you?" Al snapped.

The man, reclined on the cell's second bunk, replied easily, "I'm your new cellie."

"Like hell you are," Al bristled. "You need to tell them to get you the fuck out of here. Now." He was infuriated by the intruder's nonchalance. For almost eleven years, cell 301 in the SHU (special housing unit) at FCI Oxford had been his and his alone.

Al rapidly scrutinized the newcomer and weighed the odds of taking him. The new man appeared hardened and fit. Crude, chalky tattoos covered his arms and neck, a witness to years spent inside. Two inked teardrops sprang from the corner of his left eye—the sign of a killer depending on whom you asked. The man's hair, slicked back off his forehead "wise guy" style, was receding and graying at the temples. He appeared to be in his midforties, at least twenty years Al's junior. There was no way he'd be able to smash the younger man out of his cell.

As Al turned to address the guard, the heavy door slammed in his face.

"Hey!" he yelled. "I ain't supposed to have no cellie!"

"Yeah, whatever, pops" came the guard's tired response. Al heard the key turn. "Put your hands by the chuck-hole unless you want to wear those cuffs all night."

By policy, Al and the other SHU inmates were handcuffed when traveling to and from their cells. Their cuffs were removed by the guards through the chuck-hole—a slot in the door with a locking steel flap.

Rather than place his hands by the hole, Al crouched so that he could be better heard through the steel door. "I ain't puttin' up with no cellie," he said firmly. "Warden's orders."

"I'm not going to ask you again, Al," the guard replied, exasperated.

Figuring it best to have his hands loose, Al moved his bony wrists to the chuck-hole. Within seconds, his hands were free and the hole was snapped closed and locked.

Rubbing his wrists, Al rounded his body so that he could see the guard through the small square plexiglass window located in the center of the door. "I ain't havin' no cellie! Now get the warden down here."

"Fuck you, old man." The guard turned and walked away.

Al ineffectually slammed his fist against the door and then spun to face the man on the bunk. "Don't get too comfortable," he spat. "You're outta here tomorrow."

The man spoke mildly, seemingly unthreatened by Al's outburst: "I didn't ask to be in here."

Shaking his head while he kicked off his shower shoes, Al debated whether he should say something else to the insolent bastard, but he decided against it.

Al despised the BOP's policy of squeezing two men in a

cell in the SHU. The old days were gone, the days when *segregation* meant single cells—true solitary confinement. As the prisons filled to overflowing and budgets tightened, the feds needed to get the most bang for their bucks. If that meant cramming two grown men into a space designed for one, so be it. But for Al—he could imagine nothing worse. Stuck in a cement box twenty-three hours a day with a jackass he couldn't stand was torture. And even if Al could stand it, he knew from experience that after a few weeks, every cough, every sniffle, every smacking of the lips . . . was like a direct malicious assault on his peace. He remembered one motherfucker whose breath matched the sickening stench of his feet. Al wasn't sure what had been worse—when he opened his mouth to talk or took his shoes off. Though nothing would ever compare to the cellie who had been in the habit of shitting five times a day. That, thought Al, had been the worst. It had nearly broken him. Having to go to the bathroom in a closet-sized room while another man sat not six feet away was bad enough, but having to listen to another man shit—even at the farthest corner of the cell with your back turned—was a vile experience.

Al took a deep breath and tried to center his energy. He hadn't had a cellie in a long time. From time to time they attempted to stick someone in his cell, but Al would raise such a stink—he'd even threaten violence—that the guards would move on to the next cell before Al even had a chance to see the guy's face. This time they had moved another man into Al's cell while he showered—it was a dirty move and he'd be damned if he'd put up with it.

He stepped into his khaki jumpsuit, leaving the top button undone, and reached beneath his mattress for a comb. Barefoot, he stood in front of the stainless steel sink/toilet combo and looked at the spot on the wall where a mirror would normally hang. There were no mirrors in SHU; they supposedly served no purpose. Shaving was allowed only in the shower. Still, Al acted as if he could see his reflection. Beginning with the ends of his waist-length gray hair, he worked upward, using his free hand to clamp just above the strands of hair he combed. He leaned over the sink to get a better look at his thinning locks in the nonexistent mirror before tying it back with the string from a mophead.

He rested his hands on the edge of the sink and closed his eyes. Attempting to control his rage, he took a moment to choose his words and tone, lips moving with his thoughts. Finally, he turned to face his new cellie.

"Don't spit in the sink, don't piss on the toilet, and you better hope to God you don't snore because if I ain't sleepin', you ain't sleepin'."

Not a word from the other man.

"You got that?" Al's voice was full of menace and his blue eyes burned with manic fire.

The man sighed, "Yeah, pops, I hear you."

Al, feeling he'd asserted his territorial dominance, allowed his aggression to fade. He had been out of general population for eleven years, but prison was a closed society and a man's reputation, good or bad, often preceded him. Now that the matter of who was boss had been sorted out, Al asked the man his name.

"Martin."

"Martin what?"

"Martin Monatomic."

A sour look bunched Al's already lined face. "What the hell kind of name is that?"

"It's Greek."

With a dismissive grunt, Al asked, "You a rat?"

"Nope."

Al, his brows knit together, stared at Martin and tried to decide if he was lying. Sitting down on his bunk so the two men were face-to-face, Al said, "Me and you ain't friends. I don't like to talk, so don't talk to me."

Seeking the escape of unconsciousness, Al lay on his bunk and covered his head with his blanket before rolling over to face the wall.

The sound of a key turning in the chuck-hole lock snapped Al out of a dream, though he remained on his bunk with his eyes closed. He had been dreaming of the past, a long-ago sentence in another prison. He no longer dreamed about the free world.

"Breakfast time, pops," Martin said, stepping off his bunk.

"I know what time it is. I been doing this since you was on the titty."

"Trays!" called a voice from the hall as a brown plastic food tray slid through the open slot. Martin handed it to Al and then took the next one and retreated back to his bunk.

Still foggy with sleep, Al set his tray on the edge of the sink and unsteadily crouched down by the chuck-hole. "Hey," he said. "I need to see the warden."

"I'm busy here, all right?" came the gruff reply from the guard who was already at the next cell.

"Look," said Al, louder, "I want a request form. I'll write him myself."

"*You* look!" snapped the guard. "The warden knows what's going on. He'll get here when he gets here. Now give it a rest."

"It's fucking pointless," muttered Al. He rose, knees popping, and retrieved his tray from the sink. Two steps later he was seated on his bunk sporking lukewarm grits into his mouth. Grits and a piece of cake almost every morning. Looking up he noticed Martin staring at him. "What?"

"You got anything to read?" Martin asked.

The nerve of some people, Al thought. He waved his hand over the food that remained on his tray. "You mind if I finish eating?"

"No, finish eating. My bad."

Al swallowed a bite of cake. "What do you want to start a book for anyway? You're gonna be out of here today and you ain't takin' one of my books."

"I'll read as much as I can."

The old man shrugged. "Suit yourself." He pointed to his modest stack of books beneath the foot of his bunk.

Al followed Martin with his eyes as the guy moved toward the end of the bunk and began picking through the volumes. Al watched as Martin passed over a copy of the Koran, the Gita, some westerns . . . three translations of the Bible, a spy novel, some thrillers . . . and Al's lone Danielle Steel book for those private times.

"You get lost?" Al asked, though he wasn't really asking.

Martin stood up, a thick, tattered book clenched in his hand. "*Call me Ishmael,*" he quoted.

"*Moby-Dick,*" said Al. "Everyone wants to write the great American novel, but they're too late; it's been done." He stared off in thought for a short time. "*Gatsby*'s a close second, but that's number one," he added, pointing at the book with his spork before flicking it onto the tray. He tore off a piece of toilet paper, wiped his mouth with it, and tossed it into the toilet. The cell was so small that he was able to complete the task without leaving his bunk.

"You got the trays?" he asked Martin. The trays would

need to be handed back out through the chuck-hole when the cart returned. Usually, Al fumed until they were collected, cursing the laziness and stupidity of whichever guard was working the unit. He was ever impatient to climb back under the covers and vanish into his only refuge—sleep.

"Yeah," replied Martin, "I'll get 'em."

With no clock in the cell, Al kept time by the meals that were served. So, when a tiny square of pizza crust coated with a thin layer of red sauce and a sprinkling of a crumbly meat-like substance arrived, he figured it was close to eleven a.m. He sniffed at the undercooked white rice, overcooked green beans, and a soggy oatmeal cookie.

"They treat us better than we deserve," moaned Al, inspecting his tray.

Martin said nothing, lowering his head and shoveling food.

Al, balancing his tray on his knees, took his time eating. He chewed with his mouth closed and wiped the corners of his mouth with toilet paper after each swallow, as if he was dining in a fine restaurant instead of a seven-by-ten prison cell. He glanced at Martin who was already finished with his lunch. Next to him, *Moby-Dick* was facedown.

"Hey!" He pointed to the volume. "Use a fucking bookmark, for fuck's sake." Annoyed, he balled up his makeshift napkin and threw it down on his tray. Placing the lid over the top, he set the tray on the floor. In three short steps, he was at the sink, toothbrush in hand. "You past all that homo shit with the native?" he asked.

"Yeah," replied Martin. "They've already shipped out, killed their first whale—"

"You know that book was based on a true story, don't ya?" Al asked, cutting Martin off.

"That's what I've heard."

"Yeah, well, did you hear that in the end they all turned into murderers and cannibals? In the lifeboats they drew lots to see who would get eaten and who would do the killin'. The captain drew the straw to do the deed and the cabin boy drew the shortest straw."

Martin shrugged, picked up Al's empty food tray off the floor, and placed it in the chuck-hole. "I guess you gotta do what you gotta do."

A smile spread across Al's face. "Well, the cabin boy just happened to be the captain's nephew."

"You're shittin' me."

"When the captain got home with two other survivors, he had to tell his sister that he'd eaten her son. The other two knew, so he *had* to tell her. There's always someone who knows what you've done." He muttered the last part more to himself than to Martin.

"I know what you've done." Martin looked Al dead in the eyes. "You've got experience with killing family."

Al felt an immediate shift of power in the air as the color drained from his face. "Shut your mouth, you don't know nothin' about it."

"I know *all* about it."

Al pointed a trembling finger in Martin's face. "I did what I had to do."

"You beat your father to death with an axe handle while he slept." Martin shook his head, his face screwed up in disgust.

"The motherfucker was molesting my kid."

"But that's not why you killed him."

"Fuck you."

"You're the one who was gettin' fucked and *that's* why you

killed him. Don't lie. Not to me and not to yourself. You didn't kill him for your kid. You did it for you."

"I did it for my kid," Al replied evenly. Saying it out loud made it so and he held on to that for all it was worth.

"For what he did to you," Martin challenged.

"For what he did to my kid," Al's voice rose an octave.

"You're a liar."

Out in the hall, the other convicts, hearing the commotion, began pounding on their doors.

Martin continued, his voice low despite the ruckus outside the cell. "Come on, Al. It's just me and you in here. Admit it. You killed him because he hurt you."

"I killed him for my kid!" Al roared. He lunged at the door and latched onto the chuck-hole, knocking the empty tray into the hall. "CO!" he screamed through the hole. "CO! Get him out of here. Get this son of a bitch out of my cell! CO!"

Up and down the range the other convicts howled and banged on their doors, calling out in falsetto, "CO, *get him out of my cell*," and, "*I did it for my ki-ii-d*." Their laughter, like that of hyenas, carried and bounced off the prison walls.

Al turned to Martin, his face twisted in panic and rage. "See what you've started? You're the Devil."

With a serene smile on his face, Martin replied, "You're not that lucky."

Al didn't remember going to sleep. He didn't even remember getting on his bunk and covering up; so when he woke he was disoriented. Being careful to move as little as possible, he used the tips of two fingers to create a tiny gap between the blanket and mattress. He peered out from beneath the covers at Martin Monatomic, who sat on the bunk across from him in the same position as earlier, still engrossed in *Moby-Dick*.

The door at the end of the range opened and closed and the sound of shuffling footsteps drew closer. "Aw, man," said Al, throwing off the blanket and getting up.

"What?" asked Martin, not bothering to look up.

"It's the psyche."

"How do you know that?"

"Footsteps. Hear the limp?"

From the hall came a voice that was thin and high—male but with a definite feminine inflection. "Officer, 301, please." Keys turned and the chuck-hole opened. "Thank you, you may leave."

The sound of wolf-whistles and door banging began up and down the corridor, taunts and invitations.

The doctor turned, seemingly unable to let the moment pass, and addressed the general contained melee. "You couldn't handle this!"

Raucous laughter accompanied an increase in the pounding. Then, as quickly as the noise swelled, it just as quickly tapered off. Appearing to accept the quietness as a minor victory, the psyche smiled as he hunched down to call through the open chuck-hole. "Mr. Webber?"

Al was already positioned on the other side of the hole. "Doctor Fraud?"

The psyche cracked a smile. "Mr. Webber, besides being totally passé, Freud and his psychoanalytic theory, in my humble opinion, are totally ineffective."

Al watched as the doctor reached behind his angora V-neck sweater vest and pulled out a Montblanc lacquered pen from his shirt pocket. Opening the lavender-colored cover on his notebook-style clipboard, he made a mark on the page and then peered through the chuck-hole at Al. Smiling broadly, he said, "Sometimes, a cigar is only a cigar."

"Yeah," countered Al, "and you would know."

The doctor laughed. "You got me there. Now, what can I do for you?"

"You can tell the warden to get this guy out of my cell." Al jerked his thumb over his shoulder.

The smile vanished from the doctor's face. "Mr. Webber, we've been through this. You're going to have to deal with   "

"I ain't dealin' with shit. I've been in prison twenty-three years, eleven of it in the SHU, and I ain't never getting out. I'm going to die in here. I ain't sharing shit with nobody."

The doctor took a deep breath while making a mark in his notebook. "Look, I can prescribe—"

"I ain't takin' no more pills!" Al's voice hardened. "All you people know how to do is shove pills down our throats."

The doctor repositioned his glasses and cleared his throat. "If you'll just try something to take the edge off . . ." He was almost pleading. "There are new medications that might help, even more so than last time."

Al's voice rose: "You can help me by gettin' this fucker out of my cell."

"Mr. Webber, it's not healthy—"

"I don't need someone like you telling me what's healthy," he barked, and watched as a shade of pink crept up the man's neck and colored his face.

The doctor capped his pen and closed his notebook. "That's fine. I'll tell the warden you want your cellie moved." Before Al could respond, the doctor stood. "Guard!" he shouted. "I'm finished here."

The doctor was down the hall and gone before the guard even arrived to lock the chuck-hole.

It seemed as if no time had passed before Al heard the keys in the chuck-hole again. Funny how time was so fluid in the SHU, he thought to himself. Time in the SHU could stretch into the thinnest of streams—tiny amounts seeping by at a snail's pace. Then, big clumpy chunks seemed to squeeze together, hours passing all at once, no more noticed than a breath.

"Trays!" called the guard unnecessarily. The moment the chuck-hole was opened a sickening stench wafted through the narrow slot and into the cell.

"Meatloaf," grumbled Al. To him, it smelled as if someone had taken a dog and boiled it in its own offal. He handed a tray to Martin and took the other and sat on his bunk.

As he ate, Al realized the atmosphere inside the cell had changed since the psyche's visit—a subtle shift in the dynamic. He was more wary of the situation—warier of Martin—and guarded in his conversations.

Martin, on the other hand, had become more extroverted, almost gregarious. He licked some ketchup from his spork and then set it down on the tray. "You know," he said to Al, "you can tell a lot about a person by how he eats his meatloaf. See, a man who eats it bottom to top, saving the part with the ketchup, the good part, for last—that automatically assumes there's going to be time to eat it. What could possibly happen in the time it takes to eat a slice of meatloaf?"

When Al chose not to respond, Martin answered his own question. "Something *could* happen. Like, maybe you're sittin' at home, watchin' the tube after a long day at the shop. You got your beer. You got your meatloaf. You're about to dig into the good part—the part with the ketchup—when your wife creeps up behind you with an iron skillet. *Bam!* It's lights out, Charlie. You're no longer, and you died missin' out on the best part of your meatloaf." Martin paused. "So, what kind of person are you, Al?"

Al ran his fingers over his right brow, much like how a man would stroke his mustache. He couldn't figure Martin out; didn't know what to make of this strange intrusion. One minute, Al was barely aware of his presence. The next, he was unnerved by the creepy, implied menace that his new cellie exuded. Al had never been a good judge of character, but Martin had him totally off balance.

Al replied quietly, "I never really thought about it."

"Well, let's see." Martin leaned over to look at Al's tray. The largest compartment still held a crescent-shaped piece of charred meatloaf with a layer of ketchup on it.

"Oh Al," he tsked, "you're gonna want to watch that."

When the trays were returned and the range was quieting down from the daily routine of hollered conversations, the door at the end of the hall opened and footsteps approached, accompanied by the jangle of keys.

"Lieutenant Rios," said Al.

A few seconds later there was the turning of a key and the chuck-hole popped open. "Hey, Webber."

Al got up went over to the hole and hunched down. "L.T., what's up? How you doin'?"

"I heard you've been having some problems down here. You all right?"

"Yeah, I'm okay. It's just that I got a cellie in here and I ain't supposed to have one. I've been down twenty-three years, eleven of it in the SHU, and I deserve some respect."

"Let me ask you something," said Rios. "Have I ever disrespected you?"

"No."

"Have I ever talked greasy to you?"

"No."

"Have I ever thrown you to crazy?"

"No sir."

"Right. So—"

"Yeah, but most of those other folks . . . they ain't like you."

"I understand that you're not going to get along with everyone, but when you treat people shitty, I have to hear it."

Al nodded, though he wasn't sure if Rios was referring to the doctor, a guard, or Martin.

"Just so we're clear—"

"We're clear," said Al.

"All right. Now, what's up?"

He sighed. "I ain't supposed to have no cellie. I need this guy out of here."

Rios hesitated. "Uh . . . the warden's real busy." The man's head drooped and he scratched the day-old stubble along his jawline.

"Then you handle it," Al ordered.

Rios's head drooped further. He began to speak in a low tone, but stopped. Clearing his throat, he raised his voice. "I can't handle it. Listen, I'll put in another request with the warden."

"Thanks, L.T."

The lieutenant closed the chuck-hole and turned the key. Al sensed that Rios had wanted to tell him something, something he wasn't supposed to be sharing. A fearful creeping started up in his belly.

Al lay on his bunk, eyes closed. He allowed himself to drift back in time, long before his life in FCI Oxford. It was something he didn't indulge in often—he had trouble discerning which memories were real and which were manufactured.

In the shade of a tall tree a small child plays with a dog whose name is long forgotten. The boy's father stands unsteadily in the doorway of a nearby shed, bottle in one hand and cigarette in the other. He silently beckons the boy (there's never any sound here).

Al watches as a miniature version of himself enters the darkened shed.

A teenager with a buzz-cut sits at a scarred desk in reform school. He's not sure why he's there. He remembers a bottle and the magic oblivion it contained.

The boy is no longer at his desk, but instead stands near a window in the chaplain's office. He's told his mother is dead. His eyes are dry; the boy becomes a man.

Al feels tears prick the corners of his eyes.

A young husband dressed in workingman's clothes argues with his beautiful young wife about their future—about children. She wants them, he doesn't. The scene shifts to the young husband clutching a precious bundle to his chest, terrified at the prospect of having to protect his son.

Fear fills Al's chest with water. He's drowning.

In a flash, the baby is no longer in his arms. Now divorced, the no-longer-young husband sits at a small table in a shabby apartment and waits for his ex-wife to drop off his boy for the weekend. Gazing out the window he sees an old rusted Ford LTD—his father's car—roll to a stop. Unease sprouts in his gut. The unease turns to horror as the passenger door opens and his son dashes toward the apartment building, his tiny face a mask of shame and fear.

Al feels himself stumbling toward a blackened pit—a pit of despair and darkness. He tries to wake himself, to end the nightmare, but he continues to free-fall into what seems to be a hole with no bottom.

Thirty-five years old. In a rundown state prison for an assault he doesn't remember committing. Aggravated, they tell him, with a broken bottle. Magic oblivion. He'll be almost forty by the time he gets out.

Al's hands clench and unclench rapidly. His shoulders twitch and cords stand out in his neck. He watches as his father's bedroom materializes out of the darkness and he sees his former self standing at the foot of the bed.

This version of Al is covered in sweat and something else that tastes like copper. The room smells of rust and shit. His shoulders tremble and in one hand he grasps the splintered remains of an axe handle. Hair, blood, and bits of flesh are embedded in the tattered end that once held a blade. He drops the wood and reaches into his pocket. Removing a folded piece of paper, he rubs it between his bloody fingers. A suicide note.

It's the note Al had found next to his son's lifeless body.

"Hey, you awake?" Martin asked, his voice snapping Al back to the present. "You were thrashing around a lot, calling out." He gave Al a knowing look.

Al, breathless and covered in sweat, could see that Martin was lighting a joint with a battery from Al's radio and a small strip of foil. After inhaling he held the joint out to Al.

Al inhaled, welcoming the erasure, and passed it back.

After a few trips the joint was done and both men lay on their bunks enjoying the pleasant lift from the marijuana.

"You've been down here eleven years," Martin said. It was a statement, not a question.

"Yeah, eleven years."

"Man, that's pretty hard."

Al shrugged. "You get used to it. You adapt. A man can get used to almost anything."

"You're here permanently." Another statement.

"Yeah, I got a life sentence."

"No, I mean the SHU."

"I got in a fight and used a knife—one year, disciplinary seg. That was eleven years ago. The last ten I've been here cause I wanna be."

"You don't want to go back to the compound?"

Al was silent for a moment. "I think about it sometimes, but I've got everything I need here. Books, radio, an hour of rec if I want it, meals delivered, a shower every couple days."

Martin looked at him. "You don't miss kickin' it with the fellas once in a while?"

Al was a long time in answering. "Yeah, sometimes I do, but I don't run into too many people I get along with," he lied, knowing his standard party line was nothing more than a cop-out, an excuse for his purposeful lack of interaction with others. Too often surface relationships led to close relationships and close relationships led to self-examination. He was better off just coasting along and not having to think or feel too much. Better to play the game, even if it was only with himself; to ask no questions and have none asked of him. Better to wait out the end alone.

He'd used the party line for so many years, he'd begun to believe it. Tonight, though, with the added mellowness of the reefer, he was having difficulty holding on to the con he was playing on himself. Drifting, Al's mind latched onto an idea that carried with it the benefit of a one-night stand—namely, that the second party would be gone the next day.

"Hey, you play cribbage?"

"I play everything."

Al reached beneath the mattress for a deck of cards.

"Got anything to gamble?" Martin asked.

The question cut through his mental fog like a razor and Al sobered instantly. "That's not funny."

Martin smiled and took the deck from Al's slack hand.

"You're right, it's not." The cards flashed and flew as he rifled them back and forth between his hands. "Besides, you can't gamble what you've already lost, right?"

Al felt an avalanche of misery and despair fall upon his shoulders. Was there no end to this? He was tired—so drained that he said nothing.

"How about this?" Martin made a show of pretending to think. An expression that could almost pass for mercy settled on his face. "If you win, I go. If I win, I stay."

Al reached for the cards.

The lights in cell 301 did not go out until well after three a.m.

The next morning, shortly after breakfast trays were returned, three sets of footsteps were heard moving down the range—two pairs of boots and one pair of dress shoes.

"Warden," said Al. He looked at Martin and their eyes held an unspoken message.

From the hall came the warden's voice: "Open it. Not the chuck-hole, the door."

"But we have to cuff him up."

"Never mind that, just open the door."

"Yes sir." A key turned in the lock and the door slid open.

"Webber!" called the warden. "What's the problem here?" He was unusually short and made up for it by always speaking in a commanding voice.

Al looked at Martin again and then walked to the door. The two flanking guards stepped forward, inflated and aggressive, but the warden lifted a hand to stay them.

"Well?"

Sheepishly, head bowed and shoulders lowered, Al spoke in a voice barely audible. "Well, I was—"

"What?" barked the warden. "Speak up!"

"It's my cellie," said Al.

Amused expressions passed between the guards.

Al continued: "I was gonna ask you to move him to another cell, but I changed my mind." A bet was a bet, he thought bitterly.

The warden looked at him without focusing, as if dealing with a math problem rather than a human being. "I don't have time for this shit." He grabbed Al by the shoulder and spun him to face the empty cell. Shoving the old man forward, he rasped, "There's no one here but you!"

But Al knew differently.

The door slammed and Al collapsed on his bunk while Martin lay reclined on the other bunk, idly snapping the cards from hand to hand, fanning and fluttering with precision. He gathered the cards into a stack and held out the deck to Al.

"Shuffle?"

I SAW AN ANGEL

BY SIN SORACCO

California Institution for Women (Corona, California)

> *I saw an angel imprisoned in marble,*
> *I carved until she was cut free.*
> —A loose translation of something
> Michelangelo Buonarroti may have said

rankie lay on her top bunk listening to the boundaries of her world, the dream murmurs of her cellmates in the last hours of the night. Someone hollerin down the hall. The stomp and rattle of the changing of the guard. She wiggled her toes loose from the thin blankets, feeling the morning cold. Fuckers never put on enough heat in the winter, but in the summer the top bunk was a hundred twenty.

She grumbled. Didn't like all of her cellies, but she could deal with them. After a while inside people got slotted into categories: safe, ignore, avoid, and just-plain-nuts. Sometimes they became jailhouse friends, some maybe real friends. Never know until you got out. Everything shifted around.

She tried to set the shape of the day—like one of her sculptures, curving, smooth, and simple, or even one of her infamous hidden-compartment stashes—but jagged edges kept intruding. She was hitting the streets in less than a week. Lotta people out there she didn't like—obviously, given the conditions that put her into her present situation, there were a lotta people she couldn't deal with so good out there. She had been trying to figure out what she'd do outside, without much success. Running all the stupid scenarios through her mind: People Out There Were Generally Fuckheads.

She sat up, she was a fuckhead her own self. Not a clue. Jeez.

Inside, survival wasn't difficult, she could shut down any hostility with her clever words—if not, well, she was taller than most, stronger than most. She grinned, she was more evil-crazy than most of them. Had some backup. Had a decent rep. Worked for her.

All that would be gone when she hit the bricks. She had a couple notebooks full of designs for sculptures she couldn't do inside. She clenched her fist, felt her bicep. Meh. So she'd start with the easy shit, knock off some scary creatures. Yeah. Fangs and claws always seemed to sell. Might work out.

Or not. Most likely not.

The lights came on, the doors popped open up and down the halls. New day. Her nerves were jangled. Same day as yesterday only there were all of a sudden less tomorrows.

Besides making metal sculptures again, what would she do for money? Score a job in a drugstore maybe? Heh.

Into the dark fucking freezing cold, lips going dry, she muttered about ripped edges and hollow centers. Her kitchen crew didn't seem to mind, even when they couldn't quite understand what she was saying. Politics. Religion. Art. "The outer reaches of criminal endeavors. Where no man dares to go. Shape the world the way I want it? What a loada crap."

"What you goin on about now?" Jaykey was a large Pomo woman with a big voice. She teased Frankie, "Ya know it ain't even light out?"

"We should be in bed! But nooo, we got places to go. Things to do."

"More trouble for you ta get yourself into, angel mine."

Smiling, "There's that. Yeah."

Their feet crunched across the dead frozen grass until Charlene spoke, tiny voice, tiny girl, hesitating, "You hear bout Rodeo's diagnosis?"

They stopped. Their breath made little clouds.

"Cancer?"

"She gonna die?"

The guard grumbled at them, "Move it, ladeez. Move it along here."

Their feet stumbled forward.

Diagnosis. Never a good thing inside. On the other hand, doctors on the street, for people like her, weren't so good either. But these prison ones—these were a whole nother buncha sadists. Frankie squared her shoulders, the kitchen lights were just up ahead. She said, "Nobody gets out alive."

Charlene shivered, moved closer to Jaykey. She was in on a murder beef—killed her pimp, oh yes—getting out in months now rather than years. Fragile, timid, how the hell she ever killed him no one knew. But kill the bastard, oh yes she did.

Everyone had edges that would suddenly just cut open. Cut wide open.

And then, what? Flying free? Flying free?

Frankie said, "Fuck all. Come in onna three-year beef for dope and it's a life sentence now." She spit, watching it freeze on the side of the path. "No justice in this world." Head down, silent, plowing forward through her day. Through her life. Six days. Maybe less. Depending.

The hours shuddered forward in ritual motions, the diagnosis filtering through the air: Was it TB? Or AIDS? Lung cancer? The standard prison killer roundelay. Circle dance of the dead. Frankie thought it would be nice to smoke a cigarette, watch the glowing tip, the smoke curl up. Up and away. One day she'd learn to blow smoke rings, have a pipe with Gandalf, show him how it's done where she come from. Wherever that was, where she came from.

The kitchen shift ended with some poor broad up against the wall. A block of cheese? A missing spoon? The day was built on broken trivialities. Stupid fuckers smashed their heads against the walls. Every fuckin day it was something. Frankie returned to her cot, thinking, thinking, but to no real purpose, just mind beeps puddling up in the swamp.

She wanted to hit someone.

Curled up, face to the cement wall, fists pushed tight into her stomach. Her cellies came and went, rattling chatting swearing, incantations to push the day away. Frankie groaned. No one paid her any attention.

After deciding she wouldn't leave the damn cell until they told her to rollemup and move out, Frankie got off the bunk anyway, splashed water on her face, tottered into the common room. Couple serious card games, yapping TV, three knitting women staring at nothing, and in the corner some kinda maybe dance steps. Whee. Nonstop Good Times.

Two people looked up to greet her, saw the sleep-grump lines etched in her cheeks, nodded, and looked away. Frankie circled the small room trailing her fingers along the wall. Counted her steps. Maybe the place shrunk. Maybe her steps were longer. Size and shape were relative things in jail—and why not? Something had to shift and change. Certainly wasn't the people. Exact same ones were posted in their specific positions. God help a girl if she sat in someone else's spot. Frankie kept circling, feeling the room slither around her, tightening. Wednesday Thursday Friday Saturday Sunday Monday.

Would they come for her Monday morning? Or make her sweat through till Tuesday?

Or shove her out Sunday, push her heathen ass out on the day of their Lord?

She joined the dancers, her long body shifting through the steps with graceful curves. But she couldn't lose herself in it. Couldn't find herself in it either. Lost in a jailhouse limbo. She jerked to a stop. "We need more space. More air. Hey, let's put all the stupid furniture outside and get something happening."

"Ladies. Ladies. Turn that music down right now. This isn't a dance hall."

Frankie opened her mouth, shut it. Counting the days.

The guard had her hands on her hips, staring at Frankie. Waiting. She turned away with a smug little grimace. "That's right." Her feet thudded away down the hall back to Control.

Jaykey muttered, "Ooh, Frankie. Glad ya buttoned it, angel."

"I get real fuckin tired of her shit, yunno."

Charlene came over. "Frankie? Could you ask her what goin on wit Rodeo?"

"Not me, Charlene. I don't generally open conversation with them," Frankie said. "It's a waste of breath."

Charlene pulled herself up to her full four foot nine inches. "I gotta know. I'ma go ask her." She walked slow, looking back over her shoulder.

The guard stepped out of Control, her eyes slitty. "Yeah, Charlene? What they put you up to now?"

Stuttering, "Um. They didn't d-do nothing. I jus wanta know." She closed her lips tight, watching the guard glower at her. "What's gone happen to Rodeo?"

The guard's mouth did something odd, maybe a smile, maybe not—whatever it was it was buried by the delicious taste of her words. "What's it to you?"

Charlene stepped back. "What? What? She's my friend!"

The guard snorted. "Your friendship is unnatural." The guard showed her teeth. "She's gonna die. What you think?"

Charlene backed away, down the hall, her eyes big with water pooling in the corners. She flung herself into Jaykey's arms. "But she's supposed to get out inna few months! She's gotta date an everything."

Frankie saw the guard smile as she turned away. Bitch. Frankie folded up on the floor, put her arms around Charlene. Held her for a moment. "Who she is—what she done good in the world—that won't die."

Frankie stood up stretching, long arms out to the side, angel wings, her short light halo of hair sticking every which way, her pale oval face serious. She dropped her arms, curled her hands into fists. "I pay that bitch's salary." She looked around the dingy common room with her eyebrows arched. "We all pay her salary."

"Hey then! Let's fire her. She an arrogant bitch."

Frankie shrugged. "Ah. Now. That we can't do. But we can rattle her cage now and then." Her voice started out low, built word by word into a preaching reverb. "No cop or lawyer or prison guard has ever said thank you to me. But down in the pubic hairs of reality, the crabfact squats there: without you an me, these bastards would be out a job, on the street, suckin dogshit off their shoes."

There was a moment of quiet, a couple mumbles: "Maybe so," "Nice ta think so."

Jaykey moved Charlene around to face Frankie. She said, "Stan back. Frankie's onna roll."

"That's right," Frankie said, her voice going deep again with passion. "There's a basic shape to what we do—what we can do. But we can make it better, more beautiful. Profound.

Crime's a simple art. Our clear dedication to this art—what some people might call crime—never gets the respect it deserves. Hell, *we* don't get the respect we deserve."

"Uh, Frankie? We in here. You notice? We got caught."

"Durance vile."

"We maybe ain't the artists you think we be."

Frankie didn't even pause. "Oh yes we are. We are angels stuck in marble." She nodded, "It's true our enterprises are not always successful. But the labor and the ideas are all ours."

"Jeez, Frankie. I want some a what you been gettin into."

Frankie held out her hands. "We the ones guarantee they job security." Leaning forward she said, "They never thank me for my service. Every day I be walkin the circle, but do any of these douche bags say: *Hey, Frankie, thanks*. No, they do not."

"You be expectin too much," Jaykey laughed.

Frankie smiled back at her. "Gotta keep expectations high. We got ways. Sometimes, hey, sometimes we manage to get over. Lemme tellyas—one time I pulled off a good one."

Charlene checked the hallway, looked back at her. "Tell it."

"Long time ago a friend—not a crime partner although we did some trial by fire and jars of downsuppers coke and Mexican brown, bailed each other turn and turn about—he was doin a stretch in Deuel out by Tracy. Dead-zone flat. He let me know he was getting bored. I stumble onto a batch of vitamin cees with blue drops of LSD decoratin one face."

"You got someone out there to stumble now?"

"Fuck no. Anyway," Frankie continued, "clearly these tabs could be an agent for great creativity there in dusty Deuel. Potentially far more than on the streets, yunno." She scratched her arm, meditating in memory. "So after an interesting session at the firing range south of the city, tryin out a friend's

Smith & Wesson, I had him drive me out to Tracy. It's nasty there, so yeah, we got hammered."

Everyone remembered getting hammered.

"I felt tremendous. Powerful. Movin LSD into that prison right past those shitheads who don't know their ass from a hole—same thing t'them anyway." Frankie looked at her friends to make sure they were still with her. "But you know that feelin—powerful? Well, that is maybe not always a good thing. This was back in the far starry past an I was very young. I think those feelins happened more back then. In. Vince. Able. Anyway, I stroll through the sallyport lookin fine—ass-tight leather jeans, my moto-cycle jacket with all the chains and snaps and my smiiiiile."

She gave everyone a moment to imagine, waving her hands down her long rangy body, spinning around to shake her ass. "Bingo bang, oh you all know we wasn't born to hang, oh no oh no. I put my noisy jacket, keys, combs, rings, wallet, underwire bra—they loved to see me wiggle outta that slick-as-owl shit—into the wire basket and sashayed my fine clever self through the detectors. Hung a left at the bathrooms, plucked out several balloon-wrapped balls of vitamin cee from that easy place, headed into Visiting. Got two cups a coffee from the machine, mine black, his with cream and many many sugars. Tasted mine and went back and dumped sugar in." She paused. "Bloody hell! Serious now. They can't afford health care but day-yam, they oughta put decent coffee in the visiting room. These people are all just total bullshit."

She took a breath. "My friend strolls in, pressed jeans, white tee, yes now, a classic junkie Aztec warrior. Lookin good. We shook, formal—after all, we not lovers, just general crime friends. I push his muddy creamy coffee across the Formica. The balloons were bobbin around in there like weird-ass fish. Red green gold blue. His left eyebrow lifted and his deep brown eyes got big." Frankie shrugged. "I dunno. Thought they'd sink or somethin."

A couple women snickered.

"What'd I know? So he gives me that look and chugs the whole cup, eyes crossin. Says, *Gimme another? I'ma need it.* I totter over to the machine, tryin ta look cool but I'm waitin for the collar, ya know? He pounds it down and in hardly no time visiting is over and I zip on outta there."

"Sweat drippin, hey, Frankie?"

"Not so much right then. Just wait. I grab up my shit and head to the parkin lot, and b'lieve me, I needa cigarette. But I'm feelin real good."

She stared at the linoleum squares on the floor, glanced up at the ceiling squares, noticed they were both the same size. Creepy, she could be standing on the ceiling if she wasn't careful. She said, "Do you guys know that you can feel the blood drain from your face? It's like *whoosh*, every single blood vessel just empties. I dunno where it goes but there's no blood there. I'd put my hands in my pockets and there was the Marlboros, yeah, and the lighter, yeah." Nodding. "But rattlin around in those big old pockets was a shitload of .38-caliber steel-jacket bullets I'd shoved in there as we left the range."

Nobody was breathing.

"I looked around for my ride—nowhere in sight. I lit the cig with the lighter. My hands didn't shake."

Jaykey said, "Did too."

"Fuck you. Did not. I just fuckin de-liver forty hits of LSD into a no-torious prison with a pocket fulla ammunition! And my hands were soooo not shakin."

Charlene, who had gone back to the card game, whispered, "I be happy with the cigarette. Or the LSD. Or the bullets." She looked at her cards, tossed them on the table in disgust. "I'm out . . . That what you're in for this time, Frankie?"

"Hell no. That's not my beef. Jeez. I'm a artist. I got away with that caper. Nah—I'd say they framed me this time, but ya know what? Nobody wants to hear me whine how I'm innocent. Shit. I ain't no kindsa innocent. I did it. An inna month or whenever—I'ma do it again. Sweet sweet he-ro-in. Heart's ease. Hey, I'm not a addict—I'm a aficionado. Should that have a 'a'? Aficionada? Nah, sounds like crap."

Stretching again, shuffling her feet like a dancer or a boxer. "Sometimes I take a fall. Sometimes, all unintentional, I keep the boys in blue busy. Do any of them ever say thank you? Fuck no. But I'm in charge of my own damn life."

Charlene asked, "What happened with your friend? He out now?" Not saying, *Maybe he bring you some dope. You might share.*

Frankie sat down all of a sudden, cross-legged on the floor. "Yeah. He out. Out of all of it. OD'd within a couple months of release. Some damn release, huh? Sometimes. Yeah, sometimes I think, well, I think that nothin matters much."

Jaykey shook her head. "An how's that work out fa ya?"

Frankie stared at the floor. "Nobody gets out alive. This place just a big coffin. We don't always see it but that's what it is."

Charlene said, "But the good? The art? Like you said, that lives, don't it?"

Frankie didn't look at her. "Fuck it."

"You suffrin the short-time blues, angel. Grit your teeth and look forward."

"What I look forward to, huh, Jaykey? Ain't nothin out there for me any more than in here. It's just a bigger graveyard. Soon or late we're just bones inna hole."

"Ladies. COUNT TIME. Return to your cells for count."
Nobody moved.

"Now." The guard smirked again, watching Charlene.
"And stop sniveling. Jeez."

No one moved.

"Frankie?" The guard slapped her hands together like for
a dog. "Get your ass in your cell." She wanted Frankie to refuse. Delicate, delicate. Time was getting short. Her lips got
thin. Her mouth stretched wide. She wanted to see Frankie
crash and burn. She lifted her chin. Jerking the invisible leash.

Jaykey held out her hand to Frankie. "Here, ya silly girl.
Grab hold." As Frankie sat there thinking, Jaykey said, "Sometimes ya jus gotta take what's offered."

Frankie scowled at the big brown hand right there in front
of her face. She reached out. "Bitch. You know how to make
me feel stupid now, don't you?"

"Nah. You do that thing fine on ya own." Standing, they
were eye to eye. "Easy ta lose track in here. Ain't no reason for
you ta be like that. You got a lotta things goin for ya. Don't let
ya mind get coiled up too tight." Grin. "Shit fa brains."

The guard's greasy eyes glared at Jaykey. Another one,
nothing but evil.

Frankie whispered, "I could pop you one."

Jaykey laughed, her cheeks bunched up like winter apples.
"Yeah, ya stupid skinny-ass white girl. You could." She paused
to take a breath. "You could! You could." Her face tightened,
shining with amusement, then she threw her big arm around
Frankie's shoulders, walking her past the guard as if they were
alone, together, lovers strolling along the plaza. "Get yaself
another six months here? In the safety of ya coffin? You crazy?
Or just chickenshit?"

The guard stomped to Control, a grim graveyard keeper;

she popped the cells open *bangbangbang* up one hall, down the other. The noise proved her power. She was the gatekeeper: they belonged to her.

Frankie peered around the hallway. Gonna dance or box or get the fuck outta the ring? "She pushin me, Jaykey."

Jaykey said, "Gotta make ya choice."

"No one gets out alive." Frankie shot her eyes at the guard, measured the distance, counted the steps, one-two long roundhouse kick take her down, three-four stomp her throat. Done. Bones in a . . .

Between the legs, in that sweet secret spot—it was either wild-sex wet or piddle-piss scared. Or maybe some stupid balloons of LSD? Frankie shook herself. Oh so not-goin-to-do-THAT-again. She gave Jaykey a long cold stare, not really seeing her. "Things ta do? Cages ta rattle?"

"Asses ta kick."

"Later for you, Jaykey." A small uptilt of the corners of her mouth.

"Ya welcome ta try."

"One day. One day before we bones."

"Somethin ta look forward to. Yeah." Apple cheeks grinning.

Grinning back: "Fuck you, Jaykey. Fuck you."

"Keep dreamin, Frankie. See ya in tha mornin, angel."

Frankie moved toward her cell. "I be waitin for ya."

BARDOS

BY SCOTT GUTCHES

Fremont Correctional Facility (Cañon City, Colorado)

Attention in the facility:
work gangs in, fifteen thirty.

T he announcement is a throwback from the era of chain gangs when work details were divided up among inmates and driven with impunity by the correctional officers. Back then, convicts split rocks, worked the fields, and built roads, even the walls of their own prison. Sixteen-hour days they worked. No gloves. No protection from the high-desert sun. Water and piss breaks given at the whim of a guard's discretion. Blisters got infected. Exposure turned to heatstroke. Death wasn't an uncommon work hazard.

Now, inmates work in front of computers in air-conditioned rooms for six hours, split in two by count time and lunch. We have unlimited bathroom breaks, time off to get a haircut, and even three excused absences a month. Not all inmates have every luxury. Some work in the correctional industries, kitchen, or maintenance. But we all automatically march to and from our assignments without really understanding their meaning.

It's been a long day and I am grateful for this announcement. I head back to my cell house. Back through the same cold, dark blue-gray air. Back into the parade of inmates trafficking apathy and discontent between one destination and another. Hostile, tired, and familiar faces greet me along the way until at last I am in cell house 6. It's an odd place, the day halls looking more like a mine or a tomb—somewhere dug deep in the earth. A low ceiling and five cement columns supporting it give it all a claustrophobic, letter-box quality. The cell house is divided into four pods, each with fifty cells. At two men per cell, the day halls fill up rather quickly with disgruntled echoes and sighs. I take a seat in front of the flat-screen television. The volume is muted and the closed captioning is turned on. The New Jersey Devils won another game.

The lieutenant comes in, announces showers will be open only to fiberglass workers, then turns to go to the next pod. Fifteen minutes later, he's back to pass out mail and announce that Mr. Jennings, an older inmate I'd seen not more than four hours earlier, had passed away. The lieutenant delivers this news in the same soft matter-of-factness as the shower availability.

Attention in the facility:
count time, count time, sixteen thirty.

There have been men killed in their cells while their murderers have gone to yard, work, and chow. Some of these crimes have gone undiscovered for more than twenty-four hours. A few perpetrators have even successfully avoided justice. Now, we have to stand for count so the guards can see without question living, breathing flesh. Counts are done in two independent checks and when each guard is finished, they meet at the center of the day hall to check each other's arithmetic.

I look across the day hall as I wait to be counted, and I see cell 25, Jennings's cell. His name tag is still on the door. I can't read it from this distance, but the stainless steel plate remains hidden by the white of the tag. Through the small window I spot Jennings's cellie, Rourke, who resembles Martin Mull. I expect Jennings to pop his head into view at any moment. The anticipation is so intense, I can see him clearly. Effeminate. Quiet. Fine white hair cut close and neat, conforming to the natural, Franciscanesque male-pattern baldness. Thick black plastic frames of those state-issue eyeglasses—the ones most inmates call Chomo-nator 5000s. Signature spectacles with subsequent magnification stereotypically attributed to chomos—child molesters. Perfectly round belly. A rubbery pouch of skin for a neck. Legs as thin as Pixy Stix. That was Jennings.

The guards converge, discussing their numbers. I can't hear them, but their inflections speak of confusion. One of them has obviously accused the other of a surplus, or a deficiency. They walk back to cell 25. One guard points to Jennings's name tag while the other nods in agreement. They talk in monotonous tones, as though discussing physics equations or dismissing the superstition that counting a dead man will bring you a year of bad luck for every year of the deceased's sentence. I make out only bits and pieces, but I distinctly hear one of them say, "Died this morning." A guard strips Jennings's name tag from the door like a bandage yanked from hair and skin. The zip of the peeling packing tape shocks me violently.

Attention in the facility:
count is clear, count is clear, seventeen fifteen.

I'd seen Jennings at lunchtime, hunched at the toilet stall, ashen, making careful and deliberate movements. I offered nothing. Said nothing, except, "You look pale," to which he replied, "I've been feeling like shit all week." It was the only time I'd ever spoken to him. He shuffled out of the pod, into the sergeant's office, and begged to be taken to medical. At first they made him walk, but when he collapsed on the steps leading into the main corridor, they rushed him to the clinic in a wheelchair.

That's what hit me the hardest after the lieutenant announced Jennings had passed away—that I'd hardly thought about what I witnessed earlier in the day. From the entire time between those two moments were thousands of thoughts, and not one of them was of Jennings. I defended myself. I never knew the man. I may have seen him five or six times a day, every day for the last year—even sat with him at the chow hall—yet I never knew the man, never even spoke to him. But it was the whispers in the day hall which served as the obiter dictum of Jennings's death. It was like watching the unprepared attempt to start a fire, collectively contributing obscure memories and unverifiable facts of Jennings's life. They threw anything on top of the cold embers that might help burn away the man's anonymity.

"Who?"

"Jennings."

"Who's that?"

"The old man."

"The one that cleans the office?"

"No, that's Bill. The other one."

"Lived with Rourke?"

"Yeah."

"Didn't he work at the furniture shop?"

"Metal products, I think."

"Ran AutoCAD?"

"Something with computers."

"I heard his family was killed in a car accident a few years ago."

"Wasn't he going home soon?"

"First of the year."

There was callousness too. Jokes about his crime, or crimes.

"What did the pedophile say when . . ."

Laughter at a funeral is a forbidden release of fear. And it was fear we'd been so successful at avoiding until Jennings died. Not because we cared for him, but because we failed to remember him. And in doing so, he reminded us of how easy it is to lose everything, only to die before being given the chance to get a fraction of it back. So we hated him for it, and the laughter and the anger allowed us to momentarily hold our ground against death. Death, who'd moved into Jennings's cell and refused to be intimidated. Then the guards came back to pack out his belongings.

Attention in the facility:
cell house 1, first pull, west side dining hall,
cell house 7, first pull, east side dining hall,
seventeen thirty.

We are told that we have it easier than our predecessors. We are the last pull to chow tonight, so I watch the guards collect Jennings's possessions. They consult Rourke about ownership of small items like toothpaste, soap, and deodorant. Appliances, like Jennings's coffee pot and television, are easily distinguishable because his name and number are etched into the plastic. But canteen ephemera like bagels, peanut butter, aspirin, and candy that is left outside a foot locker is subject to the honesty of the surviving cellmate. Books, coffee cups, and other personal belongings are summarized on Jennings's property sheet—a list of what he had and was allowed to have. But it is nonspecific. Caring more about quantities than actualities. With it, a correctional officer can tell how many books you own, but not which books in the cell are yours. It's so generic, except for name and number, you can hardly tell the difference between one inmate's and another's.

The guards aren't gentle yet neither are they insensitive with the deceased's belongings. As I watch the traces of Jennings's existence disappear one by one into the stiff green duffel bag, I wonder about how easy I am presumed to have it. Canteen. Visits. Phone calls. Better medical care, if "better" means the clinic will subtract three dollars from my account to tell me they couldn't find anything wrong and shove a handful of ibuprofen in my palms. We have our radios and electric razors, hot pots and alarm clocks. I heard a rumor we'll be getting iPods or iPads in a few months, though not the actual Apple product, just something comparable in function, made in the Philippines, with a pathetic six-month warranty. I suppose that is inarguably this *progress* everyone speaks of. Progress toward a punishment devoid of cruelty and unusualness. Perhaps in a hundred years it will be impossible to distinguish between a life before and a life after prison walls.

I wonder where Jennings's belongings will go. His stuff. His things. What happens to the mementos of a man no one knows? Will the guards pick through them? I can imagine some correctional officer's home cluttered with the possessions of the dead. Maybe the unopened items get restocked in the canteen warehouse. Or do they throw it all in the dumpster before moving along to the "memorial service"? A few words by a chaplain who may not have ever set foot inside your facility. Then what? Interment? Cremation? Burial?

Something bureaucratic, efficient, and cost effective, I'm sure.

They announce the next cell houses for chow. My belly growls and I confess to myself I would have no ethical dilemma eating a dead man's food or watching his television until they came to claim it. Possession is such an absurd idea to me now, like the feeling of driving past a house you once lived in long ago. It is alien and familiar at the same time, and I doubt I will resume it when I am allowed to leave. That's ironic in a way, because it's an implicit requirement for parole—work, buy, consume, possess.

Attention in the facility:
night gym for cell houses 3 and 4,
library for cell house 7,
AA meeting in multipurpose room 1,
Catholic Bible study in classroom 6,
nineteen thirty.

In the library, I pick up a book I've had on hold for two months. *The Bardo Todrol Chenmo; The Tibetan Book of the Dead.* Only that is a mistranslation. Literally, it means *The Great Liberation Through Hearing in the Bardo.* A bardo isn't one definitive moment, but rather an age or period of time that has its flourish, plateau, and decline. It is a progression of moments before, during, and after life leaves the body, but can refer to any physical or spiritual transition. Death is a bardo, not some exact instant you can point to and say, *That is when he died.* According to the book, one's state of mind at the end of one bardo is crucial to one's disposition in the next. This series of bardos is collectively called *samsara*, the cyclic existence of beings and becoming. From human to hungry ghosts, samsara is divided into six realms, each one a metaphor for our unstable states of mind—fear being one of the most detrimental to rebirth.

When I return to my pod, cell 25 has been entirely disinfected of Jennings's death. It is conspicuously off balance. The bottom bunk is devoid of sheets. A silver, rubbery pillow sits on top of the thin exercise pad of a mattress. Half the shelf space on the wall is empty and the ledge for a TV set is vacant. An empty foot locker's lid is propped open against the wall and Rourke's fan is on the ground, slightly angled downward, rattling at high speed to evaporate the residual moisture of a recently mopped floor. In the evaporating reflections I am haunted by a memory of my father.

Attention in the facility:
count time, count time, twenty-one thirty.

I was thinking of my father's money when I signed his DNR order. I often wonder if that qualifies as being the first crime I committed. Not technically, of course, but a crime of conscience no less, and I've been plagued with guilt ever since. *The Bardo Todrol Chenmo* says that the quality of thoughts of those surrounding the dying has a dramatic effect on the transitioning process. I hated my job, despised my marriage, and was burned out from my father going in and out of the hospital those three preceding weeks. I was in debt too. Credit cards. Loans. Thirty thousand dollars worth of emotional compensation and a newborn son. First Fidelity National Bank. That's what I was thinking when I crossed that last T on my signature that authorized my father's passing.

One at a time the guards peek into my cell door window counting my body. It's not always the same two, so the countenances I see reflect myriad emotions. Contentment. Pride.

Stoicism. Self-righteousness. Judgment. I know they access our files on the department computer, reading the synopses of our crimes for entertainment. Some offer this information to certain inmates. It makes for an interesting dynamic—a hierarchy of criminal severity thriving on the economics of trickle-down loathing.

My cellie tells me that he feels like crying. He's been down for twenty-one years and doesn't see parole for another five. He doesn't miss Jennings. He feels like crying because he *is* Jennings. Fifty-six years old. Same age as my father when he died. It's the proximity between Jennings's release date and the day he died that's getting to my cellie. Dying in prison is one thing. Dying in prison less than a month shy of your parole date is entirely different. We tell each other stories of similar tragedies. A man I knew at Sterling had a heart attack while on the can. He even looked like the Mexican version of Elvis. Rodriguez was his name. Back in prison for a six-month turnaround for parole violation. A technicality. He'd served five months of it before he died. And there was the kid who got killed six hours after he stepped off the prison bus—ran across Speer Street and died on impact. My cellie told me about a convict who'd been stabbed to death in Limon three days before he was supposed to kill his number. Another man who, on the eve of his release date, strangled his best friend over a game of pinochle.

I think about my own mandatory release date, what brought me to prison, and whether there's any credibility to the theory that sometimes remorse and guilt come first, then the act which justifies it.

Attention in the facility:
the facility has been accepted by graveyard shift, twenty-two
hundred.

The overhead lights go out. The light from my cellie's television remains, flickering wonder on the cinder block walls I stare at. The lotus posture is uncomfortable for me, so I simply cross my legs casually. I imagine the light, with its spastic flashes and barely audible cathode tube pops to be the dharmakaya—the brilliance one sees when the body is ready to release its consciousness. They say there is a review of every thought, word, and action. Not like a movie, but rather an infinite table upon which the delicate knickknack moments of your life are arranged in all directions. You can see how they affect one another, and how they affect the lives of others. At any time while in this state, you can instantly examine any one of these tchotchkes of consciousness and be held accountable for every fingerprint, crack, and degradation you inflicted upon them. I imagine this is only a joyous prospect for a select few. Supposedly, while you're experiencing the pain and discomfort you've caused others, there's something of a divine presence, a feeling about you and within you that asks—not vocally but empathetically—*Have you learned to love yet?* And I go to sleep afraid and without an answer.

Attention in the facility:
the facility has been accepted by day shift, zero six hundred.

When I dream of my father, he is sick. And unlike before he died, I am aware of how little time he has left. We are in a car, one of his I'd seen in an old photograph. I am driving and my father is sitting in the backseat, convalescing. I feel the shame for having spent all his money. I sense he already knows, and that he desperately wants to talk to me. Also, he senses that I want to talk to him. But we don't speak. We just glance at each other forlornly when the other isn't looking as I drive around a foreign city searching for a bank that does not exist. I usually wake up crying.

What is it that I really miss? What is it that I've truly lost if not my fleeting perceptions? Perceptions of others. Of myself. Of who I'm supposed to be, and what I once was. For my entire life I considered Dad to be the quintessential lady's man. Tall, dark, handsome. The cool, quiet type. And gentle as a lamb. He was a mechanic and a millwright and in the 1960s he even modeled for some technical publications showcasing the latest machinery his company built. Nothing like GQ, of course, but even when he was captured in the drab beige coveralls, standing next to some drill press, it was easy to see why his nickname was Butch.

That is why, after he died, it was such a shock to discover those digital photos. I was rifling through his computer looking for information to consolidate his estate. Never in a million years could I have guessed.

There, wearing nothing but blue garters and panty hose, was the same man who taught me how to use calipers and change the brakes on my car. It was the same man who whistled at women on the beach, went to strip clubs, and was accused by both ex-wives of being the biggest womanizer on earth. And I remember being angry and ashamed. Angry because I felt robbed of my father a second time, because his secret must have been who he really was. Ashamed because I instantly recalled a moment—one of many—of my thoughtless use of the words *fag, homo,* and *pansy* over the years that probably helped to keep him a secret from me. I didn't need to experience the dharmakaya to show me this. I deleted the photos as viciously as Jennings's name tag was stripped from his cell door.

Attention in the facility:
count is clear, count is clear, zero six twenty.

In Tibet, they do not bury nor cremate their dead. It isn't something to hide. It isn't something you can cover even if you had at your disposal all the mass of the Himalayas. They have charnel grounds—hallowed stretches of mountainside where corpse, clothing, and prayer flag rot gradually over time. It is quite public and not isolated from where Tibetans live and work and play. There is even a person whose duty it is to break the body apart in a precise manner, celebrating and inviting the process in honor of the dead.

Perhaps that's why we are given time in these manage-able Pavlovian chunks. An hour here, two there. Because it's easier to choke down, unchewed, in a ravenous frenzy that leaves us salivating with anticipation for the next cold scraps of the clock's gristle and bone. Ten, twenty, even thirty years can be swallowed over the course of a few thousand bardos.

Attention in the facility:
cell house 4, first pull to chow, cell house 6, first pull to chow,
zero six thirty.

They say that when you've memorized the entire six-week menu, you've been locked up too long. It is Tuesday, and I know we're having fried eggs, diced potatoes, grits with two pieces of toast, two tablespoons of jelly, and a pat of whipped butter. I used to love this breakfast. Now I just eat it out of boredom and to avoid hunger pains while working on the rooftops fixing a heating system not even the staff know how to operate. So much effort goes into making ourselves comfortable. So little understanding about how to actually accomplish it. The talk in the chow hall is about last night's football game, tests, work, and the usual prison bullshitting.

By the time I return to the cell house, Rourke has moved to the bottom bunk and already has a new cellie. A young kid with a short property sheet, easily forgettable name, brand-new number, and a sentence so heavy he'll know what he's having for dinner two decades from now. It doesn't take long.

That's the myth of institutionalization. After your first day, you've pretty much seen all the facility has to offer. It's the days that follow that never seem to change. They've removed all the bardos, and the more this place looks like our previous lives, the easier it is to accept the facility and rid ourselves of this damned attention.

Attention in the facility:
work gangs out, work gangs out, zero seven hundred.

TRAP

BY ERIC BOYD

Allegheny County Jail (Pittsburgh, Pennsylvania)

The first night was in the processing area. I desperately tried making phone calls, but the phone system only worked if you already had a wristband with a docket-identification number. You had to already be in jail to use the phones and make calls to try getting out of jail.

Intake processing was awful. I spoke with a nurse, answering questions about allergies and AIDS. She gave me some shot and it hurt like hell. Then I stood in a line, going through a machine that was blowing puffs of air.

"What's that?" I whispered to the guy behind me.

"The machine? That's the Tin Police Dog, it sniffs out drugs. See how it's blowing air from the bottom? At the top it's suckin' the air back in and sniffin'. It works good, so if you got anything tucked, you better tuck it deeper."

After the Tin Dog, the line stood against a wall, next to a pair of showers. We were called, one by one, to step up to a desk, where a jail worker gave us our wristbands with the doc numbers and handed out a roll of bedding, three sets of red jail shirts and pants, and a bag of toiletries. The blankets looked like house insulation, and most of them were full of holes. The shirts and pants were never the right size, it seemed. Standing in line, any hope of getting out already disintegrating, I just prayed for a decent blanket and a good set of clothes; I was going to spend a year or two with them.

"Hey, I got two soups for a good blanket," I heard one of the men in line say to the worker handing out the welcome packages.

"You gonna be on level one?" the worker replied.

"Yeah, I'm just in for DUI."

"All right, two soups. I don't want vegetable. I like chicken and chili."

"Okay," the man said.

The worker bent down below the desk and pulled out a roll of bedding. The blanket looked clean, new. There was even a pair of sheets. Nobody else had sheets.

When my name was finally called, I stepped forward to the desk.

"Anderson, Fredrick? That right?" the worker asked, reading from a sheet.

"Yes," I said meekly.

"Here's your band. Number 178822."

"So I can use the phones now?"

"Yeah. You set up an account with someone outside, your woman or your family, whatever, and enter that number into the phone to make calls."

"Okay," I gulped.

The worker laid my package down on the desk. "Bedding. Reds. Soap and deodorant. Here ya go. Next: Willia—"

"Hey, man," I interrupted.

"Yeah?"

My blanket was pink, dirty, and it had more holes than material. The clothes I could deal with, but I wanted a decent blanket to sleep with.

"Could I get a nicer blanket?"

"What do you got?"

"What?"

"You got any items?"

"Like what?"

"What do you mean *like what?* Do you got any soups or anything?"

"Soups? I just got here, what are you talking about?"

"This is your first time, huh? If you don't have any soups, y'know, ramen noodle soups you bought off of commissary, I ain't givin' you shit. You'll get a nice blanket when you have some items to sell. Sorry, man."

"Are you serious? Look at this damn blanket!"

"You're stuck like Chuck, my man."

Before I could say anything more, a guard came out of one of the showers and pulled me in by the arm. I nearly dropped my shitty blanket on the ground, which obviously would have ruined it. In the shower room, the guard washed his hands after touching me and put on a pair of rubber gloves. The guy was a bodybuilder, well over six feet tall, with a beard and bald head.

"Put your shit on the counter behind you."

I tried placing my stuff down, but there was a tray on the counter with cups full of piss. For many reasons, I didn't want to touch the tray and move it; I tried putting my things down gently on the little space I had on the counter.

"What the fuck are you doing?"

"I was just trying not to—"

"Who said you could talk, dickhead?! I said put your shit down, not pretend your fucking bedding is a ticking bomb."

"Sorry."

"Strip, get in the shower, don't screw around and play with your pecker; just get in and out."

I did exactly as he said. I jumped into the shower, washed as quickly as possible with as much soap as possible, not knowing the next time I'd get to clean myself, and jumped out. Naked, dripping wet, I stood in front of the guard.

"All right, squat down like you're takin' a shit."

I bent down, almost slipping on the floor. I caught myself and squatted down.

"Cough."

I coughed. The guard looked at me. I hadn't coughed well enough.

"Come on and COUGH."

I did. It was better, louder.

"Now stand up, turn around, spread your ass."

I did.

"Okay, turn back around, look at me. Open up your mouth with your hands, show me under your tongue, behind your teeth."

I did.

"Great. Thanks. Welcome to the Allegheny County Jail, how did your ass taste?" The guard laughed and left.

Still wet, I put the red clothes on, as well as my shoes. I folded my old clothes and walked out of the shower room. A different worker called me up to the desk.

"Your clothes."

"Here." I handed him my suit jacket, shirt, and pants.

"What kind of shoes are you wearing?"

"Florsheims."

"I have no idea what that means. Lemme see 'em." He peered over the desk and down at my shoes. "Yeah, those are no good. Does that have a fucking heel? Ha ha! Why would you even try to wear those? Lemme have 'em."

I took off my shoes and placed them on the desk. The worker pulled a pair of blue canvas-top slip-on shoes, size ten.

"I wear a size twelve."

"We're out. The only bo-bos we have right now are eights and tens, a few fifteens. I actually gave someone a pair of fifteens earlier." He laughed to himself. "Well, all right, go out this door, stand over there with everyone else."

The lot of us waited as the others received their bedding and showered. After the last one finished, we were taken into a small holding cell.

Many of the men pressed their faces against the dirty plexiglass, watching for movement of any kind. Some of them looked at the people in the cells next to us, which were out-take processing, the guys who were leaving the jail. Others watched for women. Most watched for guards.

"Fuck, man," one said, "did anyone else have Housser in the showers?"

A bunch of people nodded. I nodded.

"He made me squat down and cough. I can't stand that! He only does that to people he hates. I've been to the ACJ seven times, saw Housser five of 'em, and he still makes me do that shit! I've never just had to spread my cheeks and do the *How's your ass taste?* thing; I'd rather do that than squat like a bitch."

"He made me do both," I chimed in, not thinking before I said it.

"Um. Wow. He must have *really* not liked you."

Everyone laughed.

After intake processing, I went to the fourth level of the jail, the "Shoo," where everyone went before being classified for different levels. I waited out my time, never leaving the cell I was in. I slept most of the day.

"Boy, you'd better start eatin'," Chauncey, my cellmate, said while scribbling on the walls, "or 'least come out and take your tray so yous can give it to me."

"I'll see how I feel at dinner," I replied.

Chauncey looked at me through soda-bottle glasses, huffed, and continued drawing on the walls. Then he dropped his pencil, began screaming and rubbing at his chest. Chauncey was a lunatic. He had been arrested for accidentally stealing someone's wallet; the only reason he didn't return it right away was because he was afraid the lawyer he had stolen it from might sue him. It was clearly a misunderstanding. Because Chauncey was insane, he always appeared in mental health court, in front of the same judge. This thing with the wallet was the fifth time the judge had seen him that year. Chauncey was gonna get knocked.

"Ahbubba cah! Cah!" Chauncey shouted while still tearing at his chest. I quickly got used to it. Laying in my bunk, I turned around toward the wall. The guards didn't run over anymore because Chauncey screamed so much. Not even the suicide watchers bothered checking in.

After about ten minutes he was done. "I need a cigarette," he said. He quietly left the cell and came back a few moments later with two other men. Our cell was the smoking cell; Chauncey allowed people to smoke there in exchange for a few hits of the cigarettes. If a guard saw smoke, it would ultimately come down on whoever's cell it was. Chauncey was willing to take that risk, with me along for the ride even though I didn't smoke their toilet-paper cigarettes.

"Yo, man, what's up?" one of the men asked me. He was a tall, thin, black gang-star boy with tattoos on his face and neck. Chauncey had told me he wouldn't be staying in the jail; he was going to be sent upstate in a few weeks. Triple homicide.

"Nothing much," I responded, laying in my bunk as usual. Above my head, on the wall, someone had written, *KILL ALL*

WHITES, with what looked like blood. The tattooed gang-star looked at me, then at the message on the wall.

"Shit, man," he said. "That's really *rude*."

Low-risk inmates went to level one, which had three cell-blocks, and higher-risk inmates went anywhere from level seven, which were murderers waiting to be transported to the state prison, down to level two, which was small-time repeat offenders. I was sent to level one, cellblock B. I was told that was the best cellblock because you could become a worker.

A few days on the block, I got the best job in the jail, "street gang." For some reason this upset a lot of people. Street gang was a highly sought-after job. Instead of red uniforms, we wore dark green, working from a warehouse on the bottom level of the jail, next to the outtake area. We got to go outside, eat what the guards ate, and, at night, leave the cellblock to empty garbage. I spent all of my time sitting by the trash com-pactor, the "beast." Everyone else sat in the warehouse, eating chips and watching TV. I liked being by myself, in the trash compactor room. It stank in there but nobody bothered me, which was nice; I even got used to the stink after a while. All of the other street gang workers thought I was insane.

"Hey, Fredrick," one worker, Luther, said, holding a glue trap in his hand.

"Yeah?"

Luther grimaced. "Man, how the hell do you sit back here by the beast all day? Anyway, will you throw this in for me?"

I noticed the glue trap had a mouse stuck to it, still alive, struggling. "Sure, I'll take care of it."

"Thanks."

Luther set the trap down on the ground and tried to hold his breath. I picked it up and pet the mouse; it calmed down slightly. The trash compactor room was also where county cars were parked to be washed. Every day I cleaned one or two of them, using the various soaps and sprays lined up in fifty-five-gallon drums. Some of the soaps were very harsh, could be used as floor stripper, and some weren't as bad.

I went to the drum of yellow soap, which was very mild, and pumped it onto the mouse. Rubbing the little animal, massaging the soap all over it, the glue began to loosen. The mouse started to tear away from the trap; I helped, peeling it off gently, letting it bite into my glove to pull itself further.

"Hey, did you kill that mou— Whoa, whoa!" Luther yelled. "What are you doing?"

"I'm loosening the trap."

"What? Why?"

"So he can get free," I said, looking down at the mouse.

"The fuck is wrong with you? Those things have the fucking plague!"

"We're the plague, Luther."

"What?"

"We are the mice."

"You're as fucking crazy as everyone says!" Luther shouted.

"That's fine."

"Even if you let it go, that thing'll die after a day."

"What do you mean?"

"They get caught in traps and become frightened to death." He laughed. "Their poor widdle hearts can't take it," he mocked.

"That's fine too."

Luther headed out, shaking his head.

The mouse pulled off of the trap completely. As it hung from my glove, I took it to the hose for washing the cars and dripped some water on it, rinsing it off. There was a small bend in the garage door and, on my hands and knees, I guided the mouse through. I watched it scurry away.

Despite what Luther or the workers may have thought, the guards who ran street gang liked me. I never kissed anyone's ass, and for whatever reason, I didn't have to. I kept to myself and worked as hard as I could. Nothing more. I had cut myself on used razors while emptying trash, helped clean out a flood in the jail for twenty-three straight hours, and went on road trips, hauling any usable scrap metal from the old county buildings that were being remodeled or destroyed. The county's budget must have been tight or something.

It would usually be me and one other worker, plus a guard to escort us. Once we went to an unused forensics lab; there were bullets everywhere, and a big steel water tank. Another time we went to the old morgue. We had to scrap the remaining desks, lockers, operating tables, and scalpels, and try not to get hurt. The morgue was almost empty when we got there; the halls echoed with my steps. It felt as if eyes were always on me, hiding behind the walls. I would pick up a cleaver and throw it into a box, then toss a full box into a dumpster outside. It was tedious. There were four professional scrappers, hired by the county, who were helping us; they listened to the radio a lot and ate pizza. Only one of them, Vic, actually worked. He and I were together, ripping copper wire from the walls. I tried to talk to the guy, but he didn't seem interested. Under his breath, between grunts, pulling at the wires, I heard him complain that he didn't like working with gutter trash.

"Hey, Vic," one of the other scrappers called out, laughing.

"Yeah, what's up?" Vic answered, hitting sections of wall with a hammer to get at the wire, then widening the holes with the claw end.

"Why don't you let the kid handle that?"

"Why? So he can take it back to the jail and strangle someone? I don't get why the county makes them work with us. It's fucking embarrassing," he groaned.

"Aw, calm down, he's right next to ya. After this you wanna go to the Goldmine? Two-for-one lap dances until six!"

"Damn straight."

"Anderson, come on. Lunchtime," Arnold said.

Vic and the other guy walked away.

Arnold, the guard, was a bulky, baby-faced New Jersey type. He was always joking. The other worker and I tried laughing at his jokes, but it was hard. In one of the examining rooms, he picked up two large knives from a table—the knives they cut people with. They looked like small machetes. He put them behind his back, in an X formation. He started to pull them out from behind him. "Hey, look! I'm like a ninja with these—aw, fuck!" It sliced right into one of his knuckles. There was still old blood on the blade when he did it. He ran off to clean the cut. He was so funny. We laughed. Ha ha ha.

Left alone, with nobody to help me (the other worker spent a lot of time in the bathroom, probably hiding things to steal), I grew bored. I threw gurneys down the marble steps because they were too long to fit in the elevator. It was a spectacular old building.

"This is a nice place . . ." the other worker said at some point.

I tried to smile. "Yeah. People are dying to get in." He didn't get it.

All around there were slides and Polaroids and a refrigerator that still had parts in it. I could hear Arnold screaming somewhere else in the building as the alcohol burned over. I had a few moments to look around. A lot of office furniture.

The coolers were still cold. I noticed a few lucky pennies on the floor.

Eventually, I stumbled upon a chapel. I'd heard about it before, maybe on TV: the morgue had a chapel for the grief-stricken to pray after seeing the corpse of a loved one. I opened the door and looked inside. The air swirled. High, rounded ceilings led down to walls with stained-glass windows on the right and left, dusty light sleepily floating in.

Suddenly I felt my cheeks becoming wet. I needed to get the fuck out of this place; I decided that I wanted to pray. Even though I had no idea what I was praying to, this was most definitely a place for it. When I started to step inside, not paying attention, I nearly fell. I looked down and saw that the floorboards of the chapel were missing. My hand gripped the doorknob as I regained my footing. It would have been a nasty drop. I stared at my shirt, the word INMATE printed on the breast-pocket, thumping with the rapid beat of my heart.

If the fall wouldn't have killed me, I thought, the scare still could.

A MESSAGE IN THE BREATH OF ALLAH

BY ALI F. SAREINI

Coldwater Correctional Facility (Coldwater, Michigan)

Only the fading light of day was visible through the barred window as I entered the cells at Coldwater. The shadows were silent.

"Turn the lights back on, Ali. I don't like when my cell is dark. I'm not afraid, I just don't like shadows."

"I'll turn them back on in a minute, Red. I need to ask you to do something for me. How are you feeling? Is the morphine patch working?"

"The pain isn't too bad. I'm used to it. But please, Ali, turn the lights back on. I really don't like it dark in here."

I've always found it ironic that prisoners feel comfort with darkness at the corners of their mind, but have a fear of the darkness that covers their eyes.

"Red, I need to ask you to deliver a message to Allah for me. Can you do that? I will include mercy upon you from the hellfire in my daily prayers if you take my message to Allah."

"I've already told you I don't believe in God. I've never seen, heard, or known Him. In my forty-four years in prison He has never sent me a message. If I believed in God I would send Him my own message. What I've seen, and know, is that only a hypocrite believes in God, and I'm not a hypocrite."

"That's the beauty of Allah, Red. You don't have to believe in Him for His laws and rules to apply to you. When you die, you will go before Him and He will ask you about this life. I want you to give Him a message from me. Please, Red." I'd been taking care of Red for more than a year. I believed he owed me, and what harm was there in delivering my message?

"Okay, fine. What would you like me to tell your Al Aah?"

"Thank you, Red. Maybe if I send Him my request through you, He will hear and help me. I want you to tell Allah that I've been praying for twenty-four years to leave prison, and He has not answered me!"

"Sure, no problem . . . Hey, what're you doing? Put the pillow back under my feet and turn the lights on."

"Don't forget, Red. Give Allah my message. I really need you to do this. You're my friend, so please don't forget. I need Him to get me out of here."

"Hey, what, *au augh meem meem haal* . . ." I covered Red's face with the pillow and held him down as he feebly struggled. It wasn't hard. Most older prisoners, after decades of imprisonment, have lost the will to live. The only reason they don't take their own lives is to spite, by the high cost of imprisonment, the citizens of their state. However, Red's true spite was for the families of victims, who had extracted this life and the next from him. He once said: "The victims took two lives from me when I only took one." He truly believed he had been wronged.

Maybe the reason he didn't struggle—much—was that he wanted me to give his life meaning. Of course, I didn't ask him for his life's meaning, but really, what meaning can forty-four years in prison generate in a universe that is indifferent to meaning?

"Officer More, I've taken care of Mr. Dorsey for the night. He's asleep and probably won't wake until morning. I'll be back around seven thirty. He shouldn't be any trouble during the night."

"Okay, Ali, first shift will be here when you return. Good night."

I didn't particularly care to be sent to Coldwater. The word among inmates is that you're sent there to die, or assist the dying. The whole facility is geared toward making sure that prisoners die in the least costly and most efficient way. The prison has five buildings set in a crescent formation. When an inmate walks out from any of the buildings, he is faced with a three-acre grassy yard. The yard is huge by prison standards; it has a small pond with ducks, and trees for shade. If it wasn't a prison, it would be a wonderful spot to picnic.

The facility was originally an industrial park. But during the 1980s recession, Michigan surrounded it with three fifteen-foot fences and draped them all with layers of barbed wire. Even so, Coldwater is a pleasant place to do time. The only complaint a prisoner may have is being surrounded by so many sick people. The officers are humane and abide by the philosophy that a person is sent to prison *as* punishment and not *for* punishment.

Prisoners, the world over, are conspiratorial and very superstitious; things never go their way. But because of my belief in Allah, I have avoided these two character flaws. Nonetheless, my initial thought upon being sent to Coldwater was that it was an omen that death was approaching me. I prayed to Allah to help me get transferred to another prison. When I was first assigned to help Red, he said: "I wish God existed so I could send Him a message that I need His help."

Red's words played at the shadows of my mind and the doubt in my heart. It was then I realized that ending up at Coldwater was a sign from Allah. Like the Holy Land once upon a time, Coldwater is filled with God's messengers. I was humbled, but still sought confirmation of a sign in my five daily prayers to Allah. You cannot be arrogant when it comes to God's signs. The next revelation came when I asked to work as a GED tutor, but was assigned to the critically ill and disabled unit.

As I began my job with the sick inmates, I knew that helping them die in prison, without family or friends, would not be a sign from Allah in and of itself. It's a known truth that Allah's signs are never explained in the acts themselves. The signs are always explained by circumstances; there is no randomness to Allah's signs in His three Holy Books. The Old, New, and Holy Koran testaments.

When I committed my crime, at nineteen, I was convinced that Allah wanted me to confess and go to prison. The purpose of my imprisonment was to spread His message, and thus earn His pleasure. The years added up, but I did not hear from Him. I began to think that maybe there was neither reason nor sign in the long duration of my imprisonment. I became so distraught that I wrote a letter to the warden of the Lapeer prison facility, asking:

> Why are you taking care of me? In fifteen years I've contributed nothing to society. Yet you house me, feed me, clothe me, and provide me with medical care. Why?

I received no reply.

In my twentieth year of imprisonment I began to believe there was something blocking my prayers, and that was why Allah wasn't answering me. I realized I had to change my method of reaching Him. Prayer, by itself, was no longer working, if it ever had. It couldn't be me—I did my five daily prayers religiously, did not gamble, drink prison alcohol, steal, or commit homosexual acts. I was an ideal prisoner to Allah and the prison administration. Then suddenly the idea of messengers began to make complete sense in religious belief.

After sending Red with my message to Allah, the following morning I reported to his cell as usual. I stood for fifteen minutes looking at his face, and then approached a guard. "Officer Thompson, I believe Red is dead."

He looked up from his newspaper. "Mr. Dorsey? Are you sure, Ali? I checked on him when I came in at six o'clock. He looked fine."

We walked down to cell 66, and except for a pained expression on Red's face, he looked asleep. I said somewhat apprehensively: "I checked his pulse, and he didn't have one."

Officer Thompson turned to me. "Maybe you're right, you know the policy. You don't touch a prisoner you think is dead."

Red was my first messenger, and I feared I'd made a mistake. To cover, I said: "Officer Thompson, I've been taking care of Red for over a year. He's my friend. I was hoping he was still alive."

In a whisper, because you always whisper around the dead for they can hear you, Thompson said: "I'm sorry Ali, I know he was your friend, but the rule is you don't touch him. Don't do it again." So I never touched the dead again.

However, Red's pained expression stayed with me. I knew Allah would not accept my message. I was taught that you returned to Allah with a smile on your face, because you're about to meet your Lord. A pained expression shows a lack of faith. I had to better prepare my messengers for their meeting with Allah, and I had to somehow limit the number of questions that would arise on my messengers' journeys. The limiting of questions is Allah's greatest gift to strengthen faith.

In all His Holy Books He admonishes against too many questions asked of Him or His messengers.

The medical staff and the warden were called to confirm Red's death. They too were disturbed by his face. Luckily, the attending nurse observed, "He must've died in his sleep. Poor guy looks like he was in great pain with his last breath to God." This particular nurse was very religious. She always tried to bring the dying prisoners to Christ. But she wasn't my rival, because everyone knows Christianity is a man-made religion—unlike Islam, which was revealed directly from Allah to mankind. And yet her observation forewarned that I cannot completely depend on people not caring about what happens to prisoners when they die. It would be helpful to everyone if those witnessing had a positive impression of the messenger's body after he's left with my message.

The prison staff did a cursory investigation and ruled that the death of prisoner Dorsey, #1954-44, was natural. He was twenty-one when he came to prison in 1962. After forty-four years behind bars Red had no children, but was survived by two brothers and a sister, all who had lost interest in him long ago. The prison was able to contact one of the brothers concerning Red's remains. According to Officer Thompson, the brother sarcastically said, "You must've loved my brother very much to keep him for forty-four years. So why don't you keep the body?" To reduce prison costs, John Dorsey was cremated and his ashes were scattered on the Coldwater yard. The only part of Red that left prison was my message to Allah.

I had sent the message on Friday, a day that is holy to both Islam and Christianity. Jesus was crucified on Friday night and rose Sunday morning; that's three days and three nights. Actually, it's only two nights and one day, but with the signs of God you don't hold math accountable. With no beginning or ending to God, He can't be put on a number line. It's humans who created numbers, who can begin counting with one and end with infinity. It just seems ironic that most of Allah's signs deal with some sort of numerical combination when He doesn't.

Three days later, I was ordered to Deputy Warden Engle's office. He's the one charged with the dead-men-walking unit, as it's known among staff and prisoners. (I reverently called the unit "the messengers' home.") Originally, because of my laid-back demeanor, I was assigned to help dying prisoners. I didn't mind because a dying prisoner is much easier to help than, say, a prisoner you *wish* would die. That's an inside joke among helpers that always gets an unmaliced chuckle. The messengers' home sits in the middle of the five units at Coldwater prison. It holds 157 prisoners and employs fifty-two helpers, housed separately. Only one helper is assigned to each dying prisoner.

Deputy Engle's office was situated in the messengers' home. "Come on in, Mr. Ali. Please sit down."

I sat in a chair by his desk. The deputy likes to think of himself as a regular guy; he's always quite informal. I, like every other prisoner, worry about informality but go along to avoid unwanted attention.

"Ali, I called you in to see if you're all right, because the officers' daily reports show that you and Red were friends." I immediately got nervous and silently prayed that Red would not be my last message to Allah. "I called you in ahead of the seven days required by policy before being assigned another prisoner to ask a favor. Do you know Mr. Jackson? His cell is two down from Red's."

I knew Twin—Mr. Jackson—who has a twin brother also

in prison. I knew he was very sick, hard to keep company, a devout Christian, and blamed everyone but himself for fifty-two years in prison. Mr. Jackson thought his interpretation of Christianity was the only way *not* to be a nonbeliever. When assigned to Twin, the majority of helpers had declined unless ordered. His last helper quit the assignment, which is unusual for a job that pays a hundred dollars a month. The most any other prisoner can earn on assignment is forty-five, and even that's considered high pay.

"Yes, Deputy Warden, most of the other helpers know him, but we'd rather not help him. He's very abrasive."

Smiling, Engle said, "I've heard that, Ali, and that's why I'm hoping you'll take the assignment. I think both of you being so religious would help you get along." If I played this opportunity right, Twin could be my access to a steady stream of messengers. I had to make sure the deputy remembered that I didn't want the assignment.

"Deputy Warden, you know I'm a Muslim, and I'm sure you've seen the news. We Muslims can hardly get along with each other, let alone with a fanatic Christian."

Deputy Engle sat back. "If you're refusing to be Mr. Jackson's helper, I'll understand, but that will leave an open slot for me to fill. I'm sure I can find someone who would like to earn a hundred dollars a month."

I knew his implication. At present I had no assignment, so I was the open slot. "All right, Deputy Warden, I'll be Mr. Jackson's helper. But I want it understood that he's very temperamental."

He got up to shake my hand. "I'll note in your file that Mr. Jackson is a difficult assignment and will even request that payroll gives you a one-time bonus of fifty dollars."

I never got the bonus, but I did get something far more

valuable: that day it became much safer for me to send my messengers to Allah.

There is a commonality between Allah's messengers and mine. Both of us choose men who are reluctant to be messengers and are despised by the people. Our messengers also share the trait of believing they are not special until they've been separated from the people. They don't feel different, but they *are* different.

"What incompetent person made you my helper? Plus, aren't you a Muus-limb?"

I smiled. "Twin, we've known each other since 8 block in Jackson Prison. I came to prison as a Muslim, so let's just have you believe what you believe and I believe what I believe."

He gave me a long look. "I don't need a Muus-limb's help, so you can leave my cell. Don't worry, they'll still pay you for the day." I agreed to leave and told him that if he needed help he should alert the officer, who would get me from my unit.

The following day, Twin had a callout to see the doctor. He had been waiting six months for approval to have an operation to remove cancerous cells from his lungs. I got a wheelchair and took him to the doctor's office. I waited in the hallway for only about five minutes before I was told to bring him back to his cell. I said nothing as we made our way back.

Twin was peering vacantly down the walkway when he said, "The doctor told me I was denied the operation because the cancer has spread to other parts of my body. It's in Jesus's hands now."

I didn't know what to say, so I offered to help him write a grievance against the medical provider, the warden, and the Department of Corrections.

"Ali, how many grievances have you won in your time in

prison? I've been in prison for fifty-two years and remember when we had no grievance procedure at all, and now that we do, I've never won one."

I knew he was right, but I wanted my next messenger to have hope. Hope is Allah's sign that your message is close to being accepted. I didn't need another pained expression on the face of my messenger when he stood before Allah.

For the next two weeks, Twin didn't want any help. I would come to his cell and find him reading the Bible or saying his prayers. "Twin, do you need anything today? I could take you to the yard." It's strange making such small talk with a dying man, but I wanted him to be peaceful, and hopeful.

"I've been in prison yards since 1960," he replied. "If you've seen one prison yard, you've seen them all."

An inmate's greatest fear is dying in prison. In prison you have no control. You wake up, eat, go to the yard, come back in, and sleep when told, only to do the same thing all over again the next day. I knew with only twenty-four years in prison myself how Twin felt about being told to go to the yard. He thought that, in not being able to control his life for the last fifty-two years, he could at least have some control over where he died. With great sadness in my heart, I went to the yard by myself.

It was Easter and a mildly warm sunny day when I showed up with a wheelchair at Twin's cell door. "I thought we'd go to the yard, and you can tell me about Jesus."

Twin was in bed reading the Bible. "You don't even believe in Jesus."

I looked hurt. "I believe in Jesus as a messenger of Allah, God."

Twin looked doubly hurt. "If you don't believe Jesus is the son of God, you don't believe in Jesus."

I sat down in the wheelchair and asked, "Don't you believe Jesus was a messenger who brought God's message to the Israelites? If you do believe this, then maybe you can convince me that Jesus was also the son of God."

He took my challenge and asked to be helped into the chair. I wheeled Twin to the back of the yard, where I could sit in the shadow of the trees, and he in the sun; I had to be careful to not upset my messenger. There were plenty of others in the yard, but they didn't approach us. When inmates find out someone is dying, they tend to avoid him as an evil omen of their demise in prison.

I made sure Twin faced the garden outside the greenhouse. The prisoners working the grounds provided a sense of how Allah gives life to a land after its death. I knew this scene would give Twin hope, because life being prepared to come forth always gives hope. Who has not seen a woman with child and not had hope for his own life, her life, and the life of the child?

After twenty minutes of silence, Twin asked, "Ali, do you really want to hear about Jesus as the son of God, or were you just trying to get me out of the cell?"

I pretended to be giving his question some thought. "I do want to talk about Jesus, but in stages."

He looked at me. "In stages? Like what, His parables?"

"No, not His parables, but the stages of being a messenger to John the Baptist, then a rabbi to the disciples, and finally rising from death as the son of God. I'm really interested in His message."

Twin smiled and let his body relax under the sun and the blanket on his lap. "You want to know about His ministry, and how He was a messenger of God."

I knew that those who have ministries are not messengers of Allah but messengers of prophets, and actually receive God's *calling* and not His message. Only messengers come with Allah's message. "Twin, have you ever tried to send a message to God? And has He answered you? And if not, why not?"

Twin, pleased with my skeptical expression, said, "Ali, are you in doubt that God hears you? That's why Christians speak to God through Jesus. God will always hear Jesus, so Christians have no doubt." If Jesus was a messenger, this was yet another sign that Allah would hear a message sent through him without a doubt. "You see, Ali, God hears me because I'm a messenger myself. I send the message of God to your ears."

The sign was complete! Twin was a messenger, and tonight he would leave with my message to Allah. "Twin, you give me hope."

I spent the next two hours listening to my messenger speak about how he fully understood Jesus's words. A messenger understands the message. Unlike Red, Twin believed in God, if wrongly, and Allah would correct his belief at their meeting. The yard would close at three forty-five in the afternoon for four o'clock count. After count, I would bring Twin his dinner and, if he allowed, get him ready for bed. I hoped, after our talk in the yard, he would let me help him get ready for bed.

I delivered Twin's dinner tray to his cell and helped him sit up. He did not argue and was in fact very cooperative. I watched the Christian channel with him as he ate a grilled cheese sandwich, oven-baked potatoes, and a salad. He gave me the oatmeal cookie because it was too hard for him to eat in his condition.

"Twin, let me help you get ready for bed tonight. Our talk

in the yard proved that you can help me." I needed him to feel obliged to take my message to Allah.

He didn't protest, but rather took on a childlike posture on his bunk. Twin was willing to be my messenger!

I helped him put on the state-issued orange shorts that he liked to sleep in. His sickness had created a caricatured, doll-like figure, who looked up pleadingly like the pictures of the godly men in Christian books, their faces and bodies always appearing anorexic. I lifted the sheet and blanket.

"Twin, tonight it's going to be very cold. Would you like me to place a second blanket over you?"

He nodded. I tucked the blankets tight on his left side and sat down on the mattress to secure them with my weight.

"Hey, it's okay to be in my cell, but don't sit on my bunk. Get up—or better yet, I'll see you tomorrow."

I inched closer to his shoulder. "Twin, I'll move soon. But I need to ask you for a favor. Can you take an important message to God for me? God listens with more interest to those who know they're dying. I'll leave the cell as soon as you leave with my message."

Twin peered in my eyes and probably thought, *I'll say okay so that this crazy Muslim will leave my cell, but tomorrow I'm asking to have him removed.* If any sick prisoner expresses concern that his help might hurt him, the deputy warden must remove him, or be legally liable. But that's not what happened.

"Sure, Ali, I'll take your message to God. What do you got to say to Him?"

I held Twin's eyes. "Tell Allah that I've been praying to him for twenty-four years, and He has not answered me. Please, Twin, make sure He gets my message."

I quickly placed one hand over his mouth and with the other squeezed his nostrils shut. Twin's arms were cocooned under the wool blankets, but he struggled to breathe and shook his head back and forth. I soon felt him weakening and leaned in to whisper, "Don't forget to tell Allah I've been praying for twenty-four years for an answer."

The struggle was short, but I had prepared for Twin's departure. The same day I had sent Red with my message, I'd noticed a prisoner playing basketball with a strange smile on his face the whole time. He had a mouth guard between his lips. The grin forced by the mouth guard gave me the idea of how to send messengers to Allah with smiles on their faces. I placed the mouth guard between Twin's lips and elevated his legs to force blood toward his face. The pooling blood would give him color and a peaceful-looking sleep for his journey. Nothing says peace like rosy cheeks. After several minutes, I slowly settled his legs down, loosened the blankets, removed the mouth guard, and turned off the television.

"Mr. Jackson is in bed watching TV. I'll be back in the morning to help him get ready for his medical callout." The officer gave me the peace sign and went back to the Detroit Tigers game on the radio. When he made his rounds in an hour, he would see Mr. Jackson lying there with the TV off and assume he had turned it off before going to sleep.

The next morning, I informed the officer on duty that I believed Mr. Jackson may be dead.

"Are you sure?"

I shrugged my shoulders. "He didn't move when I called his name."

The officer went to cell 64. "Mr. Jackson, are you all right?" When there was no response, he called shift command.

I was waiting in the hallway as the warden and the same nurse from Red's death arrived. She entered his cell. "He must've went peacefully with such a smile on his face. God has accepted him into the kingdom."

Her words gripped my hope that the message had gotten through to Allah and I would be leaving prison very soon.

Three days went by, and nothing. I was wondering if I had missed a sign when I was told to report to the deputy's office. As I entered, he thanked me for making Twin's last days comfortable.

"I was told, Mr. Ali, that Twin died with a smile on his face. I'm sure you had something to do with that. You did good."

"I gave Twin a reason for leaving during a nice talk we had on the day he died. He was ready to meet the Lord."

The deputy gave me a thoughtful look. "I'm glad you got along with Mr. Jackson. The daily reports say that you two enjoyed each other's company . . . Now, I need another favor, and I'll owe you." I didn't mention the fifty-dollar bonus that was still due to me. "A Muslim prisoner named Myron Woods asked to be assigned a Muslim helper. You're the only true Muslim helper I have. I know he'll be happy to have an Arab Muslim." It was a bit offensive to label me a *true* Muslim simply because I had been born as one; by implication, converts were not real Muslims.

It had been three days since I sent Twin on his journey and, seeing that I was still in prison, Allah must not have received or accepted my message. However, Mr. Woods—whose Muslim name was Abdul-Sami (Worshipper of the One Who Hears)—was not a Christian. I'd made a mistake. All of Allah's messengers were Muslim, so naturally my message should be sent by a Muslim. That's a true sign.

"Deputy Warden, I don't want to become the Grim Reaper.

I'd prefer a regular handicapped prisoner this time." I knew my request would be denied; there was no risk in losing this messenger, especially since he'd requested the only true Muslim helper in the eyes and narrow mind of the deputy.

Pretending reluctance, I was assigned to Abdul-Sami. The doctor gave him around a month to live with his liver failure. My instructions were to make sure he was kept comfortable and to give him as many morphine patches as needed to ease his pain. Ironic how the laws for narcotics with the living are reversed for the dying. When the time came for me to send Abdul-Sami with my message to Allah, all I'd need to do was place enough morphine patches on him to ease his journey.

Abdul-Sami was of my faith, so convincing him to take my message to Allah was easy. My only apprehension was the command in the Holy Koran which forbids standing before Allah in a drunken state. However, I now believe Allah exempts modern medicine because it only *mimics* drunkenness. The morphine was a mercy from Allah, it wasn't being drunk.

"Remember, Abdul-Sami, tell Allah that I have been praying to Him for twenty-four years and He has not answered me. I ask that He release me from prison. Allah may have become accustomed to me asking for this for so many years and has simply forgotten." Abdul-Sami's eyes were closed as I placed seven patches, for the Seven Heavens, on his arms and legs.

"I will tell Allah, my brother, and I'll also tell Him of your kindness to me."

We both said, "Amen." I watched his chest, for I knew my message would go in his last breath to Allah. I once again placed the mouth guard between the lips, and elevated the feet.

I have grown wiser with each messenger I've sent. Allah has

the twelve tribes of Israel, the twelve disciples of Jesus, and the twelve holy imams of Islam. I realized that it would be in keeping with His numerical signs to send twelve messengers before He would answer me. At present, I have sent the following eleven: Red, Twin, Abdul-Sami, Emmit, Michael, Joseph, Jacob, Luke, Manuel, Raymond, and David. After each departure, I have done five daily prayers and then waited to feel better than I did when I began. It's a Muslim truism that if you feel better after the prayer, Allah has accepted it. Feeling better after prayer had been easy the first three years of imprisonment. But that feeling gradually diminished until, at my twenty-fourth year behind bars, I no longer felt anything. Had Allah answered me at even the twentieth year of imprisonment, I would never have sent any messengers. It's my fault I wasted twenty years of prayers.

To present prison staff, I've become the compassionate, long-suffering, and totally selfless helper. I've gained respect among inmates as well. My cell is never checked for contraband, and I am never asked about my movements in prison. I can also request a meeting with any staff member, even the warden. Only one thing nags at me: the unintended consequence of saving the state of Michigan money. But it's also my protection, because the state never asks questions when you save it money. It costs five times as much to keep a sick or dying prisoner than a healthy one. When costs go up, questions get asked.

Thus, I've become an asset to the prison system, something you should never become. In some ways I'm the *ideal* asset, in that I save the state money and have a parolable life sentence with deportation. So I'll stay in prison until I get sick and then be deported to my home country to burden it with my care.

The eleventh messenger, David, was one of the three dying prisoners left at this place. Unless something changes, I'll have to be careful with my last pick. The twelfth messenger must be the best yet. He's the final sign and hope that Allah will release me from prison.

This morning, while jogging my five daily miles on the yard, I noticed an unusual pain in my midsection. I attributed it to runner's stress. However, being a cautious soul, I sent a request to see the doctor.

I explained my symptom to the doctor two days ago. He ordered some blood work and noticed something odd in the results. He ordered further tests and confirmed I have pancreatic cancer, a death sentence under the private prison health care. I came to the United States from Lebanon without a family, so no one will question the state about my cost-saving death.

The ironies of Allah continue. I'm the best twelfth messenger I can send. Who's better for this than me? I would never get the message wrong or forget it. Maybe the eleven messengers I've sent were too distracted by their own messages to remember mine. It's a reasonable conclusion, but still a shock that Allah would allow me to die here when I've prayed for over twenty-four years to be released. It's even more shocking than when Allah took my mother's life while I was still in prison to teach me great loss. He needed a way to balance my crime.

It's the obvious choice that I should be the twelfth messenger, but so unlike Allah's past behavior. He never killed His messengers to send His own message. Allah always protected those entrusted with His message until they delivered it. Technically, I'm sending my message to Allah, so He doesn't owe me protection. But now I need to add a new request, since being released from prison is not going to happen. So I ask for protection in the next life from the messengers I've sent there, and in this life from the illness that may earn me an abusive helper. Besides dying, nothing is scarier than being abused in prison.

I am truly the message in the breath of Allah.

PART II

CAGED BIRDS SING

TUNE-UP

BY STEPHEN GEEZ

Ryan Correctional Facility (Detroit, Michigan)

That banged-up old black tanker car got left behind. It must have been sitting there for many years, maybe decades, passing time on a split of secondary sidetrack, no place else to go. Debris and weeds choked the rails, thicker brush growing up through its wheels and broken coupler.

Fuse sat cross-legged on the weedy patch of wannabe lawn in Ryan Road Facility's big yard, just inside the pea-gravel track edged by razor-wired electric fences. Oval-walking convicts occasionally disrupted his view of the old tanker, as did the creepy crawl of a lethally armed perimeter vehicle, its skin a shiny state blue. At least you know that climbing the fence is precisely what triggers the patrol's violent assault. Fuse's psycho bunkie and his dawgs would crack an unsuspecting head for no other reason than the rumors *they* started. Like so many others in the joint, they lived the fool-rule: act stupid, put your business on front street, get yourself popped, and save face by calling the nearest body a snitch.

The daddy killdeer swooped in and challenged Fuse with a cautionary dive, then landed a dozen feet to the left and glared threats before relieving his mate at their ground nest marked by a bright orange traffic cone. *Don't step on the baby,* somebody had thought to alert other prisoners, likely some nature lover who'd just as soon padlock a human skull and stab a body fifteen times before ghosting into the crowd. The prim-looking plover fed its lone chick, then settled in to keep an eye on Fuse.

Beyond the nest, that line of counterclockwisers followed the oval's arc along the back fence, their backdrop a grassy berm blocking views of the mirror-opposite Mound Road Facility. Back-to-back job-generating prisons in the industry-pocked Eastside Detroit neighborhood must have seemed like a good idea several decades back, maybe not so much now that drugs and other contraband fence-tossings littered the yard every morning, or since a quick bolt-cutter breach proved that ten men could spurt right through and fade into the 'hood.

A train clanked and squealed its way across Ryan Road, down the spur track that ran alongside both prisons. Every day, the train delivered chemicals to a small paint factory next door to the prison, right across from the Level IV units and chow hall. Fascinated by trains as a boy, Fuse liked to sit right there most afternoons—weather and emergency counts and clear-the-yard assaults permitting—to watch the replacement of yesterday's empty tanker with today's full one. The whole process always seemed out of place, this glimpse of purpose and productivity in a rusty, falling-down city, industrious men commanding monstrous and mighty machines. Fuse's bunkie couldn't fathom the relationship between man and machine. Last night during one of his rages he destroyed their cell fan. Apparently it had been disrespecting the over-inked lunk by intentionally rattling and wheezing to interrupt another twelve-hour sleep, his rest inexplicably essential for fueling a mind that never actually shifted out of idle.

His tantrums had been escalating since two slash-and-burn shakedowns in a row convinced him a snitch must have kited about the piece of steel he'd been bragging about having handy. Hearing whispers of blame, Fuse had noticed several glares and hostile gestures.

Heavy Metal wandered over, set his guitar and battery-charged mini-amp in the weeds, then sat cross-legged and nodded with a "'Sup?" He got the "Metal" moniker for playing heavy-metal guitar—quite deftly—just as Fuse had picked up his own tag for favoring "fusion" styles during his stint on keyboard in a mishmash cover band at Adrian Regional. Wiry and muscle-bound, the long-haired metal-head claimed several names and aliases, just enough to confuse his incoming mail, though only the six digits on his door card truly meant anything to anybody who mattered.

The engine passed them and grunted as the whole train clanged its way to a stop. The engineer climbed down and joined two men walking from the rear. He studied his clipboard and the numbers on a shiny white tanker, then headed back to the engine. The other two uncoupled the tanker at both its front and rear, then switched the rails to a third side-track heading over to the paint factory pumps. The train grunted several more times as it backed in, picked up yesterday's empty tanker, then pulled it alongside the prison fence before backing into the full tanker. It coupled with a clank and hiss, then moved forward past the switch. It backed into the factory again, this time leaving the tanker before pulling out and backing up to couple with the rest of the train. Maybe fifteen minutes total, the engineer reversed the whole assemblage across Ryan Road and faded into the 'hood. Still, that banged-up old black tanker car on the other track got left behind.

The show over, Metal dropped his news with a smirk. "Mo says your keyboard's out in the warehouse, and Doug's gonna let you have it since they didn't catch on before putting in your order." The approved vendor had put a five-octave Casio with stand on sale for $79, only four bucks over the property-policy price-per-item limit, so he'd written them a letter proposing a $10 credit for withholding the otherwise contraband metal stand, and they wrote back agreeing to $69 without it. That money order to his inmate trust account from Fuse's granny right before she died proved worth saving all this time. The business office started rejecting everybody else who tried the same thing because they discovered the official sale flyer only listed the $79 deal. All his years down, this marked the only chance for Fuse to order a board with adult-sized keys.

"You still playing with that butt-kisser up there?" Metal asked, referring to Mo.

Metal used to be up in unit 4C with Fuse and Maurice— "Mo" for "Modern Jazz." Then a shakedown that turned up the program's "borrowed" effects pedal caught Metal a theft ticket and cost him his Saturday afternoon music room slot. His tat-gun and makeshift soldering pencil sent him to the hole. When he got out, he landed over in 700 building. Fuse had taken to sitting outside Mo's cell several evenings a week to play music with headphones joined by a homemade splitter. That big old black man, who looked like he'd waded into a few too many fights back in the day, more than knew how to dance his fat fingers up and down the neck of his knockoff Les Paul–style guitar.

"No, Slim won't let me use his toy anymore." Slim's two-octave *I'm a Rock Star!* mini-key by Hasbro or Mattel or Fisher-Price wasn't worth the frustration anyway.

"You put in for your own music slot?"

"Yeah—more than a year ago."

"The rappers who snaked my slot—Doug says he's gonna

cut 'em loose. Two rode out anyway, and he's pissed about smelling weed and cock-sweat every time they've been in there."

"But I don't have a band."

"Put *me* on the callout with you. Grab Reggie to play drums. Get Mo on bass—at least till someone else rides in." As Doug's music clerk, Mo could help push for Fuse to get that slot.

"You *hate* Mo."

"Yeah, well, he's the best on the compound for now."

"But all you play is metal."

"Man, I'll play anything. I just want back in."

"All original, no covers?"

"Only," Metal said, then smirked as he unpacked his guitar and plugged in his effects and mini-amp. He would answer with his hands.

"So this is how you do your time, huh?"

Metal fine-tuned a couple of strings. "It's play music or fight a lot. Oh, by the way . . ."

The killdeer craned his neck to hear.

"You need to watch your back. Your bitch-ass bunkie is still talkin' shit about you."

Even though Fuse used headphones, Psycho threw tantrums every time he tried to work on music in the cell. The mere sound of fingers striking plastic keys upset that delicate equilibrium of fixations and obsessive compulsions. Every time the doors broke, Fuse and his Casio headed for base, or afternoons with Metal in the big yard, or evenings in the doorway to Mo's cell.

"Two more weeks," Mo said one night. "Tee-Bey got paper, so he'll be ridin' to Macomb for prerelease. Ray-Ray and Westside'll make a play to keep the slot, but Doug says you been here longer. They gotta wait their turn."

Working with Mo opened new ways of approaching music for Fuse. Some thirty-odd years ago as a fish—a first-timer—Mo had fallen in with some O-head musicians who taught him the rudiments of old-school jazz guitar. Mo moved on to teach himself new styles by listening, experimenting, and playing with others who'd come and gone in the decades since. Mo offered Fuse some of his original material, meticulously charted, and taught him efficient ways to chart his own. They impressed each other, together shaping sound to conjure exhilarating new realms beyond the fence, whether to make bold statements or simply discover whatever they might find. The progressions, the patterns, the styles—Fuse picked up many, then surprised Mo more than a few times by passing along some of his own. Still, what Fuse liked most was Mo's tendency to hold back rather than diving all in.

"Don't hit that flat five every time you run down a blues riff," Mo would lecture. "Save that and the flat six, even the major seventh or minor third. Use 'em only when the chords shift, and then only maybe. Make everybody ache for 'em, wonderin' when you'll let 'em slide witchoo."

Fuse brought several of Metal's songs to their two-man sessions too, surprising Mo with how that boolshit metal could offer clever nuance and space to layer surprises, sometimes even a groove that jumped the rails and cut its own path toward whatever new places it might dare find.

One evening Mo was shuffling through his charts, looking for something to work on, when he caught Fuse craning to see the faded and creased photo of a young black woman tacked to his bulletin board, her arms in the air, apparently dancing. "That's my little girl—LaTisha," Mo said quietly. "She's thirty-four now."

Fuse nodded. "Very pretty." He had lots of questions. *You*

in touch? She live in Detroit? Ever come to see you? Grandkids? Still, he knew you don't ask, not if you really cared. Mo would say what he wanted to say.

"She was born after I got locked up. I've never seen her. Her and her mama wanted nothin' to do with me. Then her mama got cancer and couldn't beat it, so she sent me the picture toward the end, said maybe I deserved that much, see what I missed."

Fuse nodded and waited, resisting the urge to touch his keys.

Mo pulled his footlocker over, fumbled with the padlock, dug through layers of paperwork. "You ever had any kids?"

Fuse took a deep breath, not sure how to answer. "A daughter," he said quietly. "Amanda—Amanda with the beautiful smile."

"No contact now?"

Fuse shook his head.

"Her mama neither?"

Fuse shook his head again. "Nobody out in the world since Granny died."

"That sucks." Mo located a tattered blue pocket-folder. "Me neither—not since Mom's died." He pulled out two small sheaves of song charts, one set neatly handwritten, the other photocopied from the same material. "Doug made me copies," he explained, setting one sheet atop the footlocker, handing its companion to Fuse.

LaTisha's Dance, read the title.

And they played it, several times, several ways. Mo marveled at the nuance and style and layered rhythms Fuse added. Sometimes the big guy drifted into wistfulness, closing his eyes as he played, once turning away and wiping his face.

"She would like that," Fuse offered as Mo put the charts back into his footlocker.

"She'll never hear it," Mo replied, his frustration palpable. "I'm doing all day." Life without parole—a death sentence he'd got . . . the slow way.

"I'm eligible in fourteen-some," Fuse said. "Maybe I can play it for her."

Mo looked surprised, then very serious. He pursed his lips and rubbed his beefy head. "Maybe," he said.

The days leading up to the first callout on Fuse's new Saturday slot found him distracted. He worked on the first seven songs they'd selected—three of Mo's, two of his own, and two of Metal's—but often found himself also playing variations on the "LaTisha's Dance" theme. That invariably led to pondering an unwritten song he couldn't even begin to hear, no matter how deeply he listened: "Amanda's Smile."

Then his bunkie went to the hole after another shakedown, word on the yard being that he had some steel and somebody snitched. Rumors wafted back several times that Psycho's road-dawg Jack was telling people Fuse got him popped. That kind of talk might fade for lack of credibility, or escalate if more instigators jumped on board. Sitting alone late one night in his cell, the bottom bunk now empty, Fuse set up the keyboard, plugged in headphones, and began to play. He ran through all seven songs, but couldn't really remember actually playing them. He messed around with "LaTisha's Dance" a few times, but found himself distracted and frustrated. Amanda kept skittering just beyond his grasp, and for the first time in his entire bid, he realized that trying to connect with any part of his world lost beyond time or those fences inevitably left him feeling alone and afraid. He had nobody, no one to call, no one for mail, not a soul who cared whether he lived or died. With Psycho gone, he couldn't even busy his mind by hating.

The next day he sat with Metal and Reggie in the yard, running through the same seven songs while storm clouds rolled in from the west, a gusty breeze blowing cold, and an odor of rain stirring paint fumes in the air. Short and stocky with a random splay of jet-black hair, Reggie mostly worked the patterns, trying beats by slapping his legs and scatting, his mouthed cymbal-swells spraying spit. They paused to watch the train take one and leave one, even as it ignored that beat-up old black tanker. The killdeer seemed unimpressed by it all, his priorities tending toward family.

"If we have time," Fuse said, "I'd like to try a Mo song about his daughter, real personal."

Metal shrugged, honoring his promise to play *anything*. He'd proven amazingly adept at exploring other genres and styles, no doubt proud of his prowess, though loath to admit he actually reveled in material he considered beneath head-banging and metal shredding. They ran through Mo's song a few times, and Metal clearly understood what it meant, what it *could* mean. He found poetry in the images it conjured, grace in the notes, that tentative reluctance of a shy young woman yielding to her own rhythms, the yearning for a father she never met, the longing of a damaged man whose melody can't be constrained by the razor-wired electric fences.

At some point, two young black guys walked up to them, pants hanging low, dark scowls highlighted by narrowed eyes. "You on that music callout now?" one demanded.

"We all are," Metal said, setting his guitar in its case.

"That 'pose to be ours," the other insisted.

"That's on Doug," Metal said.

Reggie tilted his head toward Fuse. "He's been on the list a year."

They glared for a moment as the killdeer watched warily.

"We'll see," one said. They turned and walked away.

Reggie snorted his derision. "They wanna start somethin', *I'll* start somethin'."

"They'll try anything to get that slot back," Metal said. "We might need to take a few people and have a talk."

Reggie added, "With Jack too. He's still on that bullshit about Fuse. It's about time to tune his ass up."

"He's in my unit," Metal said. "I'll tell him shut his fuckin' mouth—or we got a problem."

Big drops of rain splattered their instruments. Everybody scrambled to pack up. Lightning flashed in the distance.

"*Attention!*" called the speakers. "*All yards are closed!*"

Never having been to the music space, Fuse followed Mo to the far end of the rec area, through the breezeway with an open-entry bathroom off to the right, then into the gym where incomers streamed in to grab basketballs and argue about the game that hadn't even started. A pair of doors in the far corner revealed a large storage area converted to a music room, Metal and Reggie already setting up. Two keyboards way better than the toy Fuse owned, real trap-set drums, amps, guitars, a bass for Mo to cut loose, more effects than Metal could channel on a hundred songs—all this had been waiting for them *right here,* so close and finally no longer out of reach.

So they played.

Fuse raced to learn all the keyboard programming. Metal tested effects to augment his new styles. Reggie tuned the drum heads and rearranged the toms until he'd placed them just right. Mo bobbed his head, sheer excitement pumping the big old guy. They laughed, got serious, honed the precision of their charts, and drifted through improvs that took them places from which they only reluctantly returned. Fuse embraced the idea of holding back, leaving holes, saving those drop-ins and blues flourishes and major-seventh jazz highlights for only when they desperately needed expressing.

And Fuse finally knew this was how he could do his time. Fourteen-some years—more if the parole board didn't yet want to let him go a personal keyboard right in his cell, real musicians gathering each week to listen to each other and sound back, a *group* of like-minders creating places and spaces where no outsiders could dictate what he dared feel.

When Reggie left to take a leak, Fuse started playing "LaTisha's Dance."

Mo went wide-eyed. He opened his mouth, but found no words as Metal quickly joined in on guitar, his chords and gentle slides first shimmering, then syncopating with delicate harmonics. Reggie came back and tried a simple rhythm. Mo shook his head and hit some bass-note beats, a catchy pattern, nodding toward the snare, the cymbals, guiding his percussionist. Reggie picked it up, embellishing with a wood block, a tom-tom backbeat. Mo added a swaying melodic bass line and quickly danced his way into the groove.

They glided through the song three times, each pass more expansive, more nuanced, more playful yet ponderous. Fuse felt a twinge of melancholy, so he dared let it ripple through his fingers. That was for Mo, and Mo understood, appreciation in his eyes. This song called out to LaTisha, and though she never knew her father, they all knew him, now more than ever, and maybe the best his little girl could ever hope would be that others might tell her about him, words or not.

Time eventually ran out, and Reggie bolted to meet someone on the walk. As a music clerk, Mo needed to stay behind to inventory the miscellany. Fuse and Metal headed out with their instruments, following gym stragglers through the breezeway.

Metal stopped to hit the urinal, so Fuse set his keyboard by the sink and grabbed a paper towel to wipe perspiration from his brow—

Bam! Bam!

The side—of his head—

He spun and fell hard, skull slamming into ceramic tile. He reached with his hand, warm blood running through his fingers. He tried to glimpse what was happening.

Feet, several feet, the keyboard picked up—

Bam!

Back of his head, spreading toward the front, his brain screaming. He tried to raise it up, but couldn't stop the spinning.

Blood all on the floor.

Metal slumped beside the urinal, eyes vacant, arm twitching, shirt drenched red, neck bleeding, hand bleeding, stabs, slashes.

Fuse laid his head in the puddle and drifted.

God it hurt.

LaTisha danced through the tableau, paused to look, then danced away; and Fuse looked for Amanda, her golden curls, those big blue eyes, sweet dimples, the smile of his adorable little four-year-old . . . For an instant he could hear her, but then it got hot, too hot, flames roaring, smoke choking him, stealing his breath, smashing him with dark regrets.

You tweakin' that shit again?! screamed his wife, bursting in through the front door. *You're supposed to* watch *her—not get high!*

But the flames, the smoke—and she kept screaming even as he found her and dragged her outside. Flashing lights raced her to the hospital, her hands and arms burned from trying but failing to reach their little girl. Handcuffs, county jail, court appearances where nobody comes, and finally word that his death-do-us-part wife couldn't figure out any possible way to go on living without sweet little Amanda, so she gave up trying.

Please, Amanda, smile for me one more time . . .

"Goddammit!" Mo bellowed, his voice echoing. "Oh shit—hold on."

Officers appeared, then stood around, waiting for health care staff to complete the paperwork that lets an ambulance into the compound. Hey, good luck. Fucking convicts.

"He's gonna need state shoes to ride."

Too much smoke, too much heat.

Hospital now. "What—what happened to Metal?"

"Who?"

"Man, it hurts."

"Sure it does."

Eighteen days in seg and the swelling subsided, gashes closed, stitches grew out. His ear would never look right, and he couldn't quiet that incessant squeal on the left side, constant noise, worse when he buried his head in the scratchy blanket.

The door buzzed open. Officer Silvestri pushed a cart holding his big green duffel into the room. The matronly black woman always looked after her guys and seemed to take it personally when something happened that wasn't called for. "Ridin' you out tomorrow, sweetie. Need to fill out the property slip."

No keyboard, no cheap-ass Chinese television, no gym shoes—just a bag full of state issue, Granny's final letters, and paperwork, too much paperwork . . .

"What happened to Metal?" he asked her.

She leaned close, sharing a secret, a breach of security. "He's still listed OTH," she said. "Beats the worst."

OTH—*Out to Hospital.*

Fuse didn't sleep much that night. He hadn't slept much at all since it happened. Head hurt too much, heat still too much to bear.

The next afternoon he stood near the back exit of the health care office while they belly-chained and cuffed him. Some prisoner barely out of his teens came in from another joint, belly chain and cuffs. He took the youngster's place in the transport van, one out, one in, then closed his eyes while they loaded property in the back.

"Run these boxes back to Mound," someone said, so instead of heading down Ryan Road they circled back between the fence and the railroad tracks. The driver stopped and rolled down his window to spend too long chatting with an officer patrolling the perimeter. The train crossed Ryan Road and pulled alongside them, Fuse's only close-up, his last chance to watch the daily ritual, take one, leave one.

Maybe Fuse would eventually find Metal out in the world—even Reggie too. They might very well rediscover the places they'd conjured together that one time in a converted storage room off the prison gym when fences stopped mattering. Probably not, though "What Could Have Been" is many a prisoner's only song.

But he would never see Mo again.

He would never be allowed to visit him, certainly never have a chance to play music with him. Fuse's instrument had disappeared, but at least Mo made sure his charts got packed. Good lookin' out.

Something got added too, for there in the duffel bag patiently waited a tattered blue folder, photocopies of a natural lifer's most personal songs, the page on top titled "LaTisha's Dance."

Fuse hoped someday to locate Mo's daughter, and he would never stop trying to remember Amanda's smile.

The train's mission complete, it crossed Ryan Road and faded into the 'hood.

As the van pulled away, Fuse turned for one last look, just to be sure.

Again, that old banged-up black tanker car got left behind.

FOXHOLE

BY B.M. DOLARMAN

Oklahoma State Penitentiary (McAlester, Oklahoma)

"Silverfox, pack up!"

Looks like I will be spending some time in the hole. Again. Edward Silverfox. Number 202859. Long-term resident of Oklahoma State Penitentiary. I remember the first time I set eyes on it. Eighteen years old, squinting up at it from a transport bus known as the "Green Lizard," acid in my throat, I thought, *This is it. Welcome to your future.* As the Lizard inched its way through the double gates of the east entrance, the whitewashed stone walls of my new residence rose up before me in warning. I mouthed the words "Dracula's castle" as we off-loaded inside the seemingly ancient, tower-guarded complex.

We were then led into the facility's common laundry site, where I was issued clothing and bed linens—two pairs each of boxers, socks, and pants; two white T-shirts; two dress shirts, two sheets; one towel; one pillowcase (no pillow); and one blanket—all inside a mesh laundry bag. My first experience with wearing used, preworn (by whom?) Skivvies had been in the county jail while awaiting trial. After checking out my linens, it occurred to me that I would be wearing someone else's underwear for the foreseeable future.

Leaving the laundry, another Native American dude and I were then escorted through another fence and delivered to another building, G-unit, or the "rock," where I was placed in the smallest single-man cell in which I've ever done time (to date). The depth of the cell was about eight feet, but the width . . . well, I could extend my arms out from each side and simultaneously touch both walls. Per correctional policy, I remained locked down there for seventy-two hours—no showers, no rec time.

Once allowed out of my cell, I was overwhelmed by the diversity of the population. I marveled that a place like this could exist right smack in the belly of a mostly white farming community. While the place was diverse, it was also very segregated, cliqued up. The blacks stayed with the blacks, though some were 107 Hoover Crips, some were Neighborhood Crips, some Red Mob (Bloods). There were the Gangster Disciples, who were whites and some Latinos. There was Old Grove. There was the Universal Aryan Brotherhood or UABs. There were a few of us Native Americans and even a couple of guys who didn't really seem to fit in anywhere.

I remember Madonna's "Material Girl" coming out of a radio as I walked through the halls. Dudes were playing poker, watching TV, kicking it in groups, waiting on the phone, or waiting on the shower. I learned that rec time would be longer on some days and shorter on others, depending on which officers were working. Some of those guards were real pricks, bringing their frustrations or personal problems to work and taking them out on inmates. I hated the rock, to say the least, and I hardly spoke to anyone. And I didn't know what to expect. I had heard stories about prison rape, and so I wanted to stay on my guard—whatever that means. *Do I just keep sitting on my ass, or what?* I had to shower, and although it was a single shower, there was only a half of a wall around it with cells right alongside. Privacy while shitting or showering isn't something a person should take for granted.

As bad as the rock was, I know now that the hole is worse. Back then I would have done anything to get out of G-unit, so when the opportunity came to move to I-unit, I volunteered. All of the other inmates told me how wild it was over there and how inmates were always getting stabbed up on I-unit. *It's gotta be better than this shit. Fuck it.*

I-unit was located under the gym and was "open dorm" (no cells). Ninety or so inmates called the place home, with its five rows of bunks and its smell—like cat piss or something, but sweet. Candied cat piss. The first and last rows were bunk beds, and the three rows between them were single beds. The rows were referred to as streets: First Street, Second Street— you get the idea. I was assigned to a bunk above a black guy who was a for-real, no-shit African. He went by the name Mac, and he worked in the kitchen. We eventually started to kick it some, and he would look out for me by bringing an extra sandwich from the kitchen sometimes. Mac had a thick accent, and you had to listen to him real close to understand. He seemed to be a good, genuine dude.

A couple of days after my arrival on I-unit I was pulled out for orientation. It was held in the gym, and I received a rule book for the facility and another pamphlet, which really struck me at the time and has stayed with me since. I was told that drugs were discouraged at this facility, but that if I was using, I needed to read the pamphlet. It had the expected stuff about HIV/AIDS, and it also had a diagram with directions on how to bleach out a syringe. *Holy shit. How fucked is this facility if they're like, "To hell with it! At least clean your shit right!"* Just one of those things I've never forgotten.

Hace hici-mokkeye. Creek Indian term for marijuana joint. Literally, it translates to "drunken cigarette." After a few weeks on I-unit, another Native who went by the name Vic

Smooth asked me if I fucked with it. I said I did. Vic gave me a joint, which we then smoked together. He said, "I notice you've been getting visits," and asked me who I had coming up to see me. I told him it was my mom and my wife. Vic nodded a knowing nod and asked, "They don't be gettin' down?" I told him that they hadn't, and asked him how difficult it was to get drugs in through visits. Vic said, "Ain't shit," and ran it all down for me.

So, at my next visit I ran it all down for my mother. "Mom, check it out. You know, I'm trying to smoke some weed to chill my ass out. I need you bring me some."

"Jesus. How?"

I told her to get the weed and take out the seeds and stems, and then to buy some little water balloons and fill two or three of them with weed. "Cut a hole in the bottom of your pocket, that way you can put the balloons in your panties, and when you go to get a snack for me, you stick your hand in your pocket and reach across your panties and grab the balloons. That way, it looks like you're digging for change."

"And then?"

"Keep the balloons in your hand. Microwave my sandwich, and grab some napkins. Come back to the table. Let me finish my sandwich, and while I'm doing that, put the balloons in a napkin and wad them up."

"I don't know about this."

"While you're doing that, I'll be wiping my mouth with other napkins and wadding them up, placing them on the table. You'll set your napkin next to mine, and when I finish the sandwich, I'll grab all the trash to throw away in the can. I'll palm your napkin in the process, see? Then I'll fish the balloons out of the napkin and keep them in my hand."

"Yeah, but what then? Geez, Ed. You can't just carry that

stuff back in. How are you going to hide the balloons once you get them in your hand?" My mom had that look of half concerned disappointment, half brokenheartedness, which I had seen before whenever I'd been in trouble growing up. I also could see that she was going to do whatever I asked. My mom raised me with no help at all from anyone, and she really tried to do her best by me. But I was her baby, and she just didn't have it in her to say no in what she perceived was my hour of need.

"Just listen, okay? You get me some peanut M&Ms. I'll eat a handful, and when I get to the last few in the bag, I'll pour them in my hand with the balloons and slap them all in my mouth at once. I'll work the balloons under my tongue. Then I'll chew up the M&Ms, swallow them, and swallow the balloons right behind them. That's the plan."

The first time we tried it, which was a couple of weeks later, it worked perfectly. I got back to my bunk, then hit the bathroom and started trying to throw up the balloons. The initial part of the process had been worrisome, but this was definitely the most difficult part of the operation. I remember I couldn't get them to come up. I tried everything. I even drank a shampoo mixture in an attempt to make myself sick. Didn't work. I used a toothbrush to gag myself and only managed to bust vessels in my eyes from straining so hard.

On to plan B—catch them coming out the other end, if they didn't get eaten up by my stomach acids. I think it took me about two days of digging through my own shit to finally get the balloons back, but I did it. It was a lot of work for just short of seven grams of Oklahoma homegrown. So Vic and I smoked a fat joint, and I gave him another for schooling me on what I'd needed to know. *Hace hici-mokkeye*. It sure made I-unit seem like a better place. Compared to the rock, I-unit didn't seem so bad, but I wasn't destined to stay there much longer.

I had met this dude we called Black Bean. He was a black guy, and his mama had named him Bert. Bert Smalley. How he got the name Black Bean, I don't know. That's what he was called though, and I had been kind of kickin' it with him and some of his dudes, shooting hoops and playing spades. So one day, Vic and I had smoked a big joint. We got stupid high, and I was cheesing my ass off. I got real hungry too. Later that night, Bean had looked out for me by giving me a bag of coffee and a rack of cookies. A dude's got to be real careful what he accepts in prison from another inmate. No matter how innocent it may seem, you just can never fucking tell. So I told Bean that I was straight, that I had money on the way, and that I didn't want to owe anyone shit.

He was like, "Come on, homey! It ain't even like that. You don't owe me shit. I'm giving you this shit, not storing it to you!" (Storing is a practice in prison in which a guy loans someone something for that same item plus fifty percent back.)

So I was like, "Cool. Good looking out."

A few nights later, I was playing cards with Bean and he asked me if I wanted some coke. I asked him how much it was, and he told that would depend on how much I wanted. I said my money would be showing up in a day or two and that I might want to get a little bit. I'd had a meth habit, and I had shot coke before, so I figured I would do a little, since talking about it had me jonesing anyway.

We were on Fifth Street, and he had blankets hanging off the top bunk to give a little bit of privacy. I was wondering as I sat there where I would get an outfit (syringe), when Bean reached down in his sock and pulled out a bundle of what looked like yellowish-tan rocks.

"What the fuck is that?"

"Coke!"

"Man, I'm not an idiot. I know what coke looks like." (Obviously, I *was* an idiot, because I hadn't known what crack cocaine looked like.)

"Trust me. It's coke." He told me to stick my tongue to a small piece, and to my surprise, my tongue became numb where it had touched the stuff. Now, I'm from the woods, and I had never smoked crack or even seen it before, so yeah, I was suspicious. I asked Bean how in the hell I was supposed to shoot a fucking rock.

"Just smoke the shit. Peep game. You's my dude, so this is what's up. We'll smoke a couple of dubs together. I'll show you how to smoke them, and if you like it, I'll sell you some. If not, then you don't owe me shit. Cool?"

Shit, you already know I was all-in on that deal. Bean pulled out a piece of antenna he had stashed from a GE Superadio III and started to put a bit of Brillo pad down inside it. I was fascinated, wide-eyed. He had something taped or wrapped around the end that he told me was the part I'd put my mouth on. He put a piece of crack inside the antenna and lit it just enough that it would, as Bean said, "stay put." Then he began heating it as he spun the antenna and inhaled the smoke. He held his breath and his nose and sat there for a second before exhaling.

He repeated that same process until the whole rock was cashed, and then handed the antenna to me. I grabbed the silver part. It was hotter than shit, so I dropped it like a dumbass, looking real stupid. Bean gave a little snort, and just nodded toward the floor. I picked it up, and then mimicked what I'd seen him do. Almost instantly, shit changed. I felt like I could see farther, hear better, and that all of my senses were really clicking. I finished the two dubs with Bean and felt like I needed to move around. He told me to enjoy it and to let him know what I thought about it later, so I split.

I remembered the smell, the sweet, sickly smell from when I first came to I-unit. It turned out that the smell was crack. Every day is a lesson in prison, just not the kind of lesson that folks want kids to learn.

The next morning, while I was taking a shower, Bean walked in and asked me what I thought about the crack. I told him it wasn't for me and that the shit had me paranoid and trippin' for real. I told him that while I was on it, everyone seemed to be acting like some straight creeps.

"Yeah, shit be like that sometimes."

I told him I was cool with that, and as I was washing the soap out of my face, I thought I heard him say, "Mmmmmm."

"What?"

Bean stepped back casually. "That's cool."

I thought I had been trippin' again, so I let it go. I finished my shower and got dressed. When I returned to my bunk, Mac had some sandwiches and a couple of boiled eggs for me. They were right on time. I felt famished. I'd worked out that day with Vic, who had seen me looking real bug-eyed and suspicious the night before. He talked shit and joked about how I'd looked.

I finished my day by shooting a few hoops with Bean. Before we left the gym, he said, "After you get done showering, swing by and we'll play some cards or something."

"Cool."

I was taking a dump a little later and had that odd sensation you get when you feel someone is watching, staring at you. I glanced up and saw Bean just standing there.

I said, "What's up?"

"Nothing. Just checking to see if you was ready."

"Nah, going to hit the shower after this and then I'll hol-ler at ya." He said that was cool and then split. Couldn't even shit in peace.

After my shower, I went to Bean's bunk, and he was the only one there. I sat in a chair, and he told me that the dudes had backed out of the card game but that we could still chill. I said that was all right with me. We bullshitted for a bit and then this young mixed kid, probably my age, came and sat down next to Bean. The kid didn't say a thing, just sat there, eyes cast downward with his hands in his lap. Bean turned toward the kid and said, "Put your leg over mine and give me a kiss."

I thought my hearing stuttered! Can hearing stutter? The kid glanced nervously at me, and then Bean told him to quit acting "brand new" and said, "Silverfox don't care."

Let's pause this for a second so I can catch you up. When I first went into prison, I didn't like gays. I guess I was what they call "homophobic." Extremely. I had never been around it, so I guess that's where the phobia part came from. I no longer feel the same way, but back then, the idea of a man being with another man in that way was disgusting to me. So anyway, I shrugged like it was of no significance to me, like I'd seen it every day, even though my teeth were set on edge, for real. So the mixed kid kissed Bean square on the mouth, tongue and all. Wow! I was definitely speechless. I mumbled that I had something to take care of and split pretty soon.

A few days later, Bean asked me if I was down to play some cards. I tried to keep it cool, like none of what had happened the other day had bothered me, so I said, "Yeah." We played spades for a few hours and smoked some cigs. After the game everyone left and Bean and I were chilling and listening to his radio.

"You know I'm in love with you, Little Daddy." Now, I hoped my ears were just clumsy, 'cause my hearing sure seemed to be trippin'.

"What?"

And this fool said the same shit! Bean's voice reminded me of the rapper Tone Loc, balding, missing a front tooth. I immediately flashed back to him walking in while I had been showering—while I had been shitting! The dude had been stalking me like a lion stalking a zebra, only with words and "friendship."

"I'm in love with you, Little Daddy."

I snapped back to reality and stuttered, "L-look, I got a wife, dawg." Bean said that he had a wife too. I told him, "Look, I'm not gay!" He said he wasn't either. He told me he was bisexual. I remembered what I had heard on a stand-up comedy routine by Andrew Dice Clay and I said, "You either suck dick or you don't."

Bean got a little salty over my joke (though I was hardly joking at the time) and began to tell me how he had been comforting a lot of these so-called straight dudes. He also told me to stay up late that night to watch all the guys who would sneak into his bunk. He told me about a white boy I knew, who always fronted like he was a hard-ass peckerwood—Willy Geegs. He told me how Willy would come and get dope from him and let Bean suck his dick and fuck him. Bean said that when they were done, Willy would go straight to the bathroom to shit out Bean's "kids" and to wipe the grease off his ass. I started to feel a little queasy. Bean reached down and pulled a small bag of rocks out of his sock and counted out seven of them. He told me I could have them if I would just let him suck my dick.

"What the fuck!"

He then showed me a slip from the inmate trust office showing that he had a little over nine hundred dollars on his books. He was very persistent, bordering on desperate. I finally found my legs and got up to leave.

Bean said to my back as I was walking away, "Stay up tonight and watch. You'll see."

I took myself straight to Vic's bunk, and told him what had gone down with Bean. Vic spat into a paper cup and nodded, seemingly unimpressed, unsurprised. "Yeah. Bean's a buzzard."

I had heard the term "buzzard" and knew it to mean a gay man who would prey on young kids when they came into prison.

"I thought you knew."

"Hell no! How would I know?

"Seven stones *and* suck your dick? Pretty good deal."

I looked at Vic all crazylike. He started to laugh. "Damn, dude." And I laughed too.

That night I stayed awake and watched from my top bunk to Bean's bottom bunk all the way across the dorm. I saw dudes going in and out, but none stayed very long. Then later in the night—early morning, I guess—I saw Willy G. creep over there. I couldn't tell you exactly how much time Willy spent in there with Bean, but it was at least two to three times longer than anyone else. When Willy came out, I watched him walk directly to the toilets, where he disappeared behind the wall. I looked back toward Bean's bunk. He was standing up and smiling at me as if to say, *I told you. This is prison, Silverfox.*

I avoided Bean after that. No more basketball. No more spades. Definitely no more kickin' it. I spent more of my time with Vic. Sometimes I would chop it up with Mac. I was starting to get more drugs more often, and I had been doing a little business along those lines. I began to read a little. I never really got into books before, but I preferred them to the television. There was never anything on I wanted to watch. All these bad-ass dudes in here for violent crimes. Gangsters. And they all watched *General Hospital*.

One evening, I was headed back to my bunk after working out, and Vic rolled up on me. "Listen, Fox. I need to holler at you."

"What's up?"

"Not here. Let's take a walk." We strolled out toward the wall and Vic told me how he had heard that Bean had been running his mouth around the unit, talking about how he was gonna fuck me before I left the facility. I asked Vic what I should do about it. Vic paused, rubbed his chin, and said, "We gotta deal with this. You got no choice here. You gotta stab him. Do it while he's in the shower. I'll post up outside the area to make sure no one else comes in. You slip in and stab him. Just like that."

Just like that. Just like that, I had found myself in what one could call a "situation." Bean was from Red Mob. They were a Blood gang. Vic and I had to have our shit together or this little plan of ours would cause real trouble, probably not just for me, but also for the Warrior clique Vic ran with. It was clear from what I had learned in prison already that if I didn't deal with Bean, I could find myself a target of all kinds of unpleasantness. (I would later learn that Warriors had beef with Red Mob. My situation was a convenient one for Vic and his clique. I guess I never questioned Vic's motive in anything.)

The next day, Vic brought me a knife. I began to wait. I grew more nervous by the minute. I found myself on the toilet, shitting my guts out. It felt like they had turned to water. After I had finished, I was washing up when Vic found me. "Come on. Bean's in the shower."

I dried my hands, slipped my crude blade (a sharpened-up old butter knife) into my pocket, and walked back to the shower. Vic posted up at the door and nodded the go-ahead. My brain was buzzing. There was no time to think about it now. Vic whispered, "Handle this shit."

I pulled the knife out and put the lifeline around my wrist. The knife had a bit of twine attached to it in a loop. Vic had told me to put the loop around my wrist so that I couldn't drop the knife. I headed into the shower and caught a bit of a lucky break, I guess, because Bean had just soaped up his face. I walked up behind him, stabbed him in the back, and at the same time grabbed him around his neck. Bean tried to spin in my grasp, as I continued to stab him over and over.

I walked away as he fell to the floor. I wasn't sure if he was alive or dead. I didn't have any idea how many times I had stabbed him. I put the knife back in my pocket and rinsed myself off as best I could, then returned to Vic's bunk, changed clothes, and gave the knife and bloody clothes to Vic to dispose of. Again, I waited. I was waiting to see if Bean would be discovered. I was waiting to see if anyone would snitch me off. I was waiting to see if Bean was dead or alive. The waiting is always the worst in anything, I think.

Bean was discovered by another inmate fairly quickly because he was still alive and was making noises—moaning and stuff. Of course, someone told on me. Whether it was Bean or one of his homeys, I will never know. But I was sent to the hole and reclassified as a maximum-security inmate. I wish I could go back to being that naïve kid who didn't know what to expect in the hole. Knowing just makes the dread of going back there so much greater. Shit, they'll probably be here any minute.

Anyway, back then I was just a kid. I remember being walked to the H-unit, cuffed and shackled, and actually feeling impressed by the site. H-unit was underground, built into the side of a hill. All that was visible was the front of the building, set into the hill, and a skylight, about six inches wide, running all the way around the hill. The cells in H-unit were arranged in a circle and in two tiers. The bottom tier held cells A–L. The upper tier consisted of cells AA–LL. The cells at the ends of both the upper and lower tiers were supermax cells. I was placed in the supermax cell on the lower tier. Cell L. The supermax cell has one door which you step through, and then another which opens to the interior of the cell. There, an inmate is kept behind two locked doors, whereas all the other cells have one locking door. The doors are heavy, solid. The bars on H block were as big as my wrist. They were all over the entire pod, and they covered the skylight. I would soon learn that on H block, there is zero inmate-to-officer contact. There's always a slider with those huge bars or a heavy solid door between inmates and officers. The solid doors have a "beanhole" near the bottom—a steel flap that opens with a key where a food tray can be passed into the cell. The officers also cuff and shackle the inmates through the beanhole before taking them out for rec or shower. H block is twenty-three-hour-a-day lockdown. Ha. Some days it's twenty-four hours straight. Sometimes it's a week at a time. The unit gets locked down for all kinds of reasons.

I spent my nineteenth and twentieth birthdays in that cell. I realized during that time that prison is the place where a man's dignity goes to die. If you wanted to recreate it, to feel what it might be like, you could move into your broom closet. Give the key to the guy who was the biggest bully at your school. Have him feed you only cheap, starchy, flavorless food. Only take a shit in full view of strangers. Never mind. There's no way to recreate it. You can't. You would never be able to fully account for all of the factors that make it miserable. Once you're on H block, there are no more contact visits. You can't hug or be hugged by any of the few people in the world who give a shit about you.

I remember during those two years that things grew steadily worse every day. It was as if the staff of the unit had regular meetings to brainstorm about more ways to fuck over the inmates. *Calling to order our monthly meeting. It has been noted in the minutes from our last meeting that prison isn't quite awful enough, terrifying enough. Anyone have any motions to present? Any ideas how we can make this prison worse?*

It used to be that rec time (irregularly given, no guarantee) was multiple cells on the ball court at once. We could play a good game. It was during those times that I almost felt human, real. I would chop it up with some of the other guys. We still had our conflicts, but damn. It was all right, ya know? We would play ball for a while and grab a quick shower. Maybe use the phone. Eventually, this officer named De Soto came through and flattened all the basketballs. Even then, we would get together and play cards or dominoes. Then another guard—Hudson was his name—took a bunch of the dominoes out of the set and tore up some of the cards. We didn't even have a full deck to play with, so we made up our own games.

Eventually they started running single-cell rec time. That meant that you could go with your cellie, if you had one. I was now supermax and single-celled, so I went to rec time alone. I started exercising during those times. At least I could stretch out a bit and move around. Isolation is a creeping kind of torture. At first I thought I would be okay. I read. I listened to music. After a while, I realized that I would probably rather die. Not sure though. Never been dead before. I can tell you, however, that it's no vacation getaway like people make it out to be on the TV.

So I guess someone must have brought up how having rec at a *reasonable* time was not a good way to make prison *worse*. So they started taking me to rec time at one o'clock in the morning. During the winter it was so damn cold and dark that I often declined to go. I began to smell bad from not shower-ing so much. I lived in an underground prison with no natural light. I was kept in a dark cell for most of the day. The tiny bit of natural light I could feel on my skin during daytime rec had now been taken away. Worse, indeed.

During the summer months, they were always working on the air-conditioning unit. It was hot. Sweltering. Sweat would run all down my face and down my back to the crack of my ass. Too hot to sleep. I'd have to wet my sheet at my little metal sink at night and hope that I would fall asleep before it dried. If it did, I would have to get up and wet it again. The cooling unit never really seemed to be up and running except, as if by some magic, on days when a tour came through or on days when the facility was having an execution.

Oh yeah. I forgot to mention: I was on H block West. H block South was death row. On days that they planned to kill one of them dudes, you could hear the men on H-South singing some kind of song all the way over on H-West. I could never make out the words, but it was the most mournful sound my ears have ever heard. In the days preceding an execution, they would clean the facility up real nice. Buff the floors. Get the AC running. The floors in the place were painted a dull battleship gray with some kind of real shiny clear coat on top. Buffed to a high gloss. Like a polished turd. I felt I was being squeezed ever tighter and tighter and that before long I would cease to breathe.

I'm still breathing, I guess. After those two years on H block, though, I never really bounced back. Once I got out of there, I was moved to a regular unit. I got contact visits, so I started up selling drugs around again. I figured out that if I ate a can of chili and drank a bunch of water before my visits in which I would swallow drug-filled balloons, it would be easier to puke 'em up later. I guess the grease from the chili made a kind of barrier over which the rest of my stomach contents would sort of float. I started bringing in meth too. That was what the people wanted, really. There was money to be made.

I carried on like that for several years, like a zombie or a dude on inmate autopilot. My wife divorced me when I was on H block. I guess she found a better deal. I started writing letters to a pretty girl named Jewel—a cousin of an old friend—a few months ago. And she wrote me back. She even came to visit me a few times. I'm sure I won't meet her again, seeing as how I am about to go back to the hole. Seems like everything there is waste and death. I don't think she could save me from all that anyway. My skin has become so pale, ain't nobody able to tell I'm a Native. Somewhere along the line, my hair turned silver. And now I get to go back to the hole, seeing as how I've killed a man. Once my case gets through the courts, you'll probably be able to find me on H block. By that time, I'll be on the other side of it. *Worse.* Someday, they'll be singing for me.

THERE WILL BE SEEDS FOR NEXT YEAR

BY ZEKE CALIGIURI

Minnesota Correctional Facility, Stillwater (Bayport, Minnesota)

T hings were different after I came back from the hospital. It wasn't just me, though; it felt like the whole joint was tilting. The night I got back, Little Bug lit a garbage can on fire. Everyone was yelling about a memo, what was being taken, what we should do about it. It was hard to process. I had already been here almost eighteen years and I thought I'd finally escaped all of what this place was.

A few years into my life sentence, an old-school crook told me that buildings are moody the way people are moody. "They have a history they can't escape, until they crumble. Sometimes these walls are depressed, sometimes they're happy and warm, and sometimes they're wicked and spiteful." I didn't understand it then. But after so many years, I think I have it sort of figured out.

I came back to familiar faces that didn't know me anymore. I was a different person with bandages on my wrists and a softened face that scared *me* enough to turn my mirror backward. I didn't do it for attention. I really *did* want to die. I didn't want to fail and come back to my life sentence and curious expressions from everyone else in the unit. Even Slick, who I went back to ninth grade with, took a few days to come holler at me. "That's pretty nuts, Clyde."

"Yeah, well, I'm no longer coming of age like when I got

here. I *am* of age. Of the age to be able to decide if this is what I want for the rest of my life."

He walked away after that.

The rest of the people who came to talk to me were not my friends. They were from the fringe—would-be predators who probably smelled something. It didn't scare me or anything, the pure predator seems a dying breed. Now they are mostly watered-down hybrids of punks and snitches, mixed with the classic features of blood and lust. When I got my property, I could smell it. Blood has a certain scent, something visceral and distinct, especially your own because it has a story you know. It was all over everything, even the notebook I'm writing this in.

I don't remember much past preparation. Standing over the sink. The razor. The first cut and the dig, the saw, the tangle of wires just under the skin, the mush of my wrist. The pink aura and the cool over my face. The other wrist, trying to gnaw just as deep, not deep enough. I remember the pain, fright that made me want to go back to before—so great as to want someone to come and undo this. My hands convulsed as though detached from me. The red mineral spouting from me might as well have been from the center of the earth. Smudges of red on my cheek—I looked at the mirror to see if it said I was ready. Instead I saw someone I would probably never see again, a face being erased, with a name and a story that didn't matter anymore. It was a mess, the last mess I would ever make of myself. I chased images of my life. My mom and dad, the alleyways in Minneapolis, from shooting basketballs to bullets. A hug from my best friend Sonny with tubes connected everywhere in her body. But the images ran from me, the backs of their heads retreating. I wanted to know why, but I couldn't get their attention.

The looks are what I remember—the pink hue wrapped around those wide, strangled, and brooding stares, uniform and collective along the walls. I didn't recognize anybody, I only saw doom in those eyes, like they weren't really people, just images. It wasn't until afterward that my therapist told me people rarely succeed when they cut their wrists. The body goes into a protection mode to save its vital organs. It mostly just *looks* dramatic, and I got these bracelets of scar tissue to say I tried, to say I was a little nuts, to say I was on fire.

Spring

They were strange times at Stillwater, the walled-in fortress of buildings sitting on the Minnesota side of the St. Croix River. We never saw the water, though, except for chance glances from the top floor of one of the old twine factories. They say the whole joint is haunted by all the souls that have gotten trapped here after they died. For almost a hundred years it has been a depository for souls trapped under the wheel. From all of our unanswered echoes, sometimes it feels like we are already ghosts, or on our way to becoming. Every once in a while there are people here from the historical society, taking pictures of the old Georgian colonial-style buildings, whose limestone has been decaying for decades. They don't visit to take pictures of *us*.

May came, but with a bite hiding under a deceptively blue sky. It wanted to be spring, but winter had been particularly stubborn this year. Another garbage can got lit on fire in one of the blocks. It annoyed most of us. Youngsters did it to amuse themselves. It wasn't just garbage cans, it was their drawers, their sheets, T-shirts, bundles of paper. The alarms went off and we'd get escorted to the hallway, or the yard, while it only took thirty seconds to extinguish the flames. They would take a couple of guys to the hole, never older than twenty-one or twenty-two, and that would be it. The administration never made a big deal out of it; they said they were just childish acts and no real threat. The old-timers just thought it was stupid.

We got locked down during a visit from the commissioner, the governor, and some kind of federal prison auditor. The visit was coupled with another memo listing a series of new policies. It made a lot of guys tense up, believing the prison could never go back to the way it used to be. I usually liked lockdowns, but this one gave me food poisoning and a throb over my right eye for three days. I was getting my sense of smell back after the incident, and I was particularly stung by the stench of rotten milk and the sweat and ass of unwashed bodies. There was an old man underneath me who ranted to himself, shouting, "The end of the world is coming!" Guys yelled at him to shut the fuck up, but he couldn't hear them over the voices in his own head.

I had to view the first really nice days of spring through a checkerboard of glass and fiberglass windows put in when the convicts broke nine hundred out in '83. I worked on the yard crew and we were supposed to be planting. Instead, we were locked in our boxes collecting the stink from bags of garbage. Men who were kids when I came here, laughing and playing grown-up, dumped my drawers into garbage bags. I was over my book limit, so I had to make a choice between *The Brothers Karamazov* and *The Count of Monte Cristo*. It was like giving away members of my family.

My only relief was going back to work. We basically lived in a hallway that attached to everything: cellblocks, chapel, gym, yard, school, chow. When they built this place they called it a "telephone pole" prison, because it connected everything through that single corridor. It was supposed to be innovative a hundred years ago. Now it was just the hallway where I followed the parade of sleepwalking zombies in boots and blue shirts, blue coats and orange caps, on their way to the factories. I was revived by fresh, cool air. For most of the year we lived under indecisive clouds—unsure of rain, unsure whether to stay or leave. I had been without sun for so long, my grill was pasty white and nasty. I'm usually pale, though, except for a couple months in summer, but I wear raccoon eyes all year round. I used to tell people the dark circles are from the pain, now I don't bother.

Our crew planted thousands of flowers and shrubs in landscaped plots against backdrops of dark old buildings with rows of squawking black crows lined up along the gutters. Every day I could look around at what this place had become—more fences, more rows of razor wire. There used to be flowers everywhere, the old infirmary building on the hill was covered with ivy and trees towering overhead. There even used to be a greenhouse within the walls, where they planted seeds for the next spring.

There used to be a lot of things, but now we had to fight to hold onto the few spaces we had left. I did most of the planting. One of the guys I worked with was an enormous black man from Mississippi who said if it was up to him, he would just lay concrete over the top of the gardens so he wouldn't have to water them every day. The other guy I worked with was a seventy-year-old, mostly unknown serial killer who didn't like to plant because of a bad back he got from his days dressing up like a woman and murdering people. I was just trying to slow the coming of an inevitable concrete wasteland. I came to understand that once things left, they didn't come back.

I dragged my untied boots through the gravel, kicking up

pebbles and dust. The blisters on my heels had mostly healed in my time off. The flock of pigeons that lived here scattered toward the old, unused coal chutes they'd made their home. I always wondered how pigeons found prisons. I see pictures of prison yards everywhere with flocks of roof rats covering the ground. Beds of red and white roses blossomed right next to the large slab of concrete abstractly painted by their feces. I wondered if they knew they were in prison, or if they were just hiding from the hawk perched on the electrical lines outside the wall.

The shop was already alive when I got there, but the wall blocked the morning sun, so it still felt like winter inside. Sawdust from the table saw danced pirouettes in the air; the welder was at work, blue flame hissing. I tried to see everything. I tried because everything has edges and people are never ready for the poke or the slice that might change their minds. I'm not even talking about from other people, I mean the edges of everything here: the dirty corners, the heavy steel tables, the slag on unsanded metal, the black mold I knew hid on the other side of the old sheetrock. In an area full of edges and blunt corners, everything was either hard or sharp. I had nicks that turned to scars all over my body from missing something I should have seen coming.

The serial killer and the enormous black man from Mississippi were talking about something in the office when I came in. Eyes turned to me for a second and they went silent. I didn't say anything to either of them, just dug around in my locker for gloves. My legs were still a bit wobbly, not used to walking on earth. And I was a little awkward starting to talk again. I was tired of explaining myself to people, and didn't feel like starting in on the recurring dream I was having before I woke up, of the serial killer coming up behind me as a shadow and clubbing me in the head with a shovel.

They were already sipping coffee that usually tasted like hot water and stale cigarette butts. The serial killer had an unusually wry smile on his face. Normally this early it was all disgust and malice in his grill. It felt like he was smiling because he knew he had just been the shadow with the shovel in my dream. He wasn't physically frightening in any way, just an older white-haired man with a hump on his back who should be someone's grandpa, still slinging dirt and holding grudges. He was excited about a show he saw on combustible engines, which made sense because his secondary vocation (after killing people) was as an engineer.

The man from Mississippi didn't talk much. He communicated mostly in nods and spooky, bloodshot stares from a face without wasted smiles. He was dark—get-lost-in-the-shadows dark—and enormous, like he could carry trucks on his back, with humongous hands that could choke a bear. He walked in patient, deliberate strides with a cup of coffee wherever he went. Even if he was chopping trees, or mowing, there was a Styrofoam cup by him collecting dust or small chips of wood. I knew, though, that his looks were probably mostly just wrinkled expressions of pain. Any real malice he had must've been locked in a tight chamber behind those stares.

"I hope the world does end," Mississippi muttered.

Serial Killer chimed in: "I'll tell you one thing: if you see me anywhere and I have another heart attack, or I'm slumped over somewhere—don't you dare revive me. Don't get help, just leave me." It wasn't the first time he'd told us this, and nobody in the room ever seemed to have a problem with his request.

I laughed a little. A simple chuckle came from Mississippi's mouth, then the cup of coffee went right back to his lips.

Serial Killer turned in my direction and, without prompt, told me: "I would have done what you did, if I wasn't such a pussy."

I gave him a plain nod and we were good.

I finished planting a bed of petunias in a plot right next to the guard shack. This was my meditation time, when I could be alone in my mind under the last two trees in the joint. I thought about my friend Sonny, before the leukemia. She was always in the garden. We'd had to chop down all the other trees a few years earlier to make space for the new segregation unit. It left an open field for the sun to burn the grass to cinders.

After lunch, we returned to work in the same procession of guys, coming back out to the dark factories on the sunny day. Some walked silent, personalities covered by the clouds lingering above. A boot flew off onto the asphalt, and two men, one spraying beads of sweat and blood from his long hair, fell into the freshly watered bed, uprooting and smashing a whole section. I just hoped the mace wouldn't taint the soil. I spent most of the afternoon with a hand shovel trying to bring the plants back to life.

I attended a group for guys trying to recover from traumatic events. The first time I went, a guard I've known for years raised an eyebrow when he saw the destination on my pass. There was another guard standing next to him in the rotunda with a German shepherd at his side, tail down, barking at anything. I think it was supposed to scare guys. I definitely wasn't scared, I mostly just felt sorry for it.

I think all the guys in the group had "attempts" too, but most didn't talk about them. Others wouldn't *stop* talking about them.

"Basically, this is hell," a mousy old heroin addict who

only showed up every few months told the group as I came in. There were seven other guys and the therapist sitting down when I got there.

"If it ain't, it's certainly one of its dimensions." There were always new guys. They would come once, dominate the conversation, and never return. Only the four of us came every month. There was Landon, who had spent twenty-two of his last twenty-six months in segregation before coming to the group. His dad played linebacker for the Vikings in the 1980s. It overshadowed his date-rape tendencies, and the fact that he was a blaster who would jack-off on the women staff. There was also Greg, a strangely overcomfortable man with a long, greasy ponytail and a mustache covering his harelip. He talked about himself as a Christlike figure, whose death was supposed to save the lives of the rest of us. His failure meant we were all doomed. He didn't ever discuss how he had doomed the two sons he molested.

I usually sat next to Rudy, a bald little white kid in oversized, underironed T-shirts, tinted beige. He had slash marks all over both arms, but not the same kind as mine. They teased him because his voice slurred, his hands trembled, and his teeth chattered. It might've been because of the dosage of lithium he took, or because before he got here, he was locked up at a place where they strapped him down and gave him shock treatments. He lived in the same block as I did but we didn't speak, though in group he was my ally. He had hung a sheet several times, but never followed through. I asked him why, and he told me: "I'm afraid of the noose, of suffocating." (They abolished the death penalty in Minnesota in 1911 because they fucked up while hanging a man named William Williams. The rope was too long and it took fourteen minutes to strangle him to death.)

Most of the guys in the group seemed way more gone than I was. Most of them were on varying dosages of lithium, I was not. My therapist tried several times to get me to take something, but I saw the other zombies. Being around them didn't stop me from wanting to die—instead, it just made me feel more alienated. But even if I didn't particularly like all of them, I related to them more than I wanted to. I couldn't be shocked by the extents they might go to—after all, I had the scars to show I could go to some wicked places myself. In their faces I saw an East Indian man I'd met in the county jail who tried to off himself by bashing his head against a steel sink. He could only do it for so long before the noise gave him away, or his neck got too tired and injured to keep going. I mostly remember the rage and fear in his purple and turquoise eyes as he jerked and flung in his cuffs.

Coming into the room it was hard to gauge individual moods. We were swept into personal tirades of whoever's mania was strongest that day. No matter what kind of topic the therapist presented.

"Lately I've been crying a lot. Is that strange? I mean, sometimes I'll be watching TV and a commercial will come on and I'll start crying, and I don't know why," a new guy told us.

An alarm went off just as we were released from the meeting, so we got stuck against the wall while guards ran full speed down the hall, handcuffs jangling, rubber-soled boots thudding, before they tackled the two guys in the main rotunda. The cloud of pepper spray misted, numbing my lips. Our eyes burned and our noses ran.

Summer

It got hot, really hot, where the heavy blue sky pressed down on me. Serial Killer, Mississippi, and I had been out in the nuclear sun replacing mulch in every last one of the mulch beds. The heat put extra rot to discarded milk and eggs in the dumpsters, and the crows stalked leftovers in the bins waiting to be picked up by the pig farmers. It was the third morning in a row I'd found a pigeon in the grass with its head missing and its belly ripped open. They often stayed cooped up, hiding from that hawk. It was so hot, the asphalt melted the soles of our boots. Serial Killer had a stream of sweat dripping down his seventy-year-old nose that looked like a melting icicle at the tip.

Flowers wilted while weeds kept growing. There wasn't any air-conditioning in the cellblocks, so the whole prison was miserable; everyone slept in sweat-soaked sheets. Even the shadows were deadly, swallowed up by the heat and made into mirages. Most of the conversations I had were with people coming out of those shadows. They said something, then fell back into them. Guys would sit on the floor in their cells and make statements like: "The world really is gonna end." It would have been fine with me, but I knew we wouldn't be that lucky.

The hotter it would get, the greater the delirium. Guys walked the tiers and their lips moved, but they weren't speaking to anyone we could see. They had stories, names of individual souls that visited them on their tiers and in their dreams. People swore the spirit of a kid who killed himself ten years before was living in one of the showers. I used to believe them, but now I don't believe anything. The dreams I have are usually either Mississippi choking me with his enormous hands, or Serial Killer shoveling dirt over my head.

End-of-the-world hysteria was going full tilt. It wasn't just the group—the whole joint had gone apocalypse crazy. After setting off the metal detector and being asked to back through, a guy just stared the guard down—"It's the end of the world, what?" It was everywhere, it was included in greetings and leave-takings. It became comical, except to the people who were coming to rely on the cataclysmic ending to their suffering, like most of the guys in the group. I was kind of hoping for it too—but I knew it would end up just another disappointment.

There were more fires. Guys in the block across the hall set a bundle of towels and T-shirts aflame in their cells. On their way out in cuffs, one of them said: "Fuck it. It's the end of the world."

When it wasn't too hot, I still went to the yard to play basketball with Slick, until a chubby Mexican guy crossed the court without a shirt on and sat down to take a shit in the old bathroom shed right next to it. Me and Slick walked the track, with the big smokestack in the background that changed positions like an illusion. We passed by the push-up squads, and watched a pair of eagles gliding over the river. An itty-bitty woman walked the gangplanks in sunglasses carrying an assault rifle that looked heavier than her. We talked about all that had changed. It meant something different to him, he was going home. The old horseshoe tournaments, the time Old Green Eyes with the cane beat up the young nappy-headed kid on the bleachers—Slick remembered things I did not. I resolved it was because he made them up.

Rudy walked the track by himself, going the opposite way. I gave him a nod as he passed; he nodded too and put his head back down.

"What's up with dude's arms?" Slick asked me.

"He's fine," I told him.

Then he asked me again about *my* wrists. "What am I supposed to tell our people in the world, Clyde?"

"We still have people in the world? I never expected this would be my life and I don't consider this living."

He told me, "Shit, I knew I was coming. Since the fifth grade people been telling me I was coming here. My dad done broke out some of them windows. I used to come here in the '80s when they had banquets right here in the yard, family and all that."

Those days were definitely gone. I told him he could break as many windows as he wanted when he got out.

At the end of the yard period, when the bats started coming out of the old powerhouse chimney, Slick pointed toward the basketball courts: "Ain't that your boy?" A line of guards were running across the yard at somebody butt-ass naked who was yelling something. It was Landon, jogging in circles. It took them ten minutes to tire him out enough to catch him. "What happened to that dude?" Slick asked me.

"That's what I've been trying to tell you. This ain't no way to live."

That night they hit us with another memo, telling us that due to the costs incurred by all of the fires, there would be no holiday meal for the Fourth of July this year. With it came division—division and blame thrown at each other. Our side hated the youngsters for setting the fires; the youngsters hated us for being passive. Even the weirdos and the punks started throwing garbage around and slamming phones. The old walls were sweating under the heat. Guys were starting fights with each other just to go to the AC in segregation. Until the AC broke and they were stuck in the death chambers. People sat on their steel toilets and flushed them over and over to stay cool. Guys were trying to corral others to do something, but nobody had a clear "what."

My friend Melanie started coming around more. She used

to visit once a year, now it was every couple of months. She said it wasn't because of the marks on my arms, but I sensed it was. We shared Sonny, who had died a couple years before I got locked up. Sonny and Melanie were the kind of people who made the world better; I was not. I thought that if they could take Sonny away, and leave me, then there was something irreparable about the world. Melanie was the only person I still spoke to outside the walls. My mom told me she was tired of explaining to people that her son was in prison. Now she tells people she doesn't have a son. She's still my emergency contact, but she never even reached out to me after my incident.

The problem with Mel was I wanted to look at her shape, but she wanted to bring me to Jesus. A guy came in the visiting room one time with a book. "What's that he has in his hand?" she asked.

"A Bible."

"People can bring Bibles in here?"

"*You* can't," I told her.

She asked me why not. I told her that if she brought a Bible, I would walk out on her. There was enough Jesus in here already. Every book cart was stacked with Bibles and tracts. I thought we were good until I brought up all of the end-of-the-world stuff and she quoted a verse from Revelation. She squinted at me, crinkling the little scar on her right brow from when her dad hit her with his belt buckle when she was young. I guess she had scars all over her body that she just didn't talk about.

Those of us on higher tiers woke up dizzy and light-headed. We came back from work one day and a water main had broken, so we were stuck without plumbing in the middle of Minnesota's hottest summer. Guys fought over the last of the ice in the machine, most of it ended up on the floor. People fought until tears came to their eyes. Most didn't know why they fought. It didn't matter to the administration, they locked us down anyway. It only took a couple of hours before the whole place smelled like shit and piss.

In the cell I usually felt safe, insulated, but in the heat I lost breath. My fan wheezed heavy air at me, its motor had run for days in a row and simply swirled heat. With no water I was thirsty, and dizzy from the smell of baking urine. I lay on the floor, hoping it would be cooler, but it had absorbed too much of the heat. At first guys started to yell in the most base kind of logic, every woman was a whore or a cunt, every man was a bitch or a fag. It only lasted a few minutes until they were exhausted and overheated. Twenty minutes into the lockdown everything was still and silent. Even the old man's voice, riled up and quoting scripture, faded to a murmur. I panicked. I swore I had heatstroke. I wanted to holler something. I wanted to yell to send a wheelchair to take me to the air-conditioned infirmary, but several people had already beaten me to the idea; when I opened my mouth no sound came out.

I woke up on the floor bone-dry with a puddle of drool and sweat around me, two guards pounding at my bars. "Clyde! Clyde—you all right?"

I wasn't sure.

A fat one, sweating heavily and holding a bottle of water, said to me: "What's the matter, you take too many pills, Clyde? You're not trying to kill yourself again, are you, Clyde?"

Wounded, I just shook my head, and for some reason, probably shame, I couldn't tell them. They left, and once I realized where I was, I was stuck to panic again. I spent the

night shivering, and throwing up a radioactive green substance I didn't know was in my body. Without plumbing, guys
threw bags of piss and milk cartons of shit out of their cells
onto the flag. One guy set a bag of shit and shredded paper
on fire and threw it out onto the tiers. Then, sometime in the
early morning, toilets started flushing. By midafternoon they
let us out. It was a zoo. I could see then how quickly a block
could transform, people's natures could change.

The heat broke for a couple days, making a lot of guys
believe it was over. The sickness had run its course and moved
on, they said. But those of us who had been here long enough
knew the sickness was always there, dormant, picking its times
to infect us.

Soon it got hot again.

We went back to work, spraying Japanese beetles and
trimming weeds until I got sand in my teeth. I came back
to the shop for water one afternoon and caught an angle of
something moving in an unlit cubby. I was aware right away of
the gas, strong but mildly sweet. I took a glance and saw Serial
Killer bent at his knees, with one of the lawn mowers tilted
to its side, the gas cap off, draining into a small bottle he held
in his hand. He didn't notice me, so I played it off and left.
But he must've heard my footsteps because he straightened
up and came back out with the mower. "I accidentally filled
it with fifty-fifty. God, what a stupid old man." I didn't need
an explanation. He did weird things every day. Maybe he was
huffing it—guys did a lot of crazy shit to get high.

Me and Mississippi were resting in a shadow after watering flowers. He was telling me that back home they had pecan
trees which hung low enough for them to reach up and pick.

"You ate them right off the tree? Damn, you is country."

"Say, what's the old man doing?" He pointed his huge

finger at a group of shrubs the sparrows used for nests and the wasps made hives in. Serial Killer was underneath one, slumped over on his side, motionless.

"I don't know. You going over there to check on him?" I asked.

"Hey, man said leave him if we found him like that. I ain't fonna have him all mad at me for saving him. Let the police find him."

The old man had made the point clear many times. We watched the stooped old body lay there for a while, then finally wheeled our hose carts back to the shop again and left them under the shadows of the powerhouse. I was envious that time might release him without a noose or lots of blood. Thirty-five years just to go away in a pine box to the cemetery out back.

When we got back inside the shop, we sat down without a mention of it between us. We just anticipated someone would find him and commotion would begin. Instead, though, the door opened and there stood a ghost. A ghost of that ornery old man with a set of hand trimmers and mulch stuck to his clothes, babbling away about something or other.

"We thought you finally kicked it."

"Unfortunately not," he answered, wiping the sweat from his nose.

"You fall asleep?" Mississippi asked.

"Maybe I did."

Landon wasn't at the next group. Apparently he was strapped to the board back in segregation for blasting off on nurses when they came to bring him his dope. A couple of the guys were so proud to tell us their doomsday preparations. They had stockpiled bottled water and noodles. Rudy was in the corner with a hand holding up his face, shaking—part tremor, part disgust at the discussion. If the rest of the joint had end-of-the-world hysteria, this group was the nerve center for it.

We were all injured, the whole joint shared it. It seemed like every day we heard the damn dog barking and boots running into the unit for something. Every day guys were hauled out for something petty. People who hadn't been in trouble for years were getting jammed up. The whole water-main thing really broke me. Staff claimed they were just regaining control, while most of us never believed we had any control in the first place. I just wanted it to be over. Throughout most of our lives, we had gotten used to being told we were like animals in a zoo or a jungle. We got used to being the kind of animals that every day thought about devouring these people, that would devour each other if we starved enough, or even ourselves if it got bad enough. It felt like that's where we were headed. I knew it would only get worse, because we were being told everything was our fault. Before too long they would have us eating out of troughs.

I lost all my faith in organized resistance after they took the cigarettes in '98. I didn't even smoke, but I'd stood with all the sour faces until they rang a bell and shouted warnings over the PA. I'd looked around and the mass that was originally gathered had thinned down to only a few of us thinking we could change something. I got stuck for a year in the hole, withering away, sleeping, and doing push-ups. The cigarettes were gone, and the joint was back to normal.

I knew my body didn't want to go through the same rigor of the blade, or look at the same ghost in the mirror I had the last time. Talking to Rudy had scared me from the noose, but I could sit around forever waiting on something to happen that never would. This was what this place *was*: a dream crusher, straps and a board.

Everyone I grew up with in South Minneapolis knew someone in the collage of their lives who had slept in one of these cages. Back then I wanted to pretend it didn't exist, but some of my friends, like Slick, had been waiting on their trip their whole lives. Its name was passed around offhandedly in conversations about where people had disappeared to, without an exact vision of what really happened there. When I got here, though, I saw it differently, mostly just shrinking space and time to make it as absurd or as monstrous as any of us wanted it to be.

Fall

I was on the phone with Mel when it happened. It was the twentieth anniversary of Sonny's death. By the end, she had broken down to bone holding onto skin. I told Mel how wicked it was that Sonny died, while I had never figured out how to live in the first place. "It's wrong how fate never lets us switch places." I was trying to tell her how hopeless the whole place felt. "You become like a robot that resets its feelings every morning." She said she would send me a Bible. I told her that people's Bibles were being stolen just so they could set them on fire. They weren't, but it sounded good.

Then I smelled the smoke, husky and chemical. I looked behind the back of the cellblock and everything was moving toward me. A wall of guards stormed the door into the commotion of bodies. Guys were coming with armfuls of things retrieved from their cells, some had made satchels with blankets. I could see enough smoke in the back half of the room to know it wasn't just a garbage can. I tried to go get my photo album, but was stopped by a guard.

I tried to see it, but there was just too much smoke. Some guys watched without regard to alarms and voices on microphones. Sirens blared in the distance, getting louder the longer I stayed. Guys ran toward the doors, some pumping their fists with crooked smiles and something covering their faces. It moved down the tiers, eating at anything flammable, ducking into cells and consuming. Staff was having a hard time getting at the closest fireboxes—they must have reacted too late, because the combustion was too strong by the time firefighters got there.

There were guards still walking the tiers to get people out of their cells. Slick had been one of the first out the door, with a blanket that could have had everything he owned wrapped up in it. I saw Mississippi leave his room in his work boots and a mug in his hand. I saw Rudy, barely holding his clothes on his body, glance back at the flames coming at his cell, then turn and walk toward the door. The smoke was too much for me to take now, so I followed the herd, who were yelling and kicking at each other's heels toward the yard. One old man whacked another with his cane for tripping him in the rush.

There was a mass convergence with guys from all different cellblocks. "Damn, the joint's going crazy!" one guy hollered. "It's about time!" The hallway was filled with coughs and gags. The yard was packed with bodies and there was a steady stream still coming behind me. The last stragglers to find the yard were mostly guards, holding up a few remaining soot-faced inmates. Slick found me; he was eating from a bag of chips he'd brought out with him. I looked around for everybody I knew. Mississippi had a spot against the wall, the flickers of light reflecting off his bald head. There were too many of us to sort everyone out. Hundreds of us standing or sitting like kids on a hill watching fireworks.

From out of the dark behind me, an old guard I knew slid down on me. "You believe this? This is gonna change some stuff—yeah, it's gonna change some shit." Peering out on the yard at everyone, like heads bobbing in the ocean, I knew he didn't mean it would get better.

Black smoke and orange flames rose into the sky. Brick and sandstone that was once so secure, collapsed, and was welcomed with applause. Let them try to save it. The water from the trucks and the hydrants attempted to stop it, but it had already burned what it was supposed to. I felt the fire—not its heat, but its history.

I was looking at that miserable old building that had taken so much more than it would ever give back. It burned for every soul this place ever held captive, every dream broken, every chopped tree. There was fire for every year it consumed, every emasculating word, every memo, every untreated illness, for every bloodred cent stolen and absorbed, every family member who passed away. It told us that for all the things we knew this place to be, even the oldest of institutions can burn, break down into ash. I was proud to watch its destruction. Sirens blared, and the ship sank. It was the moment I survived for, wore my scars for. To see the animals burn down the zoo. I swear I could see the faces of all those trapped souls escaping, William Williams dancing in the smoke. They would find somewhere for us tomorrow, but for this night, a blanket slung over my shoulders, watching flames reach up and nip the stars, I was fine. Let the motherfucker burn. There would be seeds for next year.

Afterward there were details. They said six people died of smoke inhalation, unable to get out of their cells. They said the fire started from a pile of clothes doused with gasoline, in the room of a seventy-year-old man who never left his cell. He was caught on surveillance cameras before the fire, spraying something up and down the tier from a plastic bottle. Another story came out about some dumb kid who died after being rousted from his cell; he had walked the tier, then doubled back to his room only to get back underneath his blanket for the smoke to engulf him.

IMMIGRANT SONG

BY MARCO VERDONI

Marquette Branch Prison (Marquette, Michigan)

Celso had never seen snow before. Up here it was everywhere. Beyond the fences and coils of concertina wire, there was no horizon. The sky and earth were just an endless white void.

The cold seemed to make everybody angry. The COs were always yelling at him in a language he didn't understand—and when they realized this, they'd just say everything louder and VEY-REE SLOW-LY, as if that made it easier for him.

Comprende? They always knew that word. Even the nurses who stuck him with needles and drained his blood and told him to piss in this cup and clip his nails and strip naked and stand over here, turn your head, cough, and sign this form, okay? Just put your name here, *comprende?*

His attorney spoke Spanish, but that didn't help Celso understand any of the legal jargon. The deal he signed might as well have been in braille. In any language, he didn't know how to read.

It was spring when he came to the States; summer when they arrested him. The jail didn't have any windows, so when the van came to take him to prison, he didn't know what the brown slush was on the floor. He thought it was vomit.

"It's a blizzard," the driver said, pulling out of the jail. "Total whiteout."

Celso knew that word—*blizzard*. Marichuy taught it to him.

"It means snowstorm," she said. "They have them all the time in North America."

La Ventisca. That's what he started calling Marichuy's mother after that, because whenever she showed up, Marichuy got cold. Sometimes she'd catch him in Marichuy's bedroom and would have to chase him down the dirt road with a stick. But he could always outrun her. He couldn't say the same for Marichuy's brothers. The first time, they just roughed him up outside the church. The second, they chased him through the jungle, all the way back to the farm, and knocked some of his teeth out in the bean field.

"I warned you," his father said. "Didn't I warn you? Those schoolgirls are only trouble. If you want to get your dick wet, go see Cande and her whores at the cantina. Those boys will kill you if they catch you again."

At the time, he thought the old man was just being dramatic. But when Marichuy could no longer hide her pregnant belly, and Celso came home to find the severed heads of his guard dogs laid out on his doorstep like some sort of ritual sacrifice, his father put him on the first train to Nogales.

The cellblock stood four tiers high. Celso and the other new arrivals waited in line as a young CO read off their numbers and directed them to their cells. When Celso's turn came, the officer told him to wait.

Celso sighed—more awkward translating, more confusion.

Down the block, a chubby CO was tearing down a barricade of yellow tape so an inmate porter could mop the area. The CO headed toward them, wadding up the tape into a ball.

"Fadeaway!" he shouted, as he jumped back and shot at an open trash can next to Celso. The ball came undone in midair and spilled into a tangled web of tape all over the mouth of the can. "Damn," he said.

The CO led him to an empty cell, next to where the porter was mopping, and locked him inside.

As he left, he said something that made the porter laugh. It was a high-pitched, girlish laugh. On a second look, Celso realized the porter was a woman. (An ugly woman, with greasy hair, pitted skin, and tiny breasts.) Celso looked at the floor she was mopping—a huge puddle of dried blood.

The woman caught him staring. "Hi," she said, waving her hand.

She asked him something else, but he didn't understand her. He just nodded and smiled, nervous, hoping it was the right response.

It wasn't.

Confused, she raised her overly tweezed eyebrows at him.

"Don't talk to that *maricon*," an unknown voice said in fluent Spanish.

Another inmate with a mop and bucket walked over to the cell door, this one male, Hispanic. His neck tattoo said *AZTECA* in big, bold letters. "Mexican?" he asked.

Celso smiled. "Yes."

"Guerrero?"

"Chiapas."

"What's up, brother?" the man said, extending his arm through the bars to shake Celso's hand. "I'm Flores. Listen, man, you got to watch who you talk to around here. People see you hanging with these *mariquitas* and they start to wonder."

Celso was puzzled. He looked back at the female porter. She seemed suddenly muscular. Her chin seemed stubbly. It was all so obvious now.

Flores could read his face.

"Aw, fuck no, *vato*!" he said, laughing. "What? You thought you were going to get some *chocha* in here, didn't you? Ha!"

Embarrassed, Celso tried to change the subject. "What happened there?"

Flores glanced over at the blood. "Somebody jumped, I guess. So how long have you been in Michigan?"

"Not long," he said, staring at the streaks the mop left behind. "Where are we, exactly?"

"This here is Jackson." He held up his right hand and pointed to the base of his palm. "Right here." People from here were always doing that hand-as-state-map thing.

"So how much time you got?" Flores asked.

Celso shrugged. "They said I can go home when I'm twenty-two."

"How old are you now?"

"Eighteen."

Flores lowered his voice. "So what did you do?"

"Oh," Celso said, "I didn't do anything, really. I was just there."

"So what happened then?"

"A couple of people got killed."

Flores peered at him suspiciously. "Man . . . *what*?"

Down the block, the CO yelled at Flores to get back to work. He stepped away from the bars.

"Listen, *vato*," he said, grabbing his mop bucket. "When they break the doors for yard, come find me. And bring your paperwork with you."

"Okay," Celso replied, unsure of what he was agreeing to, but too afraid to refuse his only source of conversation in months. "Hey, wait!" he said, before the other man left.

Flores stopped.

"How do you know the guy wasn't pushed?"

Flores shook his head. "Not likely. I mean, don't get me wrong, you can get killed in this bitch. But this is *quarantine*, man. This is where it starts. When that door closes, and you start thinking about all the time you got left to do . . . For some guys, it's just easier, you know?"

The sun in the desert was so much hotter than back home. Its blinding rays pierced right through the chaparral, making it a constant struggle to stay in the shade, to sleep.

Celso was exhausted. His mouth was parched and dry. But the thought of waking his cousin Eleonel for another drink of water was too embarrassing. He had already made an ass of himself the night before.

They had set out from Nogales at dusk in groups of twenty-five. They walked all night, stopping for fifteen-minute breaks every four hours. By the second break, Celso had drunk all of his water. (Meanwhile, his cousin, having made the trip before, had barely broken a sweat.) When they finally stopped before sunrise to make camp, Celso almost collapsed.

"Here," Eleonel said, handing him an extra bottle from his backpack. "But go easy on this one."

Celso didn't dare mention how hungry he was either. But he didn't have to: as if on cue, the coyote pulled out a bulb of garlic, broke it, and passed the cloves among the migrants. Everyone took a clove.

A strange meal, but Celso was too famished to complain. He frantically peeled off the skin and started chewing. He'd never eaten one whole before, and this was probably why: it had an acrid taste that burned all the way to the top of his skull and made his eyes water. It didn't so much sate his appetite as it castigated him for having one at all.

Eleonel hadn't eaten his yet. Instead, he stood up and

pulled off his shirt. He took the clove in his palm, mashed it into a paste, and proceeded to rub it all over his body.

Celso swallowed. All around him, everyone was rubbing themselves with garlic.

"Did you drop yours?" Eleonel asked.

Celso pretended not to hear him.

His cousin started laughing. "Well," he said, as he lied down under a tree to sleep, "at least the snakes won't try to *kiss* you."

It seemed everyone was sleeping soundly but Celso, even the nosy little kid from Jalisco. Miraculous, really, because the kid didn't seem like he'd ever slow down the night before. When everyone else was taking their water breaks, the boy was kicking dirt at tarantulas and throwing rocks at lizards. He ran circles around everybody.

Eleonel thought it was hilarious. Celso couldn't have thought it more annoying. The kid kept pestering him with stupid questions: *Where are you from? Where are you headed? Have you had pizza and french fries before? I have. And hamburgers. Do you know who Harry Potter is? My mom says they have roller coasters in every city in the States. Do you know what a roller coaster is?*

Still, it *was* the kid who spotted the drone. At night, the buzz of countless rattlesnakes drowned out most every other sound. Everybody was focused on the horizon, trying to spot the patrol trucks before they could spot them. But the kid kept pointing to the sky, saying he heard something. When the coyote figured it out, he yelled for everyone to take a sharp left and start running. They managed to evade the drone by running parallel to it. Later, they watched the desert light up a few miles east as one of the other groups was found and captured.

The kid hadn't moved all day. He was still dead asleep.

When the sun finally set, the coyote stood up and announced that it was time.

"Everyone get your stuff," he said. "One more night until Phoenix."

When Eleonel got up to take a piss, Celso stole a deep swig of his water. The garlic had been fermenting on his gums.

Suddenly, a woman started screaming. Everyone stopped.

"No, God!" she cried. "Please, someone help! My boy! It's my son!"

The woman sat on the ground cradling the kid in her arms, desperately shaking him.

"Let me see," the coyote said, checking the boy's limbs for marks. He found two huge red bumps on his neck. "He must've been sleeping on a snake pit." He lifted the kid's eyelids, revealing only white.

The mother just kept shaking her son. But it was no use; his body was already stiff.

"There's nothing we can do," the coyote told her. "I'm sorry, but he's gone."

Celso was flabbergasted. Why couldn't the damn kid have been more careful? The woman should've been keeping a better eye on her little bastard.

The coyote tried to pull her away from the boy's body, but she wouldn't let him. She just screamed louder.

"We can't stay," he said. "And you can't take him with you. It's too far." He paused for a solemn moment, then turned back to the crowd. "Let's go."

A few followed him. Still, others lingered, including Celso.

"Come on," Eleonel urged, pulling his cousin's arm. "We have to go. We can't help her."

The woman kept weeping.

"Maybe *La Migra* will find her," Eleonel said. "You want to stay and find out?"

Celso could only hope that was true because, one by one, they all left her there. Together, they kept walking until the woman's cries became just an echo in the wind.

Celso slipped and fell on the ice.

Flores doubled over laughing. "Easy, brother, you don't want to end up in Duane Waters."

Celso stood up and dusted the rock salt off his jacket. "Where?"

Flores nodded toward the big building that peeked out from behind the perimeter wall. "The prison hospital," he said. "Didn't you see the graveyard when they drove you in through the gates?"

Celso remembered.

"That's where you'll end up if you let those doctors work on you. That's where they bury all the lifers—all the guys who outlived anybody who'd care to come pick up their bodies. Them, and *mojados* like us." He pointed to the water tower, which stood higher than everything else. "That's why everybody's so fucked up around here. We're all drinking the dried-up corpses of forgotten criminals." He took a long sip from his plastic coffee mug.

They came to a stop at the weight pit, where a dozen or so inmates were curling rusted iron dumbbells and lifting warped steel bars. Flores dusted the snow off a preacher bench and sat down.

"Let me see it," he said, handing Celso his coffee mug in exchange for the paperwork.

The mug brought warmth to his hands again. He hadn't thought to wear gloves. Or a hat. It was a new sensation for him, being numb. It hurt like hell.

"Why do you want to read my casework?"

Flores looked at him. "To make sure I wasn't walking the track with some fucking baby-raping child molester."

Nearby, someone cried out in pain. An inmate dressed only in thermal underwear was deadlifting several hundred pounds off the ground. Two other inmates cheered him on as he lifted the bar higher, grunting, yelling. Nobody but Celso seemed to find this peculiar. Flores hadn't taken his eyes off the packet of paper.

"What does RGC mean?" Celso asked him.

"Reception and Guidance Center."

"You mean *this* isn't prison?"

"No. Well, yeah—this is prison. But you won't stay here. This is quarantine. They keep you here until a bed opens up at another joint. That, and to run psych tests and shit."

He must've been referring to the long afternoon Celso spent answering *True* or *False* to a bizarre tape recording of a few hundred seemingly random statements—from the telling (*If people make me angry, I can be dangerous*), to the ambiguous (*I can usually talk my way out of trouble*), to the downright obscure (*I enjoy repairing doorknobs*). When he was done, the proctor had handed him a blank piece of paper and told him to draw a picture of a man on one side and a woman on the other. The inmate beside him didn't seem to take the assignment seriously: he drew obscene stick figures, with a giant dick and balls on one and huge tits above a hairy triangle on the other. Celso drew a confused young man on one side; on the reverse, he drew Marichuy.

"Where's this place at?" Flores asked, indicating where the paperwork noted his previous employment.

Celso pointed to the left of his open palm. "Near Grand Rapids."

"What did you do there?"

"I killed turkeys," he said. "But I got fired."

Flores didn't bother to ask why. He just kept reading.

The report summarized Celso's life up to his crime. It told of his long ride from Arizona to Michigan. It mentioned his termination from the poultry-processing plant (his employer stated he fired Celso upon learning of his illegal-resident status). It told how he found a new job selling drugs for convicted armed robber Octavio "Spooky" Ramirez; how he started on a trial supply of marijuana, until he was promoted to cocaine, and finally heroin; how, one day, Ramirez and an unnamed man picked him up to accompany them on a prospective bulk drug purchase, set up by the unnamed man; how, unbeknownst to him or Ramirez, this man was an undercover DEA officer; how, upon seeing convicted drug possessor Alfred Burke—accompanied by his girlfriend, convicted check forger Lacey Hopkins—Ramirez stopped the vehicle (against the undercover agent's adamant protests) to follow Burke to his residence, because, he said, "That junkie owes me money"; how the party forced entry into Burke's residence, and Celso restrained Hopkins while Ramirez repeatedly struck Burke with his fists; how Ramirez, visibly agitated, produced a Glock 9mm pistol and placed it inside Burke's mouth; how there remains a dispute as to whether the trigger was pulled deliberately or accidentally, but upon witnessing the shot, the undercover agent drew his own weapon and demanded, in a clear and loud voice, that Ramirez put down his gun; how, according to the agent's testimony, Ramirez turned to fire on him, but was promptly shot twice in the upper torso by the agent; how Celso was then placed under arrest for home invasion, conspiracy to purchase and distribute a controlled substance, and later, felony murder for the deaths of Ramirez and

Burke; and how his court-appointed attorney later pled down the substance and home invasion charges.

In the weight pit, a group of inmates had gathered. They weren't working out and they weren't talking. They were just waiting.

"That still doesn't make sense," Flores said, flipping through the packet.

The group was staring at a lone inmate doing bench presses, completely oblivious to anyone else.

"Oh, here it is," Flores said, stopping at the final page. "You must've just misunderstood."

One of the inmates grabbed a small dumbbell. He tested the weight in his hand. Not satisfied, he switched it for a heavier one.

"It doesn't say you get out when you're twenty-two, *vato*," Flores said.

The inmate with the dumbbell walked toward the man on the bench, the rest followed. They circled around the man.

"Look," Flores said, referring to the paper. "It says, *Twenty-two-year sentence minimum.*"

The entire weight pit went silent when they heard the crunch.

Back home, death was an event. It was a small town; when somebody died, if you weren't grieving them, you were comforting someone who was.

Up here, death was routine. Maybe, because there was so much of it, people were numb to it. Even at Celso's sentencing, he had to wait in line. He had spent the week leading up to it rehearsing his speech, but when the moment finally came, and he stood in the crowded courtroom, it just felt like he was wasting everybody's time. The way the judge got irritated and slumped back in her chair when the attorney mentioned he would need to translate; the way the stenographer paused from typing to take a sip of water; the way the other convicts scoffed at Celso (who was struggling to remember the right words) and kept looking at the clock like they had somewhere else to be; the way the prosecutor yawned and picked the lint off his tie—it all seemed so banal.

This is what the turkeys at work must've felt like. They were unloaded off trucks and hung by their legs on a conveyor belt. His boss showed him where an electric spinning blade slit their throats. The turkeys coasted by in an endless waterfall of blood.

"No matter what," his boss had said, "the line's gotta keep moving. You have to pay attention. Every once in a while, one of the birds is too short for his neck to reach the cutter." He had drawn out a long knife with a narrow blade and handed it to Celso. "For when that happens."

At first, it had been easy. The knife was so sharp, the gullets so thin—if not for all the warbling and death throes, Celso would hardly have felt complicit in the deed. And there were maybe only one or two turkeys the machine didn't catch for every dozen it did. But then, out of nowhere, there came a bevy of dwarf turkeys—each one of them flapped and squawked and put up a fight. It turned into a melee of blood and feathers, absolute carnage. Celso could do nothing but try and keep up, furiously slashing away. (They were so small, for a moment he thought maybe they'd switched to chickens.)

When he'd paused to catch his breath, he noticed one of the birds looking at him. Its black, beady eyes were impossible to read. Did it even understand what was happening? He could see them all, staring at him, accusing him. He'd lost track of time.

Then an alarm had gone off. The line came to a halt.

Celso panicked. How long had he zoned out?

Down the line, past a huge, long metal vat filled with water and a wall of steam, he could hear his boss yelling.

When he'd arrived at the commotion, everyone was watching. His boss was ripping bird after bird off the line and throwing them into a pile on the floor. Soaked from the water, their feathers came right off.

His coworkers were circled around the pile, their smocks still pristine and free of blood. Eleonel was standing among them. "What'd you do?" he asked his cousin.

Celso kept staring at the pile.

When his boss saw he was there, he picked up two of the birds to show Celso the difference: one's skin was clear and white; the other was dark pink. The pile was mostly pink ones.

"Not *bueno*!" his boss had shouted at him. "This is not *bueno*."

And for the most part, Celso had agreed with him.

When a letter came, Flores offered to read it to him. "It's from Mexico," he said. "Some girl named Marichuy."

Celso smiled. But then he thought about it again and stopped smiling. "What does it say?"

"It says, *Dear Celso, I can't believe what has happened to you. I've tried speaking to your father, but he has been very sick since you left. Your cousin wrote him about everything.*" Flores paused to read ahead. He turned sullen.

"Keep reading," Celso told him.

Flores hesitated. "*I'm not sure if I should tell you, but I lost the baby. My mother said I should just—*"

The intercom cut him off. It was five minutes to count.

Flores handed the letter back. "I'll finish it afterward."

But he never got the chance. Before count was over, they announced a bunch of ride-outs. Flores was one of them.

As hard as he tried, Celso couldn't make sense of the letter. The words were just an indecipherable mess of squiggles.

At some point his door opened and the CO told him to pack his things. "Cell transfer."

Outside his cell, the transsexual porter stood by and waved hello again. But the cell wasn't for him; he was pushing a decrepit old man in a wheelchair. As the porter wheeled the guy through the door, the chair got caught on one of the bars. The tranny rammed against the back of it, his breasts bouncing up and down, until, at last, he forced it through.

"To where I go?" Celso asked the CO.

The man pointed. "Top tier."

Celso never knew he was afraid of heights. But as he stood on the narrow catwalk, four flights up from his previous cell, his legs trembled.

Just as the CO was about to open the door for Celso, he stopped. Something was happening on the base floor. The CO turned and ran back down the stairs, shouting something into his radio.

Celso worked up the courage to peek over the railing. Far below, an inmate was trying to shield himself and run as another inmate stabbed at him with a sharpened toothbrush. They all seemed so small from up high.

Slowly, Celso crept all the way to the ledge. It would be so quick, he thought, nobody could stop him. Two seconds versus two decades. A quick, merciful slice or a long, boiling dip.

He thought awhile about it. He thought about it for days and weeks and months and years.

* * *

It wasn't until they were on the bus that the driver told everyone where they were going. He said something about the market.

The inmates all scoffed or rolled their eyes at what he said, disappointed.

Celso turned to the man next to him. "Is far, the market?"

The man was confused. "Huh? No. Not market—Marquette. That's up north."

Celso held up his manacled hand as far as the chain on his waist would permit and offered his palm as a map to chart on.

With one of his fingers, the man drew a line from the base of Celso's palm far beyond his fingertips. "Way up there," he said. "Over the bridge, 'bout a twelve-hour drive, maybe twice that in this weather."

Celso understood. He'd taken a long drive before. At least this time it wouldn't be hidden in a trunk with three other Mexicans.

Then a thought occurred to him. "Is more, the snow up there?"

The other inmate looked at him like he had just asked for his hand in marriage.

He chuckled. "No, buddy. No, there's no snow up there."

RAT'S ASS

BY KENNETH R. BRYDON

San Quentin State Prison (San Quentin, California)

They can't write me up, my parole hearing's next month."
Rick and I headed down concrete stairs. We were on
our way to San Quentin's lower yard.

"Yeah, Jason, that's fucked up."

I felt like shit on what was otherwise a sunny Saturday
morning. An ancient craggy wall towered on our left. Assorted
old pipes hung there serving no purpose. An earthy smell
came from the various mosses and small shrubs hanging off
the wall. They'd been growing for decades longer than my arrival ten years ago.

We walked in a wide-open path. "I gotta do something!"
It felt like the walls were closing in on me. The both of us wore
shorts and tank tops; mesh bags slung over our shoulders held
water bottles and towels. Rick had talked me into working
out. "I am completely fucked."

Our steps brought us down the first flight onto the flat
middle walkway. On the right side stood a shiny chain-link
fence; through it, our reflections showed on the end windows
of the huge new hospital. Rick flexed his pecs while I spit at my
image and watched the white blob catch on the thick wire. In
another eight steps, we started down the second set of stairs.

Rick asked, his voice jittery, "How'd they bust you?"

My head rewound the visit. The rookie prison guard had
stuck his face up close to the mesh over the door bars. This

son of a bitch looked around the cell before his eyes landed on me. I'd held my breath, waiting for his next move. The staring contest was brief, and he then turned and left. I'd cut loose a loud gasping moan.

"The cop smelled it," I said to Rick, recalling how he suddenly reappeared. His chin pressed against the mesh to get a good whiff of the lingering odor of fermentation. "Augh, shit," I'd mumbled as he pulled the door open and ordered me to step out.

Rick and I turned at the bottom of the stairs, making our way out onto the yard. On his arm were crude tattoos mixed with others showing a degree of artistic talent. I'd done some of the best work he had, covering up some of the shitty stuff from the Youth Authority. Rick stood five ten just like me, and his workouts had put almost as much solid meat on his chest and arms as mine had. We were both blue-eyed and had short, slicked-back blond hair. Rick put a lot into that skin color, but I thought it more of a problem in doing business.

"How much he bust you with?"

The memory was kicking me in the ass. It kept going to where they ripped up my place and carried the containers away. When you're busted, they toss your cell so bad it'll take hours to put it back together. My jaw flexed; I'd paid a lot to the kitchen worker for fruit and sugar.

Rick glanced over at me a couple of times. I could see he was waiting for an answer. Finally I barked out, "Ten fucking gallons!"

"Shit, Jason, were you gonna invite me?"

It ain't as if I owed him anything, so I didn't respond.

We walked along in silence. Making "good" prison wine was an art, and I had it down. A tumbler of my shit was like two or three of anyone else's. I'd line up to buy some good weed with what I didn't drink; even meth if anyone had it. We were moving along in the shadow of the hospital with the yard opening up in front of us. The sounds of basketballs pinging and people shouting and laughing didn't do much to stir me up. Still, I was going to get a workout.

"Hey, check it out!" Rick said, pointing to the tennis court. Two women were there with inmates as partners. The match had a large audience, and all the attention was for the one young gal. She presented a nice view leaning forward, preparing for the coming serve.

"I didn't even get to enjoy the shit." A deep breath brought the salt smell of the Frisco Bay to me; it only made me sigh deeply. "Man, I'm through. The board will hammer me!"

My words didn't register with Rick; he was fixed on the tight feminine body in knee-length shorts bouncing around on the court. I'd seen a lot more skin on Wimbledon, but this was one hard body. When her return landed in the net, a collective sound, "Oh!" came from every direction.

I stared at my so-called buddy. "Hey, Rick, I heard they're giving away bags of dope up in North block."

"Yeah, that's cool," he answered, sounding like a dude dumbed-down with meds. He remained transfixed with the tennis court, eyes glazed over. Any other time we'd both be drooling, but I needed my ass covered before enjoying this one.

"Fuck!" I said, thinking of my daughter Sheila. "I've got to fix this." I'd written her for five years before she finally answered. She'd just started bringing in my grandson to visit; we'd even made plans to take him on his first trip to Disneyland. The thought of never seeing her or Jimmy again opened up a pit in my guts.

I looked about the yard, and ahead of me I spotted David,

of all people. He wore gray sweatpants and, even in the warm sun, he had on a blue sweatshirt three sizes too big. The billowing sleeves were cut at the elbows. Coming toward us past the cop's shack, he also turned to check out the girl playing tennis. David had the same stupid grin as Rick. "Hypocritical punk," I said.

"Yeah, I'm there," Rick answered. It was bad enough that David would handle the paperwork for this write-up, but seeing how his wife Sherry had gotten close to my daughter, it was certain the motherfucker would rat me out. I grinned. It wouldn't be a problem to return the favor, telling his wife about him leering at the court cutie.

Another chorus of "Oh!" came up, including Rick.

I smacked him on the chest. "Hey! Come on, how do I beat this shit?"

"Fuck, I don't know." Rick gestured at David thirty feet away. "Go talk with that asshole. If anyone can do it, he can."

"I'm not speaking to that maggot, he'd tell on me just for asking."

"How's it get worse?" Rick asked. His head twisted back to tennis. "You're fucked. What're they gonna do, put you in prison for life?"

I stared at the back of David's head; earbud wires reached up on both sides. I said softly, "A lotta help you are." Rick laughed, but it was at someone stumbling on the court.

David's bald head bobbed a little to some tune. My vision blurred as I glared at him. I did some stupid telepathic shit in my head, as if I could make him agree.

"You know he did it already?" Rick asked.

"Yeah," I nodded, "he probably did." I pictured him taking the report written by that snot-nosed cop, laughing as he typed away. My jaw was tight and my teeth squeaked.

"You've got that cocksucker in a couple of groups, right?"

My voice came back whiny: "That don't mean shit." I pointed at Dave. "In fact, he'll fuck with me at the next AA meeting."

"So tell the punk how sorry you are, and you'll never do it again if he'll help you this one time." Rick turned and walked backward, eyes fixed on the tennis court.

"What makes you think he's got the juice to do shit like that?"

"Come on! I've had shit squashed." Rick turned back around, and we stopped walking. "You mean you've never had a clerk make things disappear?"

My head shook, still focused on Dave's back. "He doesn't fuck around. This guy's as square as they get." My eyes closed, and I turned to peer at Rick. "He's never done a thing for anyone."

"What's to lose? I'll kick the dog shit out of him if he tells on you."

Normally Rick and I turned here, and we went down a slope to the dip and pull-up bars. We could see the rest of our workout crew, Ron and Keith, there waiting for us. I really wanted to bust a good sweat, use the buff to distract me from this fucked-up situation. My shoulders dropped. "I don't want to talk with him!" I looked over at Ron and Keith. From their expressions, it seemed like they knew our talk was about something serious.

"Yeah, whatever," Rick said. He put his hand on my shoulder and shoved me forward. "Go!" David had just turned onto the main road inside of San Quentin. The road ran all the way from the vehicle gate, up past the top of the stairs we'd just walked down.

I tossed Rick my bag. "I'll be right back," I said. The other half of our crew watched; Keith had his arms wide, asking, *What?* My head nodded toward Rick who was headed down to them.

"Don't blow it, Jason," I said out loud. It felt stupid to be talking to myself, but my lips kept moving. "Just play it cool." From the way David's head bobbed, I knew he couldn't hear me. I stepped quicker, almost running.

I caught up to him behind the backstop of the baseball field. He didn't see me at first. *"Hey Joe,"* he sang, *"where you going with that gun in your hand?"* His head kept moving as he checked out the visiting baseball team from the streets. David played on the San Quentin Giants last year. This year's team was on the field all decked out in the San Francisco Giants' old practice uniforms. They stood in groups stretching and swinging bats. *"You know I'm going down to shoot my ol' lady, you know—"*

Catching sight of me, he abruptly ended his bad karaoke. For a moment it looked like he'd taken a bite out of a shit sandwich. "How's it going, Jason?" he asked while reaching down and turning off the clear plastic radio clipped at his waist. He was close to eye level in height.

"Pretty good," I answered. "How're you doing?"

Gray eyes flashed and the same turd-eating scowl came again, but he took a deep breath. His hand waved across the entire yard. "You remember when you got here?" he asked. "What the lower yard used to be like?"

"Yeah," I said, nodding, "twice as big." For a moment I lost myself in that memory. It had been better; more space for guys to hang out. Now, on the other side of the baseball field, what was once a part of our yard area stood the school modules.

David sighed loudly. "I remember when we still had weights, even family visits." He turned to look at me. "You ever make it out on a family visit?"

I shook my head. "Naaaw, after conviction my old lady dumped me; the boneyards were done for lifers when I made it back to the joint."

David nodded, and his head kept going up and down while he looked forward. I'd decided to not ask him for anything. I opened my mouth to tell him goodbye, but he suddenly turned back and looked at me. "So, Jason, what do you want?"

"I, uh . . ." The walls were coming in again. "I . . . Why do I have to need something?"

"Because, Jason, you don't say squat otherwise."

"What, can't a guy just come and say hi?"

I didn't like the way he laughed at my question. "Yeah, you could, but you never do."

"Oh, man, that ain't right!"

His head moved like the music was still on. "Yep, that's for sure; you took the words right out of my mouth."

"I don't do that!"

There was that fucking laugh again and a smirk. "So, Jason, what can I do for you?"

I wanted to slap that smug look off his face. "Can you talk to the lieutenant for me?" The perimeter track turned left here off the pavement, and now we walked on a gravel road, which was also the home run area for the baseball field to our left.

With every look, I was getting more pissed. He was sticking his chest out now, strutting around like a rooster. "What did you do?" he asked.

"What's with all the fucking condemnation, David?"

He turned to stare at me with real anger in his face. "You know, Jason, I really love Hendrix." He reached for the radio. It was a little smaller than a cigarette pack. "We can forget this conversation." David fumbled with the front to get his finger on a switch.

"They busted me for pruno!" I said, a lot louder than I meant to. We'd made our way next to some tables on the right side of the road that a number of my partners hung around. My attention stayed on David, pretending that my "road dogs" hadn't heard shit, but they were all eye-fucking me while checking out my company.

"You mean you finally got caught?" He said this loud enough to be heard by my fellas.

My voice lowered. "What's that supposed to mean?"

More of that laugh. "Dude," he said, "you're as dirty as they get."

At least we'd passed the tables. "You saw me doing what?" He didn't know shit; he never came around where I did my business.

His eyes rolled. "Come on," he said. "You and your cellie were busted, what, six months ago for pruno?"

The gravel on the road ended, and we turned left onto a dirt path next to a chain-link fence. On the other side were the education trailers. Home runs here would land on top of the module classrooms.

"My cellie owned it! He told the lieutenant it was his!" I knew this was lame, but my mouth kept going. "The lieutenant found me not guilty."

That laugh again. "But this time you didn't have a cell-mate to dump it on, did you?" One of his eyebrows rose up like fucking Spock in *Star Trek*.

"Yeah," I replied, staring down. "He took the heat for me." The kid had said he didn't care and agreed to ride the charge in my place. The fact that he had to serve another month didn't bother him too much.

Dave's face was a fucking stone. We walked a couple of steps before he asked, "Remember what the cops used to do to guys making hooch?"

"Yeah, they poured the shit out in the fucking toilet." Recalling that pissed me off even more.

David raised a finger. "The first time, they poured it out." He let that settle for a moment. "The second time," he held up two fingers, "they poured it on your bunk. It went all over: your blankets, sheets, and mattress. Your crap got soaked!" His hands went behind his back, and he spoke slowly. "What'd they do the third time?"

This asshole was giving me a headache. "They pissed in it." My face felt flush, and I didn't dare look at him.

Another fucked-up laugh. "Which one would you prefer, Jason?"

No point in speaking. I saw it a toss-up: drinking wine fortified with a guard's piss, or going through this shit. I might as well be on my knees, with him behind doing me. My shoulders went up and down in a shrug.

"You know," David said, "you really need to find yourself another crowd to hang out with. Most of those guys are half your age."

"Why? What about 'em?"

David's eyes rolled. "You're kidding, right?" He rubbed his forehead. "In the past six months, your crew's been busted for one thing after another."

"I'm schooling them." I'd told myself as much many times. "So they don't get all screwed up."

"Schooling?" he asked with a big grin. "Was Big Rick sticking that shank into Skunkweed graduation?"

I'd had enough. "What's so fucking funny?"

"You really don't know, Jason?"

"See, David," my hand waved about, "that's why I don't bother talking with you. You come off with this holier-than-thou bullshit."

"And you interrupted my walk *why?*" Now he was angry too. "To see how I'm doing?"

We'd come around to the far side of the baseball field, heading left again down a dirt path in foul ball territory. We turned right onto the blacktop. "I can't afford a write-up, David. Can you help me or not?" We walked straight toward the hospital.

"You can't afford it?"

"Yeah," I answered. Our direction took us past one end of the basketball courts where the San Quentin Warriors were playing an outside team. On the other side were the tennis players.

"You can't afford a write-up?"

"What the fuck is your problem, David!"

"Right this moment," he said, as we started up an incline that brought us into the hospital's shadow, "my problem is you being a pretend friend." He breathed deeply a moment before adding, "Selling me this piss-poor version of you being a good guy with really bad luck."

"Who the fuck do you think you are?" I was wasting my time with this fool.

"I'm a nobody." We finally came back to the point where Rick and I had entered the yard one lap before. "But I've busted my ass for twenty years now." We walked a couple more steps before stopping. "Where were you, Jason, when I got serious about my life?"

"Not in prison," I answered.

"Right! While I'd been about changing my life for over ten years, you were still robbing, stealing, and killing." I stared at the ground, wondering if one of my dogs had a big fucking mouth. David continued, "I got up next to lifers squared up about changing, and I listened." He stuck out his thumb like a hitchhiker, aiming at my buddies. "Not like a bunch of kids still playing cops and robbers."

"You ain't a fucking saint," I said. A couple of guys walking close glanced over but quickly returned to their own business. "I've seen how you treat guys—like they're trash. You should hear what kinds of assholes they call you!"

"You should know," he countered. "You're the one doing most of the talking." David stopped suddenly, closing his eyes and taking a deep breath. His hand came up in a fist, and he pounded lightly on his forehead. "Yeah," he said calmly. "I can be a perfect asshole . . . I gotta own that." He let his arm drop down, then turned and looked at me. His right eye had a twitch. "But when you walk into that boardroom, Jason, it's nothing . . . You're nothing but a fake and a fraud."

"I don't need to hear this shit!" This punk needed correcting. "I'm getting ready to say something I'm going to regret." Hitting him in the throat would've fixed things real quick. My hands were balled tight; I'd done the math for launching on him.

"Oh, I think you need it." David swayed back slightly as my body leaned in a little. "And all those thoughts about a sucker punch." His right eye fluttered. "Seeing how Sherry just dumped me, I'm feeling like I don't give a shit about consequences either." He took in a deep breath through his nose. "You may find your back dirty. You think you know me?"

The punk-fuck had called me out. I needed to do something, or start eating humble pie. I couldn't blow it . . . not yet. "And you're supposed to be a Christian!" I said.

David's mouth opened at that, grinning as if I'd just told a good joke. "You didn't go there!" He covered his mouth with his fist, trying not to laugh. "This is what you say to get what you want?" In a moment his eyes became slits. "And you, Jason, aren't you this *solid* Alcoholics Anonymous member?" He shook his head as his fingers made the quotes sign. "Sober ten years now? Isn't that what you've been saying at the meetings?"

"I'm a fucking convict," I said. "Don't think you can say whatever you want."

"Tell me, Jason," he responded, his hands on his hips, "where do you put 'convict' on a resume? You really think that means shit outside of these walls?"

"David, what is your problem?" Fuck it, I'll bust this fool in the mouth. He glanced down at my hands, and I got satisfaction that his eyes went wide a moment.

He stopped, closed his eyes, and took a deep breath. David grinned as his eyes opened slowly, then he reached out his hand, palm up. "Jason, you still want me to help you?"

"Yeah," I said, exhaling deeply. My body relaxed a little. Maybe he'd do me right after all.

"Then I want you to say to me, *David, I don't give a rat's ass about you, just help me!*"

"I'm not saying that."

"Oh yeah, you're going to," he shot back, his voice rough. "All this running your mouth, acting like you're something you're not." His anger was coming up again. He raised his hands, his fingers beckoning. "Come on and say it."

"What's with this ignorant bullshit? Are you going to help me or not?"

"Sure," he said, "when you tell me, *I don't give a rat's ass about you, just help me.*"

A gust of wind suddenly hit us, and David went into this

weird look. There was something like insanity in his stare. We stood in silence for a moment. I thought he might be about to jump my ass. But as the wind backed off, the craziness seemed to leave.

My feet were glued to the spot, wondering what David's twisted mind was thinking. After ten seconds, I shook my head and said, "This isn't right."

"What ain't right, Jason, is you strutting around here claiming to be a model prisoner to one side and a gangster to the other. You sign up for programs that other guys are dead serious about, and you laugh about 'em and talk bad about the guys in them."

"Fuck you, David!"

"Perfect!" he said, smiling big, his eyes bright. "Now say it."

He wasn't making me his parrot, but my mouth began to twist. He raised his hand up next to his mouth, coaching me. "I . . ." My voice got tight. ". . . don't give a rat's ass." After that my mouth slammed shut. I wasn't going to play his fucked-up mind game.

He dropped his hand a moment and then brought it back up next to his mouth. He opened his pinched fingers a little as he said, "Just . . ."

"Just do the fucking thing!" I blurted out. "Do it, punk motherfucker! I don't give a shit about you!" Trembling, I thought my knees were going to give.

David stuck out his fist, offering me a knuckle bump. "Congratulations, Jason," he said. "A baby step to an honest man!" This dude was really messed up in the head.

I ignored the fist. "Don't talk to me like I'm some fucking kid." I did my best to hide my shaking legs.

"And don't come at me, Jason, like I'm a scared punk you can walk over to get what you want."

A whimper came from deep within me. "Come on, David, will you help me?"

He looked up toward the top of the hospital, staring as if he saw something of interest. In a moment he said, "Don't ever ask me this again."

"No!" My hand rose up like I was swearing in court. "First and last time!"

In spite of my promise, he peered at me with arms crossed, showing doubt. "If you tell your 'puppies' I helped you," his thumb went in their direction, "I'll deny it. That'll make them wonder who you snitched on to beat it." David watched me for a moment longer. "I'm putting my ass on the line for you. I could go to the hole behind this."

My fingers were running across my lips before he finished speaking. There wouldn't be a thing said to anyone, except Rick.

A thought hit me. "*I'll pay you.*" That was easy enough. "Give me a list . . . fifty bucks?" It didn't look as if David was buying it. "How about a hundred?" He still wasn't smiling. "I could get you two hundred in a couple of months." Still nothing.

He crossed his arms again, his chin resting on his thick chest. His workouts showed in his muscled arms and shoulders. In a soft voice, he said, "You just don't get it, do you?"

"Get what? Tell me what you want, and I'll take care of it!"

David shook his head. Glancing down, he kicked at a rock. "I didn't do it for you."

"Didn't what? Didn't do what for me?"

The yard seemed suddenly quiet. "I'm doing it," he finally said, "because I couldn't stand seeing your daughter and grandson spend another ten years visiting your sorry ass." David was a statue; his eyes fixed on me.

"I . . ." I sputtered while looking up at the sky. Sheila and Jimmy's faces came. "You're right," I said, my voice hoarse.

David stepped up close. "Knock off the crap, Jason!" He grabbed me by the shoulder. "I'll see you at the Saturday AA?"

I nodded. "Yeah, sure." I still couldn't look at him. "I'll be there."

"Why don't you ask your daughter about the Bible she reads while waiting for you?" He squeezed my shoulder tight a moment, then smiled and said, "By the way . . ."

"Yeah, what?"

"It's already taken care of." He winked. "It's a done deal." David turned and headed for the stairs back to North block.

My teeth squeaked as I raised my hand to eye level and turned it palm up. I closed one eye while sticking my middle finger up. I used it as a target site, aiming for the middle of David's back. In a whisper I said, "Blam! Blam! Motherfuck! Blam! Blam!"

PART III

I Saw the Whole Thing, It Was Horrible

MILK AND TEA

BY LINDA MICHELLE MARQUARDT

Women's Huron Valley Correctional Facility (Ypsilanti, Michigan)

Sometimes the most significant moments in our lives happen when we make no choice at all. This was one of those moments. Her feet must have been only two feet from the ground as her body dangled like a rag doll from the door hinge. There was chaos: screams, officers running, hands shaking, fellow inmates praying, everyone watching with morbid curiosity as her limp body crashed on the cement floor, cracking her skull. Not that it mattered; she was already dead.

Damn! I was jealous. If only I didn't have amazing sons, parents who love me unconditionally, and friends who have stood by me. They are my curse that binds me to this prison. They are the people I continue to try to please, the ones whom I emulate and love. They are my ties to earth and this current hell. If only they knew how long twenty-four hours is in here. How years slip by, but a day can feel like eternity. Time is not real, but it is the only real thing I know, the only real thing I have that is mine.

My neighbor, three doors down, was carried away in a body bag. If only I could escape as she had, like the seven others before her. It's almost a certainty that this prison, Women's Huron Valley—what I call "Death Valley"—is cursed, that there's a dark prophecy about it that hasn't yet been fulfilled. It's not just inmates hanging themselves; seemingly healthy officers are hauled away in ambulances, never to return. One was pronounced dead from a brain aneurysm. Strangely, no one noticed her car parked in the middle of the lot, wrecked by a crash she was involved in on the way to the prison. It was as if she needed to arrive here before the fog of death in this valley sucked out the last of her breath. Visitors drop dead in the visiting room without explanation. No more visits with that inmate's sister. Death surrounds this place, and I crave it like iced tea on a summer day.

Death brought me here, and death could set me free. It's been ten years to this very month since I've killed.

Click, click, click. That damn gun was empty, yet I could still hear him screaming, *You fucking bitch!* deep and harsh, echoing in the room.

Adrenaline like I have never felt rushed through my veins.

Get out, get out, get the boys out! my only thought. *There's no turning around this time.*

Never would I have imagined me—a Catholic schoolgirl raised in a loving, middle-class family with a stay-at-home mom, college-educated, mother of three children—becoming a murderer and a prisoner. But some of the most significant moments in our lives happen with no choice at all. There are many like me sprinkled among the addicts, the criminal-minded, and the socially inept. We keep the balance and are a testament that the most horrible things can happen to the kindest people, and the kindest people can do the most horrible things. I did a horrible thing.

It is a mother's most basic instinct to protect her children, and that is what turned me into a killer. There was no choice. The morning I shot him to death, we were up before sunrise, fucking. I was on top, straddling his body, riding him as rhythmically as the waves crash onto the shore. His hands were on my hips, thrusting me a little harder, both of us sweating to the grind. He suddenly lifted me off his fully erect dick and rolled over without a word. Dead silence filled the room, except for the sound of our heavy breathing.

Are you kidding me? Not this again.

His favorite mind game was to make me feel guilty because he could not get off. The routine was to kiss the back of his neck, slither down his body, and finish him off with a blow job. Five times a day he demanded sex, which seemed excessive for a man who couldn't cum. Like clockwork, every day, it was my duty, and always my fault.

On that day, I got up and left him to tend to his own needs. I could hear my oldest son pouring cereal downstairs, and I went to join my children. Big mistake—huge!

Earlier that year, he had taken me to a total of four gynecologists, trying to figure out what was wrong with me. I used to sneak into the bathroom and place K-Y Jelly up as far as I could, because God knows I could no longer get wet with him. When all the doctors insisted I was perfectly healthy, he felt humiliated, still insisting I was the problem. Once he finally admitted the doctors were right, he tied me up by strapping my arms and legs to the dining room table. I was bound, naked and trembling, and beads of sweat bubbled up on my stomach when I saw him plug in the hot glue gun. That glue dripped onto the inside of my thigh, and I screamed as if I was giving birth. Next came my vagina. I was gasping for breath, pleading, twisting like a fish on a hook.

"Please, please don't. I'm sorry. It'll get better. I promise, I'll do anything. We can do it right now! Please, please don't do this!"

* * *

To this day, that pain is indescribable. But it was not nearly as painful as what came next. He sliced that dried glue from my lips as if it were rotten sushi. I passed out.

Apparently, he had decided that if I wasn't "working" properly for him, I was never going to be attractive to anyone else, ever. As if I wasn't faithful. Hell, I had three young children, worked, and put up with all of his madness on a daily basis. Over 2,102,400 minutes of nonsense. The glue incident took only about forty-five of those. I was exhausted.

I'm still exhausted. Every day I try to bring something positive into my life and into someone else's, even in here, at the Valley of Death. For years I was a positive role model for those less equipped, but it seems impossible lately. I'm even losing my sense of humor, which has always been my favorite coping mechanism. After a decade, here I am: sarcastic, crass, cynical, and impatient. I can hardly stand myself.

The daily routine is easy and familiar. Like an abusive relationship, prison is full of the mentally ill, there are officers on power trips, and there are strict structures that lack any form of common sense. Even though you are never alone, you are lonely. No one is able to speak the real truth about what is happening or about how they are feeling. Worse yet, you are unable to help others in any natural way. There is no comforting, consoling, or human contact allowed. You learn that all souls in prison are damaged and there is not one person you can trust, even yourself. There is nothing normal about hell except death.

Three Doors Down was lonely. She didn't last eight weeks here at Death Valley. My bunkie at that time had lasted thirteen years of her life sentence. Still, she has unsuccessfully tried to take her life at least five times that I'm aware of.

When I first moved into the cell she was quiet, living mainly in her own mind, consumed by her thoughts of what was and what could someday be. Slowly, we started to talk. She shared intimate details of the abuse she'd endured as a child—graphic details similar to those in the book *A Child Called "It."* We became like sisters: shared food, shared secrets, shared the TV, laughed and cried together. She became my prison family and gave me an odd sense of purpose.

Then one day, out of the blue, after two years of living together, it all changed. The significant moment that I had no control over happened. She stopped talking, started sucking her thumb, started banging her head against the wall at lockup time. Her tantrums grew violent. The officers gave her tickets, not expecting this behavior from her. She lost over fifty pounds within two or three months. She looked like a walking skeleton, and I pleaded with the officers to call mental health. Together, we colored pictures with crayons to relax. I made a swing out of a sheet and would swing her at count time so she would stay in the room. I cooked three different foods, and when she refused each one, I fed her milk and cookies. These episodes would last days, sometimes weeks.

On the days she was an adult, she was increasingly frustrated and angry. Overwhelmed by all of it, she took a handful of blood pressure pills. That was her first suicide attempt. She was fine, and only received a substance abuse ticket. I continued to plead with the officers to move her to the mental health unit, telling them that she was a danger to herself. Finally, she was cuffed and moved. I watched as she looked at me with contempt, as if I had turned her in for the murder she is serving time for. I felt relief then; now, I only feel regret. She wanted her iced tea like I crave mine. I didn't save her like I thought—I tied her to this hell.

Six months later, she was diagnosed with dissociative identity disorder. That made sense. At Death Valley, she attempted suicide four more times. The last time, she hung herself with a bra and was cut down by the brain aneurysm officer. She is now on medication. She walks around like a zombie on good days and remains violent on the bad ones. She's a shell of the person I knew, truly the epitome of the walking dead. Now a level-four prisoner, she is considered strictly a management problem instead of a mentally ill patient. There is no true help in the penitentiary. I bet she hates me for saving her.

I hate him for not killing me. Odd that this is my reason for hating him, after all the other reasons he's given me, but it's true. He is resting in peace and I am separated from my sons, which is exactly what he wanted. Either way, he won. I am still as trapped as I was with him; I'm just here at Death Valley. I am so exhausted lately, the same way I was at the most intense time of his abuse. I believe the Monster realized at some point that his torture was just not working anymore, that I was too tired and it didn't have the same effect. He needed to harm those I loved to get a reaction from me.

I recall him telling me that lions will sniff out the cubs that were sired by another and then eat them if they are not their own. My two oldest sons were from a previous marriage, and he acted as if I should have known he was out in the world, waiting for me to find him. Somehow he believed I was a possession that he owned, and that I had wandered off before I'd even met him. I was perfect and damaged all at the same time. He convinced himself that if I were to get rid of my two sons, we could somehow live happily ever after with our own child. Twisted realities filled my world. They still do.

* * *

My current bunkie is also mentally ill, a time bomb. She has extreme highs and lows. Unlike my previous bunkie, she never gets tickets for her behavior. Since crazy is the norm for her, all of the officers tolerate her outbursts. It seems unfair and unreasonable to the rest of us, but there is no logic applied here in hell. This lady sings nonstop all day long, which is why I call her American Idol. It's the nicest name I can come up with.

Her greed drives everything she does, and she hides behind some false sense of Christianity where she truly believes Jesus has saved her and only her. He will someday heal her from all her medical and mental issues; the rest of us are confused dykes or lying crackheads. She refers to people as "humanoids," as if she isn't human herself.

One of American Idol's favorite testimonies is when she was on crack and the Holy Spirit came down and raised Big Mike up, levitating him as she preached. She said it didn't matter that she was on crack. She is a "head cracker" and a servant of God, even with the drugs. I couldn't care less about her religion or her past—I am not judgmental—but living with her makes me question if I am becoming the killer I am accused of being.

This bitch won't stop singing. She wakes up from her sleep to make noise, and I contemplate crushing up her blood pressure pills to quiet her. American Idol is enough to drive a sane person crazy, and I'm pretty sure I should be there already, considering my past.

Looking back, I see the progression of it all. Having our son is when the most significant change took place. Still, there were early signs I had missed. Apparently, if you're an educated person, this can be held against you, as if there is some Abuse 101 course in college that prepares you to recognize the warning

signs. There isn't. By the time you are in an abusive relationship, it is harder to escape than most people realize. I tried
many times.

Once I attempted to get away, but he threatened to kill
my parents. I remember him saying, as sweet as can be, "I
know I'll at least see you at their funeral, baby. You might as
well come home now."

I did. I naively longed for a happy, blended family, and
I did everything I could think of to fix him and us. I begged
for us to attend counseling, for him to seek help with his depression, for us to work through things together. We took va-
cations without the children, and I never burdened him by
leaving him to take care of them. They were never alone with
him at the end, ever. I followed all his rules. I was faithful and
obedient, and eventually feared him to the point where I lost
all reason.

The year after we had our child, he needed to travel home
to Georgia. He'd passed the bar exam and was being sworn
in. Did I mention he was a licensed attorney in three states
and had a master's degree in medical anthropology? Still, he'd
never had a job—he died at the age of thirty-two and had
never worked a day in his life.

Right before he left, he explained to me how we should
get married. He told me that I needed to give my two oldest
sons away, that I should just forget they were ever born and
start a new life with him in Georgia. He wanted to go back
to his home and "rule the country." He believed he could be
somebody there and I could have a big Southern home and
everything would be perfect. The part I never understood was
the fact that he was so kind and patient with my boys when
we first started dating—it was one of the most attractive qual-
ities he had. How did he become this beast? When it came to

the children, I never bit my tongue, and the very idea of abandoning them was insane. This, of course, provoked his rage even more. I told him he was being absurd. He said, "Those fucking cum-crunchers you call sons are going to go one way or another!"

I thought he had walked out to calm down. I heard the sound of liquid pouring, so I assumed he was making himself a Jack and Coke. He snatched me into the kitchen and I realized he wasn't calming down at all. When I yanked back my arm, he kicked me into a wall and I fell on the floor. Next thing I remember, he was explaining to me how easy it would be to remove my skin when I was dead.

The Monster was lying on top of me with my elbow in a bowl of boric acid. My teeth were clenched, my eyes watering uncontrollably. This was new—not the pain, not the torture, not the reason, but the method. He was creative. I lifted my head toward him, groaned from the pain, and began kissing his neck, slowly twisting my tongue around his bulging vein. Then I bit.

"You bitch!" He released my arm.

I ran into the bathroom, not knowing what to do with the acid eating my flesh. I rinsed it in cold water and the sink filled with blood. He came in and said, "Baby, let me take care of you." He placed ointment on gauze, wrapped the wound, and gently tended to it with seemingly genuine concern. I didn't say a word. Tears continued to stream down my face. He made popcorn with extra butter—my favorite—and we watched a movie as if nothing had happened. Today, that elbow has the softest skin on my body.

Of course, these days I can't even see my body. At Death Valley, there are no mirrors. American Idol never leaves the room; therefore, there is no alone time to care for or tend to myself. Every day, I drag my clean clothes into the shower area since there's no privacy in my cell. Naked in the shower, I'm surrounded by women. Four other showers are running at the same time, women are coming in and out and in and out, calling for a spot, humming, arguing, complaining. Fuck!

If she would just leave the room, just for a while, maybe—just maybe—I could regroup. Maybe I wouldn't be so tense when that spine-chilling noise comes out of her mouth, that noise she calls singing to the Lord.

My neck pain is beyond chronic from all of this tension. I keep telling myself: *She is ill, it's not her fault, this is temporary.* The problem is, "temporary" can mean years in prison. The reality is she's not moving, I'm not moving, staff is not empathetic or accommodating, and neither of us is going home anytime soon. I am trapped in this cell with American Idol at Death Valley, and I cannot take it.

The Monster couldn't take my rejection of him. He lay there quietly—too quietly—as I wrapped my robe around my naked body. One day I chose to be a mother first, not his sex slave. I got up and didn't get him off. It felt amazing.

Before I even got to the second step to go downstairs to the boys, I could hear the *click, click* from him cocking the gun. I stood still, my stomach in knots, my throat tight. I looked up at him standing at the banister, naked, his eyes crazed with rage.

"Baby, what the fuck do you *really* think you're doing?" he said.

I could barely breathe, much less answer. As I turned to walk back up the steps, he grabbed my hair and pulled me into our room.

"I asked you a question, baby. What were you thinking? You're choosing those cum-crunchers over me? No one comes before me, no one!"

I still didn't speak. I just stood there with my hair in his hand while he waved the loaded gun in my face. Every time he asked me a question—and every time I didn't answer—he became more enraged. My throat was too tight. My hands were trembling. This felt like the moment he had been waiting for, the reason he had purchased those bullets.

"Guess what, bitch? You chose the bastards over me, but you won't have that option again. Whichever one of them hasn't drunk the milk in his cereal bowl, that's the boy who gets it first."

The Monster had a rule that the boys needed to clean their plates no matter what. This included his own son, after a year: if he didn't eat all the food the Monster prepared, he would force-feed him until he puked, then get pissed and say his son was becoming too picky, just like the other cum-crunchers of mine. I made every effort to serve food everyone liked just for this reason, but no one, including me, ever drank the milk in the cereal bowl if we could get away with sneaking it into the kitchen and pouring it down the drain. We had the oddest rules in our house.

The Monster shoved me onto the bed and went on and on about how I had betrayed him, how this isn't how things were supposed to be, how the kids had made me impure. Nothing made sense. He went to put on a shirt and laid the gun on the nightstand. Without a thought, I picked it up and simply shot him in the back of the head.

He turned around and laughed at me.

Holy shit! This was it. My life was over. I held on to that gun like it was my own hand. We weren't going to make it through this. His fingernails dug into my hands, but I was not going to let go. He was not going to get my boys. He was screaming, and I must have kept shooting.

The rest is like a puzzle. Pieces are missing, and no combination provides me with the entire picture. Even now, a decade later, I stare at each one, waiting for closure. I shot him seven times and only recall three. Logically, I know I did them all, but I just can't remember. It's like being in a car crash—you know something happened, you recall some parts, but most of it is a blur.

I told my attorney he had purchased quiet bullets to kill us with. The attorney told me there was no such thing, that there must have been a silencer. There wasn't, and I knew this for a fact because the Monster used to play Russian roulette with me if I didn't have the laundry done on time. His schedules and his rules took over my life. Since the Monster's clothes were not to be washed with the boys' clothing, I would run late. On those nights, Russian roulette became the norm. Once the weapon clicked and I was still alive, he'd keep playing with his guns, cleaning them and shooting them out the backyard, trying to hit the basketball, as I finished up the wash. I was very familiar with the quietness of the bullets. He told me he purchased them specifically to kill us so that the neighbors would not hear. I had no reason not to believe him, all things considered. I had never known him to make an idle threat. He always followed through.

When the ballistics came back, my attorney apologized. The bullets had no gunpowder and are illegal to purchase; this is why they made so little noise, and likely why the Monster laughed at me when I shot him. The first shot didn't even pierce his thick skull. After that first shot, I believe karma, fate, luck, or just a mother's sheer will to protect, took over.

* * *

There is no fate taking over my present situation. American Idol's psychosis is getting worse, and my sanity is teetering. A hospital run would give us some relief. We need that. Eighteen days ago, I stopped taking my blood pressure pills.

Twenty-eight days the Monster lay dead in our bedroom before I buried him in the backyard. Thirty-two days it took me to clean up our room. When it was all clean, I knocked on the police station's door and turned myself in. Before that, I forced myself into that room for one hour every night after I put the boys to bed. I puked every time I entered it; the stench was overwhelming. Our last morning together would flash over and over in my mind like a film on repeat. I wasn't able to sleep, I was short with the boys, I wasn't able to function except to clean up this mess from the Monster, just as I had been doing for years. Every time we fought, I cleaned the room, cleaned up my body, hid the bruises, fixed the broken doors, fixed the chairs. I cleaned and cleaned and cleaned.

Once everything was done in the bedroom—the carpet removed and replaced, the bed thrown out on bulk trash day—I put up wallpaper, bought a peaceful rocking chair for the room, and just sat there. I never cried; I just sat there. I didn't know what to do. What I did know was, if something had happened to any of my sons, no matter what, I would want closure. I would want to know what happened to my son even if he was a beast. I couldn't live with the Monster's parents always wondering what happened to their child. They deserved some peace of mind. I spent one last weekend with my children before knocking on the police station's door. After that I took a plea, and ended up here at Death Valley.

* * *

Lately, Death Valley has been entirely too much for me. The constant noise from American Idol is like bugs crawling in my ears. I wonder if that is how the Monster felt about the boys. All I know is, one way or another, I need to have some peace. Thirty-six pills I crushed up with my lock and stirred them into the chili. One bowl has beans and one does not. The bowl without the beans has the pills. American Idol's greed may very well be the death of her. Two bowls: one for her, one for me; her choice, my treat. I mix up a glass of Nestea iced tea and offer her some chili. This significant moment is mine.

ANGEL EYES

BY ANDRE WHITE

Ionia Correctional Facility (Ionia, Michigan)

F ish! Every day they come in younger and younger. Pretty soon they'll be babies, and I'll end up having a work detail changing diapers. I'd rather shine shoes than smell shit all day and hear their crying. Oh, they'll be crying when they get behind the wall, the whole lot of 'em, whining all day—mama can't help now! They all look the same too, when they first come inside: stretched face, locked lips, eyes out of sockets, looking up and 'round the rotunda, dumbstruck on how big and old it is. Ain't no pictures on the walls and ceiling. No saints, no angels, just cracks and chipped paint, dirty gray and filthy white, ugly 'nuff to be a sin. God ain't in here, oh no, only all kinds of religious groups. Some of 'em fishes gone be on their knees serving with their mouth, others gone be carrying a flat piece of steel in the name of a group. Some don't make it a day and run to Blue Hoe Card. Getting on protection won't help 'em none—what they're running from is there too, or can get there the same way.

Oh, 'em fishes would come in and see a lot of guards at the rotunda—keys jingling and boots stepping hard on the concrete floor, moving in a hurry—having their fish heads spinning and hearts jumping, feeling so safe, and for good reason. It's a setup for failure though. When they get behind the wall, eager feet to the rescue is the last thing they'll be hearing and seeing; they'll be scared, and for a whole 'nother reason. They'll see me shining guards' boots—the white man's. I know what they be thinking, Jabo Tut's a house nigger! Before long, a whole lot of 'em wished they was shining shoes instead.

I was once like the one or two young bucks of a batch that ain't a cur. Oh, I 'member wings in my stomach flapping 'bout when I done my first stretch, was eighteen years old and ready for whatever.

I'd seen some wild ones come through that bit hard, like a piranha in a fishbowl. One stood out, I mean this boy gave a helluva first impression. Had the kind of face that drew you in: clean, forever young, an innocence begging you to corrupt, to violate him. Take it for yourself or ruin it for others if you couldn't have his youth and 'thusiasm, good looks and 'telligent features. Oh no, a look that a certain type of convict—*Henas*, what I call 'em—took as feminine; they'd scavenger hunt for someone easy to slide up on, spit in their ear, isolate 'em, and later have the fish walking 'round with his finger latched onto his belt buckle. I could tell this kid's 'pearance was deceptive, had the doo-doo chasers fooled from the get-go. He was medium height and build, barely legal, if not still in high school; probably living with Mama, baked chicken and potatoes fed, baby fat over muscles hungry for the weight pit, a rare treat for the Henas—so they thought. He had a piss-yellow 'plexion, like his mama laid him in her bladder spill for a while. It was his eyes, though, blue as a late Joplin sky, that had the Henas yapping over. It wasn't normal for his skin and was something exotic, a prize. I could see that this boy had something else other than Massa's genes behind those baby blues. Oh, it was vicious, nasty in a bad way, just waiting to come out.

Our eyes were different colors, but we saw the same old raggedy castle, Michigan Reformatory—Gladiator School! In

Ionia—"I Own Ya" what it's called—oh, need Harriet Tubman to get you out of that prison town. All was built on swampland, in the middle of the wilderness. A city boy won't find his way out these dark woods; endless trees blocking the light, every way winding back to the starting spot, confusing you, and Billys riding around in pickup trucks with double-R sixes and year-round license to shoot a nigga on sight. Frustrating 'nuff to have you stay behind the wall and take your chances in the concrete jungle.

Didn't recognize the building in front of the rotunda was the chow hall when I first got here. It was all bricks and a set of steel double doors. Seagulls lined the chow hall's ledge, waiting, watching, and swooped down on anything put up in the air, swallowing it whole. They had no fear of people, shitting on convicts at will. I was given a bedroll and simple 'nuff directions. "J block, that way," the guard said outside the rotunda, pointing at a building 'minding me of the abandoned ones I used to play in at the commercial district when I was a rascal. I had looked straight ahead, not at J block but what was in front of it: all the blue coats and black shoes, like I had on, all either standing or walking or working out or playing basketball inside the gated projects. Oh, it wasn't like no projects I'd seen before! All of 'em, I mean every single one of 'em, stopped and stared at us come in carrying our bedrolls under our arms. These guys was big—swelled chests, pumped shoulders, muscles busting out their jaws—and was mean mugging us out of habit. Some of 'em stepped to the fence that separated the yard from the walkway, straddling it, and made remarks 'bout us being fish, trying to scare us the way vets do, picking out the weak ones.

I was forty years old then, far from a fish. Done twelve years already in Missouri State Penitentiary, five years in the fed joint. You couldn't tell like most half-breeds—smooth skin, good hair, see, look good for seventy-eight, huh? Oh, still'll give 'em a run for their money. Done the type of crimes that kept me in big ole houses, fancy apartments, with mighty pretty women, a crew of gorillas. Scared, oh no, I was dangerous! My eyes was charcoal, gasoline pumped through my heart, and I had three bodies under my belt. The sort of build that brought strength your way to check what you're made of.

I came up out of Missouri earth, hard nuts and no give, the only way my manhood gone get took is cold and loose; they have to kill me first! I couldn't wait to make an example out of anyone who tried. And I did: just six months in, a flabby nickel-and-dime prison loan shark had overcharged me the going rate. Oh no, I wasn't paying extras for nothing! Him coming on strong meant *or else* to me; either blood on his knife or shit on his dick. I ain't never ran from a fight—brought it to your doorsteps. I didn't sneak up on him, I walked up with a bone-crusher, stabbed him twice in the neck and once in the heart, putting his dick to the dirt for all to see. And they had; watched all six foot four, 270 pounds of dead meat hit the ground jiggling. I spent five years in the graves, came out the wrong nigga to fuck with.

Oh, Henas was riding the fence too, always smoking over fresh fish and dropping lugs, hoping one would bite. A whole bunch of lugs was dropped on D.T., the blue-eyed lil' brotha. Yeah, Henas was already trying to sink their hooks in him. J block connects to I block like a right-angle math symbol, the prison yard slap dead in the middle of them. So was the fence; Henas walked the length of it up to J block's entrance, doo-doo chasing, howling through the gate, mostly at some white guys, particularly one they called Suzanne Somers, and also

Angel Eyes (the name that D.T. became known as, oh, for a-whole-'nother reason).

Inside, J block looked as industrial as it gets: stripped concrete floors and walls—stained with bleach from half-ass blood-spill cleanups—and rusty iron rails and bars, shit brown, a decay that ate away your sight, eroding your emotions to a numbing oil base, with time drying out hope that's brushed away like dandruff. Oh, a factory as any I've seen. But its finished product came out an assembly line of cells, in state blues and bloodshot eyes. Narrow steps and rails corkscrewed to each floor, five in all, and D.T. was assigned to cell 36 on J-5, the pen-house, better known as Predator's Row, the same floor I was on, oh, would you believe he wound up my neighbor. The rock, long as a city block, had rows of barred cells, faced a depressing gray wall and dirt-shaded windows, tinting the already bleak forest. We was near the end of it. Guards would only make their rounds when we was locked in our cells or during chow—when everybody was gone—never when the cells was open for mass movement.

After the rock cleared, the guards could see the slain bodies on the floor. Sometimes during chow they'd make a round and find a body or two dead in their cells: some under their blankets with their wrists and heels slit, bleeding out, others butchered on the floor. Those near death usually was took to health care, got their cornholes sewed. Oh, you'd keep your eyes and mouth closed and keep moving 'cause you'll know better than to do anything but. You didn't have to be con-wise to know you was on your own on the rock. Guards gassing the meat wagon wouldn't come and pick up the man down till it was over. They knew better. The first look down to the other end of the rock made your knees wobble and your johnson yank back: it was far, narrow—a long desolate tunnel to hell.

No way out 'cept past a world of trouble, ever present like stink on shit.

It was quiet when Angel Eyes walked down the rock, passing each grim and grimmer mug popping out every cell. They watched to see if he'd look. Henas had their hawks stuck outside the cell bars, staring at his backside. The kid had done good not to look in anyone's cell. He walked straight, head up, attitude in his shoulders, 'nuff not to come off too cocky. It would have been took as a front. Had that happened, had he done that, they'd thought he was looking for something, what else 'cept sausage and hard-boiled eggs. Oh, he was already in for rape. No reason was good 'nuff reason for 'em, it'd tickled their fancy, raping the rapist—a white girl! Daddy's lil' girl was the daughter of L. Booth Peterson, Oakland County's top district attorney, I hear one racist son of a bitch. A blind man could see D.T. ain't did that. He should have known better not to cross 8 Mile, fooling 'round with those devils.

D.T. had to feel like a giant inside his cell, a birdcage. You can't even spread your wings without touching the walls. The toilet and sink was elbow to elbow in the back corner, jamming your legs and arms together, feeling like you're taking a shit in a phone booth next to a coffin for a bed. Rust poured out the sink bowl, and the cell's floor was scraped and mutilated, like a cat's work to the side of the couch. D.T. knew better, Heathcliff ain't sharpened nothing, it was somebody who knew what time it was. The kid had to suspect it wouldn't just be his freedom he'd be fighting for, but his manhood.

Morning always cleared the dark cloud for a minute. What a sight to see: fishes shooting out their cells before the door closed back for breakfast, like cowboys, tossing their coats and shoes out the cell and hopping in the stagecoach. They'd come out pulling up their pants, tripping over shoes, shit face, crusty eyes, and hot mouth; turning the breakfast table's 'mused faces salty and mean, mugging 'em fishes for a-whole-nother reason—John Wayn'en. It's what they called it, a really bad look on a fish. 'Least a vet done 'nuff time not to give a Jim Crow anymore 'bout hygiene. Henas would be up before the rooster, watching 'em hard. Maybe it's the idea of catching a fish with his draws down that have 'em willy-nilly; maybe not? Same difference to Henas, they have the ups on their prey, it's all that matter to 'em.

Opportunity comes when the cell doors break open. Most Henas on our rock talk a fish out his draws, all 'cept Gorilla Black. Oh no, he liked taking it . . . forced entry, 'specially to punks acting like they're tough. He got off on proving they ain't thoroughbreds but sissy boys. Gorilla Black was a bona fide predator, all head and shoulders, black as motor oil, ugly 'nuff to deserve the name *Tracey* to soften his 'timidating 'pearance, a stocky fella, built like a Sherman tank. He was nasty as a rattler and hung like a palomino. He'd put a hurt'en on a seasoned whore, D.T. hadn't a hope or prayer and was in a world of trouble. Gorilla Black laid on D.T., telling other Henas the boy was off limits, that Angel Eyes was his! Those Henas knew better than to step on Gorilla Black's toes. I didn't know better, I ain't no Hena—Gorilla Black knew better than to cross *me*, a big-game hunter! I'll cut him into lil' pieces and feed him to the gulls. D.T. was a sharp one though. He would leave his cell for breakfast already dressed, groomed, on his Ps and Qs. When he didn't go to breakfast, he was up, made bunk, reading a book: business, law, oh, had a good lawyer and strong appeal in court. Him and the girl had been fooling around; there was no evidence of rape. The girl's best friend sided with D.T. Oh, you'd never catch him sleeping when the cell doors broke open. He 'minded me of myself.

Almost—he hadn't been tested yet, but it was coming.

One day I had went to the counselor's office, Ms. Bitchard—actually, Prichard; the other name was what they called her. I went to her office so she could straighten out 'em taking me off the special diet line—they know I'm a diabetic and can't eat that other shit! They rather see Jabo Tut dead than spend another dime sending me out to the world hospital. I'll check out when I'm ready—I'm gone write the final chapter! And it ain't gone be nothing nice. D.T. was already in her office when I got there. I waited right outside the door and heard 'em loud and clear as a church bell. Said things 'bout him enrolling back in college. Didn't recognize her voice though; she was all sweet on him like nobody else. You'd 'spect a house to fall on top of her mean ass, evil as she was. But not to him: she was giggly, gibberish, asking personal questions, oh, twirling her fancy gold ink pen. She never unlocked the armor gate and let prisoners inside her office. All business was handled through the bars since she was back there alone. Oh, they had something going on 'tween 'em; he was in her system, probably didn't even know it. His mother was sick, the cancer had got hold of her, he was hurt in the worst way over it. I took a peek and saw her eyes, green as a leaf, wide as all outside, taking him in: his pain, frustration, helplessness, 'flecting off her plump cheeks ripe with sympathy, lips that was usually thin and pink had swelled to Kansas strawberries. Her orange hair, pear-shaped as could be, had never looked so good, 'specially the way she stared at him, into those eyes of his.

Shining shoes got me all 'round the prison, access to everywhere. I moved like water through cracks and crevices, leaking out where I wanted. No one 'cept a few, here and there, knew what Jabo Tut was really moving. You wouldn't believe where I was getting the dope from, oh no. Bo Jangles has benefits, I shined shoes as a sideshow. A turnkey named Mohlerson was an unusual one, not the regular white folk: average height, full beard, fading red whiskers, a stubby version of that fella, ah . . . the brawny man. He hated everybody, even his own kind. Other guards alike, they didn't want to work with him, a shit starter. He was always trying to talk up on the 'pocalypse, killing everyone 'cept him and ole Yella, his dog. All he was was ornery, a wretched piece of shit. He'd made a routine of stopping me going to work to shine his boots, right there outside the rock on the stairway port. Putting his beat-up boots on the rail, the rubber all worn, tips faded, he'd kicked plenty of people when they was down. I had a leather shoeshine box that Old Man Howard made for me at the hobby craft shop. It was like a real toolbox: when you opened it, drawers came out like a step ladder, filled with different color polishes, wax, shoe taps, and other stuff.

Ms. Prichard had come back from somewhere one time and was headed to her office way on the opposite end of the rock. Mohlerson stopped her, talking out the side of his neck, making no damn sense. No wonder he was a hermit: he didn't know how to knock a broad. She was a country girl, not simple 'nuff to wear what you eat. If what he was saying wasn't stupid 'nuff, the tobacky bumping his gums made him sound stupider. Her response was dumb too. Oh, he'd dummied her down, and she didn't like it one damn bit. She was past ready to go like two shakes and a rattlesnake. I felt the awkwardness; I'm always ready to hightail it out when I see Mohlerson.

The phone had rung; it was her opportunity to make a clean break, and she took it. Oh, she was still stepping even though he had told her to wait. Sour face and all, she made it to the door, opened it up, and all that loud from the rock came out. Mohlerson called Demonte Taylor on the intercom for a visit. She stopped dead in her tracks. Mohlerson stepped to the walled control panel; it was all lever action till they installed electric cell doors. Mohlerson pushed the button for cell 36.

D.T. came out of his cell ready, shining like a new penny: shirt, slacks, shoes—not gym shoes, dress shoes!—fresh out the box and spit-shined. He looked sharp and dapper. Ms. Prichard's eyes had lit up. She was diarrhea at the mouth, all of a sudden talking to Mohlerson 'bout D.T., well, nice and neat guys in general, "model prisoners," oh, she matched 'em. I could tell Mohlerson's grill was heating. She went on and on 'bout D.T.

Red and blue veins popped up out of Mohlerson's neck. "There's the pass!" he said, nodding toward the desk. Another pass was stuck to the control panel across from the desk.

"Which one?" D.T. asked.

"Right there!" He pointed to the one on the control panel. "It's simple as white and black. Don't you know the difference?"

D.T. ignored him with every part of his body 'cept his eyes. He cutted him deep with them and picked up the pass. Ms. Prichard whipped out her fancy ink pen and signed it. 'Parently, she didn't know the difference either, she left too, same direction as D.T.

D.T. got a whole bunch of visits from his mama and sister, even from white folks from the college he went to. He had church support too. Oh, I could tell something awful was 'bout to happen; good people going through troubles always have the buzzard's luck. And I'm no stranger to the angel of death: I outlived everybody, including my children. Couldn't even go to the funerals, murderers ain't allowed. Can't tell me this ain't hell.

I had left work one afternoon, took the hallway from the rotunda to I block, like walking down a snake's throat, wide 'nuff for one fat man or two skinny fellas squared together like dice. Bare pipes taped and patched like a busted spine hung loose and crooked from the ceiling, a skeleton on the walls. I stopped at the med line window. Didn't have nothing to pick up, just wanted to see Nurse Betty, the only thing good in this shit hole. The window was closed shut. Oh, the railroad ahead wasn't, it was wide open, two Henas had Suzanne Somers in the corner running a B&O train on him. That white boy and Angel Eyes was tight as flea pussy: walked the yard together, hung in the library, the gym, had came through quarantine together. All they knew was each other. Oh, birds of a feather don't always flock together. Henas think so, 'specially Gorilla Black; he never took his eyes off D.T., watched his every move: where he went, who he 'sociated with. Gorilla Black had to have him for hisself, with nowhere to turn, make D.T. his bitch and like it.

When I got back to the rock, Gorilla Black was dust-mopping the floor, moving like molasses on sandpaper, circling the same area by D.T.'s cell. The kid had got an intercom call to go and pick up legal mail. He came back from the control center happy. Gorilla Black's face was tore up, he didn't like that D.T.'s appeal was looking good. Gorilla Black stopped in front of D.T.'s cell, stood there silent as could be. The kid flagged his good news with a goofy 'pression, didn't bring no noise. Gorilla Black dug a Snickers bar out his pocket and tossed it on D.T.'s bed and left. Oh, D.T. was stupider than me. He ate it for a-whole-nother reason, thought Gorilla

Black was being nice. I wish a nigga would cut into me 'bout it; no damn candy bar better be on my cot. I'm eating it with my bone-crusher by my side.

I was on my way to work another time and saw Mohlerson looking out the window, staring down at something. It was my shot to duck past him down the stairs. I made it too. Passed D.T. on my way . . . saw Ms. Prichard ahead of me on the walkway. Oh, I'd be a broke-dick dog if I hadn't forgot something, can't 'member what it was, but I had to get it. On my way back up the stairs, Mohlerson had D.T. hemmed up. He was at the top of the steps talking real greasy to D.T., blocking him from leaving. Even pulled a picture of a boat out his shirt pocket, saying, "Me and that bitch gone be on it, and you gone give me the six months." D.T. didn't know who or what he was talking 'bout and blew him off. Oh, Mohlerson was on to his and Ms. Prichard's thing, whatever it was. Wasn't gone be no mulattos running 'round his woods, not on his watch. Mohlerson intended to push the kid's buttons and provoke him to lay hands on him; he'd get six months off with pay for sure. D.T. would catch a case, sit in the hole for years. Probably turn into a savage. Mohlerson knew he couldn't get Ms. Prichard on his boat—long as he cock-blocked D.T. and her from shacking up, all was right in the wild. Oh, he was a piece of shit!

I had been ripping and running nonstop, sunup to sundown, had to take the day off—and it wasn't my regular off day. I was tired, too tired to care if all of 'em ever got served, got a shine; too tired even to yearn, tired of all this shit! Tired of being tired. Something sweet in the air had woke me up. It was Ms. Prichard's perfume. She was at D.T.'s cell, probably been there for a while; had a dream about some home-cooked meals: chicken dumplings and peach cobbler. Oh, she had the whole rock smelling good. I couldn't hear 'em, a bunch of radios was going, blasting that bip-bop nonsense. I had put my ear to the hole in the wall, a dick hole; most cells have them. Even took a peek and saw that fancy gold ink pen of hers sliding up and down his bare chest. I knew it! He pulled her, the lil' squirt. I stuck my mirror out the bars, saw her big wide ass in tight white jeans, looking like moon pies. I saw Mohlerson too, coming up the rock. She wasn't paying 'tention; her hand was still inside his cell. Mohlerson's eyes jumped out his face like a chicken bone got caught down his throat. She finally saw him and eased her hand out, but no fancy ink pen, probably left it on his chest. She didn't move or stop talking to Angel Eyes. Mohlerson had no words either, just made his round.

The next morning, Mohlerson turned up the heat, searching the kid's cell for no good reason, hitting it like a hurricane and leaving his stuff everywhere, all out of order: papers and pictures on the floor, floating in the toilet; took his Walkman and TV, lying in the report that they were stolen goods. Ms. Prichard saw the game Mohlerson was playing and would give D.T. his stuff right back; she threw out all the false misconduct tickets Mohlerson wrote against him. Mohlerson hated that, went as far as cried to the brass 'bout her not backing his plays. They must've just let him vent, that's all. He came up with another way to try and get D.T. off his square. "Want to kick it, want to kick it?" Mohlerson asked just 'bout every time he passed D.T.'s cell, 'plying the kid was a rat, turning other inmates against him. It didn't work.

Then Mohlerson shook down others' cells, taking radios, TVs, beard trimmers, clothes, property they either bought or strong-armed from another inmate. Oh, they'd be pissed off, and Mohlerson would blame it on D.T. Convicts know better than to let a turnkey buzz 'em up, pitch you against another inmate. No one bit 'cept Gorilla Black. He cut into D.T. hard and raw 'bout some stuff Mohlerson had took from his cell. It was probably a play too. D.T. said he ain't have nothing to do with it. Gorilla Black told him that he owed him anyway, and he'd pay in due time.

I 'member that morning like it happened to *me*. D.T. was tired of it all: tired of the courts jerking him 'round all these months, of prison politics; tired of his mother putting it in God's hands. Oh, tired of crud, black mole, oh, the shitty mood always here. D.T. came out Ms. Prichard's office with nothing 'cept dried streaks on his face. His mama's 'dition had worsened; he'd let some of it out in there. Ms. Prichard came out right behind him, dabbing her eyes with tissue, had papers for him to sign. She handed him another fancy ink pen to use, a silver one. She told him she'd get him transferred to a prison closer to home, be near his mama.

Later that day, I had finished polishing the deputy warden's shoes at my shoe stand, and Gorilla Black was coming out the barbershop, talking with Hully Gully, a notorious homo thug. Gorilla Black said he was gone "tap that ass tonight." I took it to mean D.T.'s time had run out; either was gone fight, fuck, or flee to Blue Hoe Card. I left the rotunda in a hurry, wasn't sure why at the time, just did. I stopped by D.T.'s cell, went against my long-standing practice to never get 'volved in prison bullshit, and interfered, to even things out. D.T. didn't see what was 'round the corner—a monster. The one and only time I done that, got burnt trying to save a boy who wound up having sugar in his tank after all. Angel Eyes was different, worth saving, was from good stock, decent upbringing.

Up till then, I hadn't spoke a word to him. I told him to hold onto this, and handed him a single-edged flat piece, eight inches of steel coming out of a tape-and-shoestring handle, strong 'nuff to blow holes in any tank.

"What I need this for?" D.T. asked.

I told him for trouble.

"What trouble?"

I said no trouble after you use it, and I walked away, leaving him dumbstruck. Oh no, he didn't give that shank back though—he wasn't no fool. He tucked it in his pants, probably carried it everywhere he went.

Turns out D.T.'s mama had died, didn't make it past noon. Oh, Ms. Prichard called D.T. to her office, then she came out by herself, reckoned to give him some alone time in there. He came out sometime after . . . passed my cell puffy-eyed and blank stare; aged some too, was thin from water loss and looking empty; the worst had finally come out. In spite of it all, it felt good, I know: getting shit out, shit off your chest, the suffering over with. I'd been there. How was he gone deal with it, his loss, now knowing how to not hold back no more . . . All's left is rage. Oh, I truly was him before. Ms. Prichard had 'mediately got to work 'ranging for him to attend the funeral. He had a better shot than I'd had to make it.

Nothing in here surprise me no more. Saw big-timers bow down to pipsqueaks; killers broke over like a double-barrel shotgun; some had their manhood taken, but not their dignity— their heart! Saw wardens crooked as scoliosis, guards taking bribes for a blind eye. I never mind 'em, tend to my own business like a full-time job. Seems everybody 'round here need their nose cut, instigating trouble for kicks, playing the dozens like seagulls, watching, waiting to see somebody in a jam, gobble it down, then laugh and gossip like old women. Guess you gotta make it your business though to help a guy trying to do good, trying to help himself. Oh no, can't fight for 'em— give 'em a stick, is just as good. Only Henas and black-hearted folks eat babies, shit on everything they touch; fucked up their life and hate to see others with a future, a soul. They been had their souls sold for rotgut spud juice and 'perimental med pills to cope with the time. Some come fresh off the streets strange fruit; hide behind a bush till someone shake a leaf, bring it out 'em, have him on his knees shining knobs.

Oh, D.T.'s friend ain't no kind of business of mines; that was a hopeless cause. I turned my back; the warm shower water took me to Ozark Creek. D.T. came in the showers, got all undressed. Stepped 'round the wall blinder, saw his buddy with a throat full . . . D.T.'s look was a shattered glass; pieces of his face fell to the floor. His buddy's was different, caught like a deer in headlights at D.T.'s blues, bright, spellbinding. The pale hand guided his face back to position. D.T. shook his head, grabbed his stuff, and left.

I got back from the shower and saw D.T. sitting on his bunk in the dark, staring at the wall. He turned, looked right through me like glass. Those eyes was midnight . . . a dark you don't go out in; you wait till they brighten up; nothing 'cept death was in 'em. He truly died that day, woke up in hell for the first time where he was all alone, was too full of hope to realize before . . . it was all gone now: the scholarship, his freedom, his mama. They couldn't take nothing else from him 'cept his manhood. Since he already had hell, they'd have to pay with their lives for his asshole. Oh, he had hell to give from what I saw that night; it was exactly what Angel Eyes was gone give 'em.

Gorilla Black came dust-mopping again, waited at the end of the rock for the cell doors to break open for night yard; soon as that happened, he rushed D.T.'s cell, plugged the door with a piece of rubber so it wouldn't close while he was inside. He stood over the kid with a shank in one hand and his dick in the other, then said, "Shit on my dick or blood on my knife?"

D.T. didn't hesitate and gave him what he'd asked for—blood on his knife. Oh, it was D.T.'s knife that was dripping blood. Wasn't what Gorilla Black 'spected, him being so fast, a beast! He had sliced open Gorilla Black's wrist—the shank came out the guy's hand, but D.T. still had his; had a sword fight, chopping Gorilla Black's dick down to a stub. Gorilla Black cried like a bitch, hightailed it out of there, bleeding like a hog. D.T. stayed on top of his head, whacking away!

Gorilla Black made it back to his cell, tried to close it behind him. Oh no, Angel Eyes wasn't having that. He pulled it back open, went inside, and stabbed Gorilla Black all over: his face, neck, head, everywhere. Gorilla Black hollered, screamed, *wah, wah, wah*—oh, what the babies gone do? You ain't never heard a man cry till his balls get cut out his sack. Gorilla Black begged for his life, would have put shit on the kid's dick for him to stop. But Angel Eyes wanted the bloody knife. Had to stop him before he killed Gorilla Black, he wasn't worth getting a life bit over. He came to his senses and gave me the bonecrusher, then we went straight to the yard. The guards made a round and found Gorilla Black covered in blood, twitching on his floor, butchered half to death.

A couple of days passed; no guards came marching in hockey suits to take D.T. to the grave for the stabbing. The kid was too new to worry; he'd never seen 'em come before. Even so, he was still drugged off stabbing all his troubles away to see the world hadn't been dropped on his shoulders, yet.

The prison's alarm blew like a tornado warning through foghorns. The whole place went on emergency lockdown; everyone was rushed to their cells. Teams of guards ran to Ms. Prichard's office. No sooner, a bunch of nurses came; one had a big ole medical bag, two others carried a stretcher. All the big brass came running: warden, deputy warden, assistant deputy warden, who not. They all came out Ms. Prichard's office. She was lying on the stretcher: heart machine, IV bag, oxygen mask, all was laying on top of her body. Suits and uniforms had their hands on the stretcher, racing her to medical. But Ms. Prichard was DOA, strangled to death; Mohlerson had found her on her office's bathroom floor. The whole prison was on lockdown indefinitely.

Three days went by before they fed us—one bagged meal a day, cold cuts and an apple. They had done a mass shakedown, tore up our cells, threw all our personal 'fects on the rock: pictures, letters, clothes, got it all mixed up, trashed most of it. Oh, they was pissed over Ms. Prichard's murder; had another reason to hate prisoners, mess 'em over.

Mohlerson searched D.T.'s cell and came out with Ms. Prichard's fancy silver ink pen. They took the kid straight to the graves: hog-tied him, hands and feet cuffed together, slammed his chest to the floor every step of the way, brought blood out his nose, then tossed him down the stairs, all five flights. They whooped him some more when he got to the graves, put him in an observation cell, a plexiglass vestibule. They whipped him like a slave, a lynching, cuffed him to the cell's bars, left him hanging like that a whole day. Didn't feed him for a week; when they finally did, Mohlerson made it his business to give D.T. the meals—spitting in his tray, then shoving it through the food slot to the floor. Mohlerson would fuck with D.T.'s head, told him he poisoned his food, 'jaculated in it, put all kinds of shit in it, shit even, wouldn't put it past him. The kid went long as he could without eating before his will broke. Ended up eating the food loafs, whole rations mixed together into a log, dabbed with some of Mohlerson's foulness.

Guards wouldn't give D.T. his mail—'specially Mohlerson, he'd tear it up right in D.T.'s face: letters from his sister, friends, Mama's obituary. They turned all his visits away, lawyers too. Oh, D.T. was at a place worse than death, was in a living hell, a place no one should ever be, buried alive, alone, no reason or answers for it. No penance or closure, just an open wound, never healing, always pain. He hadn't been able to see his mama for the last time; convicted of a rape he hadn't done; accused of a murder he didn't commit; his teen life snatched away like that, had him in a world of misery, suffering, beyond relief, way past vindication, too far gone for vengeance.

D.T.'s lawyer was a fighter, got a court order to have the brass 'range for him to visit his client. All they done was let D.T. talk to the lawyer on the phone, didn't want anyone 'portant to see the hurt'en they'd put on him, turned his face black and red. The lawyer hadn't a what's what 'bout the murder and all. Just had good news to tell D.T.: that the courts had overturned the rape conviction, that he would be back in court in a couple of weeks. D.T. wasn't 'cited, caught the lawyer by surprise, told him all what had happened, blew the lawyer's wig back. He jumped right on the case, told D.T. to hang on, he would get him transferred. Oh, he should've been got took out the gut of the beast.

The lawyer made some waves, had them give D.T. all his property: legal documents, notepad, and stuff. Gave him his reading glasses and case; the fancy gold ink pen Ms. Prichard gave him was still in it. Mohlerson kept fucking with D.T., playing in his food, tearing up his mail, taunting him in the worst way, saying God don't like ugly, 'plying him and Ms. Prichard was coupling up. Mohlerson had a picture of D.T.'s sister, stuck it down his pants, then bad-mouthed his mama. Said he rather see Ms. Prichard dead than with D.T.'s nigger ass and was glad he killed the filthy whore. D.T. was 'furiated, a mad dog, wanted to kill that cracker!

I was over at the graves, shining shoes, working my way to D.T., had something 'portant to tell him, had a care package for him too: snacks and hygiene stuff, snuck it in my shoe-shine box, heard how they was treating him. Made it just in time and saw D.T. get his wish. He caught Mohlerson off guard, too busy rubbing D.T.'s picture 'cross his nuts, and for the last time. The kid reached 'tween the bars and got hold of Mohlerson's shirt. Oh, drew that fancy ink pen and stabbed Mohlerson in the neck over and over, screaming, "Same thing make you laugh, make you cry!" Those blue eyes was cold, reptilian, no moist, gleam, only a blue so black, soulless.

Mohlerson fell to his knees, clutching his neck, trying to hold it together. Blood gushed out, squirting horror on the glass, spilling to the floor. He stared up from the pool of red death into D.T.'s eyes, evil and unforgiving, watching him wallow in agony, waiting fiercely for Mohlerson to die. Oh, wish I could've threw his carcass to the gulls.

I was ear hustling at the rotunda, heard 'em say the murder case against D.T. had been dropped. Oh, I had took the bloody ink pen from him, stuck it in my waist, and waited . . . It was a good 'nuff chapter for an ending.

HOW EBAY NEARLY KILLED GARY BRIDGWAY

BY TIMOTHY PAULEY

Monroe Correctional Complex (Monroe, Washington)

W hen it was announced that the Green River Killer had been apprehended, most people assumed he would be tried, convicted, and executed in short order. Based on the sheer volume of bodies he had stacked up, it was difficult to imagine any other outcome; even his legal team didn't have much hope for him.

One of Bridgway's junior lawyers, however, had a vision. He was just a couple of years into his career and was basically brought along to take notes, but he saw the bigger picture in a way others couldn't, wouldn't, or hadn't even considered. To Martin, being the guy who saved this monster from certain execution would be an excellent springboard from which he could launch a lucrative law career. With that in mind, he began some informal discussions with a colleague in the prosecutor's office the day he was assigned to assist on the case. It was a long process, but Martin felt certain he had the leverage to see his vision to fruition.

Mike, on the other hand, was having a run of bad luck. His identity theft ring had just been busted, and he was booked into county jail with a bail he could never raise, not to mention the prospect of ten years in prison looming ominously over him. Just in case he had some question about how mad they were at him, the guards assigned him to a cell in the highest-security section of the jail, three doors down from Gary Bridgway. He'd have to have been a complete idiot not to get that message.

When Mike called his wife from jail, he tried to avoid talking about his case. All that would do is depress her, so he casually mentioned that he was living practically next door to Gary Bridgway. Molly's reaction was quite unexpected and caught Mike off guard. She seemed very interested in the fact that Mike was a neighbor to the most notorious serial killer in the history of Washington State.

When Mike called Molly again the next day, she almost immediately brought up Bridgway. He filled her in on the details as best he could, but there really wasn't much to tell. They spent the majority of their lives locked in cells, so even though Bridgway was in close physical proximity, there was little opportunity to interact with him, even if Mike actually wanted to do so. Toward the end of their conversation, Molly asked Mike if he could get Bridgway's autograph for her. Mike was repulsed by this and almost hung up, but Molly was quick to point out that Mike hadn't exactly left her financially secure. After the cops were done seizing all of his stuff, there was almost nothing left but bills. Eventually, Molly admitted that she'd done some research and discovered that a Bridgway autograph was currently selling for four hundred bucks on the Internet. Mike ended the call, assuring her he'd see what he could do.

Meanwhile, Martin was getting close to arranging a deal, and it was time to pitch the idea to Bridgway. Seemed simple enough: trade some bodies for his life. Bridgway was screwed anyway, so what did he have to lose? After an hour talking with Bridgway, however, it seemed that the small degree of trust necessary for him to get on board with the idea was lacking. Understandably, Bridgway was leery of a trap and reluctant to agree to the deal unless his fears could be put to rest.

Bridgway had only been back from his attorney visit for a few minutes when Mike showed up at his door. When the tier porter had been caught smoking, Mike, with only a series of identity thefts on his record, was the logical choice to replace him; if the guards had to let a prisoner wander around outside of his cell, everyone was more comfortable with a guy who'd passed a bunch of bad paper than with the other, more violent prisoners on the tier. Mike was hired the same day the tier porter was fired. His first mission was to get his wife a Bridgway autograph.

The problem was, Bridgway didn't want to sign. He found it hard to believe anyone would want his autograph for anything other than to screw him over, so he refused all of Mike's pleas. Every day Mike would try another angle, and each time he'd get the same answer. Every evening, when Milto called Molly, he'd catch hell for failing to produce.

Tuesday afternoon, Mike had a brainstorm. He was pushing the dirty dust mop down the concrete tier when he noticed a piece of paper sticking out of Bridgway's door. It was common practice for prisoners to slip written communications through the crack in their doorjambs; the guards would eventually pick them up on their numerous daily walkthroughs. As soon as Mike saw the paper sticking out of Bridgway's door, he quickly scanned his surroundings to see if anyone was watching him.

Upon closer inspection, he saw that the paper was a store order. This was the method through which prisoners were able to purchase snacks and personal hygiene items. The procedure was to list the items one wished to purchase, then sign the bottom to authorize jail staff to take the necessary funds from the prisoner's jail account. Mike made three more passes along the hallway, each time looking out of the corner of his eye through the small window in Bridgway's door to see if the guy was paying any attention to him. He appeared to be reading a book, so on the next pass, Mike reached out and snatched the store order on his way by, stuffing it down the front of his coveralls in the same motion. Nobody appeared to notice. That evening, the first Bridgway autograph was in the mail to Molly.

Friday afternoon, Bridgway went to meet with Martin again. Martin had nearly convinced him to agree in principle to the verbal arrangement he'd hammered out with the prosecutors, but Bridgway left the visit without actually agreeing. Martin could tell he was close, but there was still no deal.

When Bridgway got back to his cell, the guards had already delivered store. He asked about his, but they informed him nothing had come for him. Bridgway was pissed, and the moment he got back to his cell, he wrote an angry kite to the store officer. An hour later, when it was time to pass out chow, Mike couldn't believe his good fortune when he saw the kite sticking out of Bridgway's door. When he came out to help distribute the trays, Mike crouched as he passed Bridgway's window, snatched the kite, and then continued on to the food cart. Soon, another four hundred bucks was in the mail to Molly.

The following Tuesday, as expected, Bridgway put his store order in the crack of his door. This time he ordered large quantities of everything. Having experienced difficulty with the processing of his previous order, he was preparing for any similar episodes in the future. His order was so large that it took two forms. Mike was ecstatic when he got back to his cell and discovered he'd scored two autographs instead of just one. Molly would be very happy about this, and Mike couldn't help but smile as he put Bridgway's order forms in with his letter to Molly and sealed the envelope.

That Friday, Bridgway stood with his face in the window of his door as soon as he heard the store cart rolling onto the tier. He waited in patient anticipation as the store officer opened the door of the first cell and handed its occupant his purchases. The process repeated three more times before she got to Bridgway's neighbor. The door next to him clicked shut, and Bridgway's face registered an expression of shock mixed with anger as he watched the cart roll past his cell. Before the store officer even reached the next cell, Bridgway called out, "Hey! Where's mine?"

Officer Finkel tried her best to just ignore him. Everyone knew who Bridgway was. Some of the officers gave him grief any way they could, but most just tried to treat him the same as every other prisoner. None of them, however, had any desire to get close to Bridgway. They dealt with him as quickly and professionally as they could.

When Bridgway began hollering and banging on his door, nobody was anxious to be the one to have that conversation. Even though he was locked in a cell, this man had dozens of murders to his credit. Now he was having a psychotic episode. Officer Finkel passed out the remaining three bags on her cart and got out of there as quickly as possible. The moment the door shut behind her, Bridgway began pounding harder and yelling louder. "I want my store, you assholes! Give me my shit!"

The jail staff believed Bridgway was a psychopath, the likes of which no one had ever seen. Whatever his problem was, he could put it in a kite like everyone else. All his screaming and carrying on did nothing but further instill in the staff the

226 // PRISON NOIR

desire to keep their distance. The less they saw of Bridgway, the better.

Eventually, he calmed down. Every time an officer would walk past his cell, Bridgway tried to engage him or her in a conversation about his store problem. Each time, he got the same response: "Put in a kite."

For lack of any other recourse, Bridgway sat down and wrote kites to everyone from the mail commander all the way down to the store officer. There were eight in all. He meticulously described his problem, signed his name, and put them in the crack in his door.

When Mike saw the thick stack of paper in Bridgway's door, his delight was hard to hide. He bit his lower lip to keep from laughing out loud as he pushed the dust mop down the tier. Each time he passed the cell, he'd sneak a glance through the window, only to see Bridgway sitting on the edge of his bunk facing the door. For fifteen minutes, Mike continued sweeping and mopping the tier, waiting for the opportunity to make his move. It was starting to look like that opportunity would not come, but Mike couldn't let a whole stack of kites get away.

When he finished cleaning the tier for a third time, Mike rinsed out the mop, hung it up, and headed back toward his cell. As he neared Bridgway's cell, he heard a toilet flush. A quick peek through the window allowed him to see Bridgway moving to his bunk with his back to the door. Mike ripped the kites from the door crack, stuffed them down the front of his coveralls, and hurried back to his cell without so much as a glance in the direction of the cops. If they saw the move, so be it. It was his last chance, and he wasn't about to let this opportunity slip through his fingers. Either they didn't see or they just didn't care. Whatever the case, Mike made it back to his cell with no reaction from the cops.

On Monday, Martin arrived at the jail right before lunch. The prosecutor's office was ready to officially offer Bridgway a way out of the death penalty if he would agree to lead them to the unrecovered bodies of his victims. The papers had been drafted. It was time to meet with Bridgway, and Martin was confident he'd locked in the deal. Now all he needed was for Bridgway to sign on—and how could he refuse?

When he and Bridgway were alone in the attorney-visiting booth, Martin proudly laid the papers on the table and grinned as he extended a pen to the inmate. "We did it!" Martin exclaimed. "They're ready to make a deal. It's now or never."

Much to Martin's dismay, not only did Bridgway not take the pen and sign the papers, but he also ranted on for the next thirty minutes about his store and about how "those people" could not be trusted. Try as he might, Martin was unable to steer the conversation back in the direction of signing the papers. Bridgway seemed obsessed with his store and some problem he was having with the jail staff. The visit ended with Martin assuring Bridgway he'd see what he could do to resolve the problem.

The next day, Bridgway filled out another store order and put it in his door crack. Shortly thereafter, Mike collected it, and that evening it was sealed in an envelope and sent on its way to Molly.

On Wednesday, a memo was circulated to all jail staff. The commander explained that they were now required to go to Bridgway's cell and ask him for his store order form; they were also to ask Bridgway each evening if he had any mail or communication he wished to submit. These instructions generated a considerable amount of resentment among jail staff, but they came from the top, so everyone reluctantly complied.

Actually, the jail commander wasn't any more pleased about this situation than they were, but the King County prosecuting attorney himself had personally made this request for cooperation, so what could they do?

When the officer approached Bridgway's cell that evening and asked him if he wanted to submit a store order, the serial killer was more than a little surprised. At first he told the officer he'd already submitted his order, but when he was informed that if he wanted store he was to give them an order now, Bridgway sat down and hastily filled out another form.

That Friday, the store cart stopped at Bridgway's cell. In fact, it stopped there every Friday from then on. Much to his dismay, Mike no longer found any four-hundred-dollar bills sticking out of Bridgway's door, and Molly's popularity on eBay waned. Shortly thereafter, Bridgway signed the deal, and Martin did become known as the legal mastermind who saved Gary Bridgway from certain execution. But for a time, Mike, Molly, and eBay nearly got Bridgway killed.

3 BLOCK FROM HELL

BY BRYAN K. PALMER

Jackson State Prison (Jackson, Michigan)

Allow me to introduce myself: I'm Bo Carr, I'm a serial killer. Not just any serial killer, but the best one. Oh yes, I'm bragging, and I am not a dictator of a foreign country or even a depraved lunatic doing it for sexual thrills. Does that surprise you? Does it offend your delicate sensibilities? How many have I killed? One hundred and ninety-eight men. Each one of them deserved it. You don't believe me? I'll let you be the judge.

Who was the first? Nepo Shyler. I can still see his face clearly: his bald, shaven head, his untouchable, smug attitude! What did he do wrong? Are you serious? Did you not hear who I said? *Nepo Shyler*? Murderer extraordinaire? He was locked up for the first time when he was thirteen years old for burning his grandmother to death because she wouldn't give him money to buy ice cream. He was found in the basement playing with her eyeballs like they were marbles, with a gallon of melting Neapolitan ice cream dripping between his fat legs. He's been in and out of psychiatric hospitals, juvenile homes, and prison all his life. He is a true product of his surroundings. I saw him come in and out of Jackson Quarantine five times during my stay there.

Jackson Quarantine, as you probably know, is where all the circuit courts in Michigan send their prisoners after sentencing. It is here, at Jackson Prison, that each inmate is screened for security classification before being sent to his primary prison. It could be anywhere in Michigan, from a prison camp in the U.P. or even to Gladiator School in Ionia. It all depends on what the paperwork tells the prison officials here in Jackson. It's why I loved being there. I got to see everyone as they came through the bubble. We called it the "bubble" because the scene, as it unfolds before your eyes, bursts your bubble when you enter 7 block and hundreds of men whistle at you and the other fresh fish walking across the gallery floor in your underwear, holding your bedroll tight against your fragile chest, as if that will protect you from the predators salivating from their psychopathic lips with every step you take. For the seasoned prisoners who are returning, it's like homecoming week: seeing the same sissies who sucked their dicks in the shower, the drug dealer who gave them their fix of brown heroin, the female guard who smuggled them a cell phone up her snatch. These are the men I cannot stand, and Shyler was my final straw.

Whenever a prisoner leaves on parole, he always says, *I'm never coming back,* or, *If I do, it'll be in a body bag,* or some other ridiculous remark to sound tough. The fact is, the recidivism rate is over 50 percent, so for every two people who leave, one of them is coming back. It is sound mathematics, not personal. Honestly, how many chances does a person need before we finally say, *Enough is enough!* I'm doing the public a great service.

The *system* is what should be placed on trial, from the judges who hand down pathetic, soft sentences, to the parole board that buys into every social-reform excuse. *I grew up poor, my father beat me, I was sexually abused as a child, whaaaa, whaaaa, whaaaa!!* Do you really think these same things haven't plagued other people since the beginning of time?

How is it that other people can get on with their lives and not commit crimes, but people like Shyler can't? Why should the public be saddled with the taxes to let prisoners lie on their lazy asses and watch TV for twenty years? It's an unfathomable system that I could not tolerate any longer. So I did what any good citizen would do: I threw Shyler's fat ass from the fourth gallery on the Fourth of July and watched his head splatter like a watermelon. I swear, the spray went so high you can still spot the pinkish stains on the ceiling. To anyone who asked, though, I didn't see a thing; the official story was that Shyler jumped from depression at finding himself back in prison again.

It's a devastating concept for most people to grasp, but the sound of that cold, iron cell door shutting behind you each and every night is gut-wrenching, like the finality of a coffin lid being closed. The clanking of hundreds of doors closing at the same time, echoing off the porous cement block walls, is eerie, to say the least. It is a sound I will promise myself to never hear again if I ever get out of here—but still I stay behind, as others get to leave time and time again. How would you feel to experience that every single day for twenty-three years?

Of course, I chose to be here. I will not excuse my own actions, not like the rest of these conspiracy theorists, crying that they are here because "I'm black" or "someone snitched on me," "my judge is a bitch," "they lied on me," etc. It's never "I got caught because someone snitched on me, but I did the crime." It is so rare for a person to come in and say, "I did it, and this is why." Or if they do say that, they don't change their lives while they're here. It's sad, to be honest, to watch these prisoners lie to themselves and the families who wait for them.

I did what I did not only for the people of Michigan, but

out of a sense of compassion for the families these prisoners use each and every day. What do you mean, how did I get away with it? Do you know how many prisoners try to kill themselves every year? Thousands, and half are successful on their own. I'm just tipping the scales a little heavier on my side. Ever since they initially expanded Jackson Prison's quarantine to 1, 2, and 3 block, to go with 7 block, the number of suicides has risen, enough that no one asks any questions. And to be honest, who really cares if a prisoner offs himself? It's usually the sick pedophiles who fear retribution from other prisoners, or the husband who can't live with the guilt of having brutally murdered his wife. There is always some ghost haunting every one of these inmates. Jackson Prison is *filled* with ghosts. I've only added a very small percentage to that: the ones who refuse to stop coming back to prison after they are released.

I've given the willing bedsheets already torn up, slid razor blades into cells, and thrown at least twenty-five men off the top gallery. It has never been an easy decision to make. Even without a family to return home to, I was still very aware that I would never leave these walls if they caught me. As my months turned to years, it became well worth it, and I like my chances of a jury finding me guilty for doing what they think of every day when someone they love is victimized by a repeat offender. Tell me it doesn't bother you to see a young girl raped and murdered by some scumbag who has been released from prison with prior offenses? I couldn't take the guilt anymore when I laid my head down to sleep at night. It's not that I think I'm better than them or that I have a God complex, because neither of those things is true. I care very deeply about those outside these prison walls—and those inside them as well.

I'd be lying to you, though, if I didn't say that I have a mor-bid fascination and I get an intense satisfaction from seeing the face of a prisoner after he has hanged himself. It's almost like watching *Willy Wonka and the Chocolate Factory*, where Veruca Salt turns blue and blows up like a balloon. It's the same effect: their faces get all puffy, eyes bulging out of their sockets, blood leaking from where tears once flowed, and they turn a wonderful blue color, at least in the beginning, while the body temperature is still warm. It's better than someone who simply slits his wrists. That's boring, and it takes so long for them to die. (It's fulfilling in its own right, though. I get to hear them babbling their apologies and then beg God for forgiveness as the Devil's own hand reaches up to snag them into Hell.)

In my early days, after Shyler, I was scared that I was go-ing to get caught. But after a while the fear left me, and it was replaced by the calm assurance of one who is doing the right thing.

What other ways did I kill them? Besides the hangings, wrist-slittings, and throwing them off the tiers? It's not easy to murder a prisoner, especially in the twenty-first century—too many outside bleeding heart agencies looking in. I had to get more creative. I remember one time there was a prisoner always going to medical to get injected with insulin to keep his diabetes under control. Each time he went, he would just grab a needle and insulin bottle, and inject himself. This was completely against the rules, and they let him get away with it. He kept doing it, so one day I grabbed a bottle of insulin when no one was looking and replaced it with battery acid from the maintenance shop. It was incredible to watch the guy strut in and grab the bottle, and inject himself. At first I thought he was going to be fine, but as the acid entered his bloodstream

234 // P<small>RISON</small> N<small>OIR</small>

he looked like he had indigestion. Then an expression of terror came over his face as the acid ate his veins away and blood filled his organs. When he collapsed, I ran over to help the female nurse get him up, and in the process I pocketed the bottle and threw it away before they found it. Of course they figured out what killed him, but they couldn't prove who did it. There was even a national recall from the company that produced the insulin. It's still listed today as an accident and not a homicide.

Last month I killed another one. This time it was Angel "Southpaw" Granger, a forty-five-year-old degenerate construction worker who kept defrauding and fleecing his customers. He would get a down payment for supplies and start the job. Then, when he got another partial payment, he would take the supplies, sell them back to the same Home Depot he bought them from, and never return to the site. He had been back in prison at least three times for the same thing. I wanted it to be particularly degrading with this guy, for taking advantage of senior citizens. I waited until he got a work detail as a porter cleaning the nasty-ass showers where sexual juices flowed daily. I broke a mop handle in half and buried it through the back of his neck. He was dead before his body hit the cum- and piss-stained tile floor. It wouldn't exactly be the first time a prisoner had a hit put out on him. Could have been some political dispute from before he came back to prison, a dope deal gone bad, or he simply bumped someone the wrong way.

Do I feel bad about it? Are you kidding me? For the first time in my life, I feel like I have done something for someone other than myself. I can look at myself in the mirror at night and not be appalled by the reflection that stares back at me. I believe God will understand what I did. After all, it's in the

Bible: *An eye for an eye.* I am giving these men two chances to get their lives right. The third time, I am taking things in my own hands. It's not as if I'm forcing them to make their choices. They do everything of their own volition. It's the consequences that I dole out.

The prison system has changed. I remember when I first came to Jackson in 1989. I was scared and unsure of what prison was going to be like. At first I had high expectations of the state. There were good programs to help prisoners. Prisoners were paid a good wage. But then, as the inmate population grew, the economy collapsed and the first things to go were the good programs. With each program cut, the recidivism rate grew. I got tired of seeing it happen every day. If ten thousand prisoners come into Michigan every year, at least 50 percent are repeat offenders. Of course I can't get every single one of them. There are quite a few I've had to let slide through when the heat got turned on too high and investigators came asking questions, but there's always a next time.

I remember when the state started to close these blocks one by one. What was once the greatest prison in Michigan, and possibly the whole United States, was slowly and bitterly made smaller. 11 and 12 blocks, 4, 5, and 6, and then even 7 block closed for good. Jackson Prison is but a shell of its former self. Now all that remains are the prison hospital and 1, 2, and 3 blocks. The rest sits there, looking out the windows, accusing every passing car of neglect and abandonment.

Get back to the story? This *is* the story! And if you want to hear it, you'll listen to me tell it my way and on my own time. Now where was I? Ah yes, the poor empty blocks. Sometimes when the wind is just right, I swear I can hear the hinges crying for companionship. Do not take lightly what I'm telling you about the ghosts of this place. They are very real. Too many people have died here under suspicious circumstances. What about the guards? you ask. You know as well as I do that the guards, screws, turnkeys, officers, or whatever else you want to call them are just as guilty as prisoners, bringing in their dope, cell phones, and tobacco (after they banned smoking in prisons). They are sometimes worse than prisoners. You think so highly of these correctional employees, as if they are so much better. Look at the cops on the streets who take bribes or misplace evidence; you think the guards are any better in here?

Prison has become a joke, a business where money and head counts take precedence over making inmates better so they don't victimize innocent people again. *You* are part of the problem! You close your eyes and turn your head even when you see something wrong, and for what? It's all fun and games until it's your family being victimized. Then you're in Lansing campaigning for tougher prison sentences. But it's not the sentences; it's the lack of programming. You think these kids are going to get better by playing basketball or cards all damn day in prison? In here, they get to hang out with the same set or gang they did before they arrived. They are coming home worse than they were when they entered. March on the Capitol with *that* change!

Have I killed guards too? No, I never even touched a guard—until Richard Tracer. Tracer was the worst of the worst when it came to prison guards. There wasn't anything he wouldn't do to make a buck from inmates. I watched him smuggle in drugs, vodka in water bottles, tobacco, porn magazines, even weapons. He gave protection to prisoners for a price, and that's where our paths crossed the wrong way. I had my eye on a pedophile from Oakland County. It was his fourth time in prison for various crimes: child porn, using a computer to commit sex crimes, criminal sexual conduct, and then the big time on this trip—he was caught in a human smuggling sex ring. They would buy, sell, and trade kidnapped kids like baseball cards.

Harold Spivey was his name, and as soon as he arrived he began strutting around like he owned the joint. He immediately had his family send Tracer a Western Union moneygram. A thousand dollars for protection. Spivey knew he was going to have his prison number run on OTIS, and within a day or so someone would shank him or give him a beat down. I can't say I blame Tracer for taking the grand, and if it had stopped at protection, then I would have let Spivey slide again. I didn't need any beef with the guards.

One day, however, I was walking around and I saw Tracer pass Spivey a magazine. The cover looked innocent enough, like a *Maxim* or *Playboy*, but I knew it had to be a front. Spivey didn't like girls or boys that old. So I followed him to his cell and saw him staring at the magazine. He was so engrossed that he didn't even notice me walk up and glimpse the contents: ripped-out pictures of children from a J.C. Penney's catalog and other computer-generated pictures of young kids. I threw up in my mouth just imagining him playing with himself to those pictures. I wondered how much he had to pay Tracer to bring those in.

The next day, I got my answer. I was working my way from the fourth tier down after the block had been let out for lunch, and I saw Tracer duck into Spivey's cell. That in itself was nothing to be suspicious about since guards always do random cell shakedowns looking for contraband. But then I heard Spivey's voice: "Hurry up and take it off!" I peered around the cell bars and saw Tracer pull his pants down, and then Spivey got on his knees and started sucking Tracer's dick

238 // P<small>RISON</small> N<small>OIR</small>

while the pages of the catalog fluttered open on the concrete floor. Now I knew how Tracer was getting paid for the pictures. I could not allow that to continue.

Even as I'm telling you this, I can see Spivey's oily black hair bobbing up and down, his acne-blotched face turning red with excitement while peering at his catalog. I can still smell his bad breath as it fogged up his chomo glasses (state eyeglasses). I blame myself for not getting rid of Spivey before it got to that point. I didn't take lightly the killing of Tracer; he probably had a family who, like most, was living beyond their means in this debt-ridden country. Again, it's the system that's to blame.

I tossed and turned for days trying to find another solution. I thought about just killing Spivey, but what if Tracer did the same thing with another prisoner? What if I killed Tracer and let Spivey slide? But of course I couldn't do that— I couldn't depend on another prisoner to kill Spivey. So the only option left was to take both of them out at the same time. I would watch them and get a schedule of their frolicking, and then, when I sorted out the timing, I would off them both.

I wasn't sure how to do it, though I knew it had to be instantaneous. The only thing that made sense was fire, and I would need an accelerant to speed up the process. I soon determined that their rendezvous took place at least three times a week, and always when the block was called to chow.

So I got to work: I siphoned gasoline from the maintenance generator and added a little paint thinner. I placed the concoction in a latex glove and tied it in a knot. Now I simply had to wait for them to get together again.

I remember it was one thirty p.m. when 3 block was called

for lunch one afternoon, and I hung back long enough to see Tracer climb to the fourth gallery. It must have been a long weekend at home because he practically ran up the stairs, which is surprising because guards never run unless a PPD (personal protection device) goes off. I climbed up the stairs with very little trepidation. Before approaching the cell, I turned the lever off that controlled the fire sprinklers. When I approached Spivey's cell, I cautiously looked around the corner, and there was Tracer, sitting on the bunk with his eyes closed in ecstasy as Spivey swallowed his member. I ripped a hole in the glove and threw the flammable liquid on both of them. The expressions on their faces were priceless. The shock at seeing me, and then the slow realization of what was happening, spurred them into action.

Tracer jumped up with his cock dangling and slapping against Spivey's cheek. He began to protest in vain. The feeble excuses came fumbling out as I lit a match and threw it between them. They went up in an amazing blaze, one that would make any arsonist proud. I wasn't expecting the stench, and I have to be honest, my stomach churned as the flesh and hair fell from their bodies like rubber from a burning car. I wasn't prepared for the sound either, as their screams echoed up and down the block. It wouldn't be long before the guards from the other side of 3 block came to investigate. I took one last look before scurrying down the stairs. I managed to escape the block before I heard the guards' walkie-talkies starting to chirp like crazy.

In my defense, I have to state the obvious: if Spivey had died on the scene like Tracer, you still wouldn't have found out about me. But Spivey hung around just long enough to whisper my name to an investigator. Even then you didn't believe it. It wasn't until state police checked out the security camera footage and saw me enter the maintenance shop, then saw me climbing the stairs before the sprinkler system was activated (but didn't work). Then there were my fingerprints on the sprinkler valve itself. Even so, the evidence is circumstantial at best. It's my job to check the sprinklers' functionability, and I always walk up and down the blocks. The truth is, you have nothing on me, except what I freely admit here. I am past the point of caring if I'm caught. I'm ready to tell everyone about how much money I have saved them: almost $660,000 so far. I, Bo Carr, have been saving the citizens of Michigan from being victimized by these repeat offenders. Where's my medal, my praise? You look at me with disgust, but let it be *your* family who is affected, and you'll be ready to tear down these prison walls to get to the perpetrator.

Would I do it again? Have you not been listening to me? At what point do we stop coddling these monsters and paying for their mistakes? When will you people learn? You can't change these cretins! They fill you with their sob stories, their woes of a terrible life, and you want to fix them. I understand that. I, too, used to be that way, until I saw them in a different light. A saner light. I know not everyone is amenable to such a shocking change of protocol, but before we had these bleeding-heart liberals, we killed by electrocution, hanging, beheading, and even caning. These punishments had a profound effect on criminals. They dreaded those severe punishments, and they were deterred. Not completely, but enough. Today you want to put them to sleep like we're living inside some fairy tale. What I did got the job done! You can't cure crime, and your system is so corrupt from the bottom up, any other solution would fail miserably. You can let me back out there and we can work as a team, or you can continue to suffer the injustice of the "justice system" you rely on so much.

You think you're putting away a bad man today, but tomorrow or next month, when the prisoners keep coming back, you'll think of me again and again.

"Thank you, Mr. Carr, for your cooperation and for enlightening us on your criminal philosophy," said the older of the two men across the table from me. "The director of corrections, as well as various government officials, will be privy to your statements and ideas. Is there anything else you would like to add before we're done?"

What was the point? They would never get it, or if they did understand, they were too cowardly to step up and fight the system. I shook my head as he turned off the tape recorder, then watched them walk out of the room oblivious to my greatness.

The door to the interrogation room slammed shut and the FBI special agent in charge of the field office for the region looked at Detective Jose Rivers and said, "Do you really believe this guard has been a serial killer all these years?"

Without answering, the detective flashed his state police badge at the gate to be let out. The buzzer sounded, and he walked down the steps of the Jackson County Courthouse as flashbulbs and questions from reporters came at him from all sides. He had no idea how Michigan was going to restore confidence in its criminal justice system, not after this. Maybe they should have continued turning a blind eye to what Carr was doing. It had to be better than facing these vultures.

"Detective Rivers, how is the state responding to the class-action lawsuits filed on behalf of the murdered prisoners' families?" a female reporter called out.

"Detective, will the director of the MDOC be stepping down?"

another reporter asked, causing the rest of the press corps to erupt in a flurry of additional questions.

It was going to be a long day.

THE INVESTIGATION

BY WILLIAM VAN POYCK

Florida State Prison (Raiford, Florida)

T he five men in the cage should have felt crowded, but familiarity of circumstance had long ago erased any such sensation, leaving each instead with a certain economy of emotion. The old man in the wheelchair sat still as a heron, bearing the weight of one who has made peace with the narrow dimensions of his life. A brown rubber surgical tube snaked out from his pant cuff, draining cloudy urine into the clear plastic bag hanging from the chair. With some effort he braced himself and carefully shifted his weight, his handcuffs forcing him to awkwardly use his elbows.

"I ain't even going to talk to him," the tall, thin, black-haired man said, showing his bad teeth. "He can't make me talk, ya know? Ain't no rule says I gotta talk to him."

"You'll talk to him," the old man grunted, shifting his weight again. The metal frame of the chair creaked in protest.

Cotton stood in one corner, mildly irritated with the cloying, caustic odor of institutional disinfectant that permeated the entire hallway. He idly watched the black Cuban sitting silently on the bench, intent on his chore of hand-rolling cigarettes with his even blacker tobacco-stained fingers. Occasionally, Cotton glanced up the hallway at the closed door behind which, he knew, sat the prison investigator. To Cotton's right was a smooth young man with straight blond hair cut in perfect bangs, his delicate fingers absently picking at the worn, knotty pine bench running around the inside of the cage.

"I've been through this shit before," the tall man said, waving his cuffed hands for emphasis, momentarily ceasing to be self-conscious about the shiny scar tissue covering both arms.

"It was horrible," the blond boy whispered to nobody in particular.

The old man snorted. "Get used to it. I've been here at Florida State Prison over thirty years, and this one wasn't no more horrible than any other." The man paused, looking around before adding, "More or less."

"It was still horrible."

"That's a cliché."

"Huh?"

"A cliché, horrible. Hell, life is horrible. Why should death be any different?"

"Well, I don't ever want to see anything like that again. All that blood. And the moaning. It *was* horrible. Just horrible. And I hope to God I don't spend thirty years in a place like this. I would kill myself first."

The boy stared at the floor as though he was unable to conceal from himself his own unimportance. He had a refined, gentle voice, pleasing to the ear, its delicate tenderness incongruous in this cold, steel-reinforced kingdom. Cotton secretly enjoyed the sound, much as he once delighted in the lusciously perfumed letter a guard had mistakenly passed out to him. Cotton recalled how he rubbed the scented pages across his pillow before returning the letter, and how that night in bed the feminine fragrance stirred long-suppressed memories, flooding him with powerful emotions. Cotton wept that night, so many years ago—that is why he recalled it so clearly. It was the only time in his adult life he had cried. Or perhaps the fourth.

"You don't set out to do thirty years, son. That's how they get you. You start out with hope—that you'll be out in a few, see your girlfriend, your wife." The old man paused, glancing at the boy. "Or maybe just see your mom and dad. You know: get out, go straight, start all over. But they don't let you out. So it just grows on you, one day at a time, little here, little there, until one day you wake up and the hope is all gone, and all that's left behind is you."

"I heard you were once on the row. Two times, in fact. Is that true?" Even the clinking of the boy's shackles somehow sounded delicate.

"Yup. That's a fact. But they keep letting me off. Hell, I only killed convicts." The old man laughed hoarsely, then began to cough and sputter.

"You should put your faith in God," the Cuban interjected as he licked another cigarette paper. "If you really and truly believe—if you have the faith—God will see you through."

"Yeah, right," the thin man said, jerking his hand up. "Where was God this morning when Cisco cut Bobby's guts out and left them smeared all over the dayroom floor? Huh? Bobby was a good guy. He didn't deserve to die like that."

"Who does?" the boy wondered aloud.

"Do you believe it matters how you die?" the Cuban asked.

"Well, all I'm saying is, God don't seem to be too concerned about shit like this, about convicts like us. Shit happens all the time," said the thin man.

"*My thoughts are not your thoughts, neither are your ways my ways, sayeth the Lord.* God was there. He saw it all," the Cuban intoned.

"Seeing it and doing something about it, that's two different things. That's all I'm saying. God could have stopped it. Why didn't God stop it?"

"*You* could have stopped it. Why didn't you stop it?" The Cuban cocked his head.

"Bobby wasn't really my friend. I didn't even know him all that well."

"Are we not our brother's keeper?" The Cuban stared at the thin man. "We are all instruments of God's will," he added softly, turning his face.

Cotton's fingers absently brushed at the halo of thin gray hair that crowned his head. It seemed as if his thick mane had fallen out almost overnight, though in truth it had taken years. Cotton stared at the thin man's arms, which he knew had been burned when another convict threw lighter fluid on him some years ago. Cotton saw it happen. The convict thought the thin man had stolen something from his cell, but later it came out that the thin man was not the thief. The skin on the arms was parchment-thin, shiny as wax, with purplish white gnarls streaking from shoulders to wrists like some hideous octopus trying to skulk away. Cotton knew it could have been fixed up a lot better, with skin grafts or something, but that did not happen. It was like when Cotton fell off the kitchen roof fourteen years earlier while carrying shingles up a broken ladder. The convict orderly set his shattered ankle badly, and when he finally saw a real doctor five weeks later, it was too late—or too much trouble—to do it right. Now the joint was fused and he walked with a painful limp, his ankle making a clicking sound with each step.

"Cisco killed him over a ten-dollar pocket debt. Man, you don't kill nobody over ten lousy dollars," the thin man said.

The boy raised his questioning eyes.

"How much do you kill someone for, then?" the old man asked, cocking his head.

"I'm just saying."

"All this talk of killing. It's so negative," the boy said softly, mostly to himself. "Please stop."

"It wasn't about no ten dollars, any more than Jackson got killed over a piece of fried chicken, or that guy who got killed in the gym for stepping on some other guy's shirt. It was about respect. He disrespected Cisco in some kind of way. Must have. Or at least Cisco thought he did. Maybe he didn't. Maybe it was all a misunderstanding. It happens." The old man shifted his weight again and the wheelchair groaned, its spokes popping loudly.

"Respect God. Only God is worthy of true respect." The Cuban stared ahead.

"Yeah, great advice. That will get you killed in here," the thin man said. "I say respect the big knife and big balls."

The Cuban glanced around the cage.

Thus sayeth the high and exalted one who inhabits eternity, whose name is Holy: I dwell in a high and holy place, but I also live with those who are broken and humble in spirit, to revive the spirit of the humble, to restore the courage of the broken.

The Cuban almost seemed to be speaking to Cotton. "Isaiah 57:15," he said.

Cotton glanced up the hallway as the investigator's door opened and a young, sullen-looking black prisoner silently left the room, staring straight ahead, his leg chains scraping the shiny linoleum floor. A guard appeared with a large brass key in his hand. He opened the cage door and motioned to the Cuban, who followed him to the investigator's office. Cotton caught a dim glimpse of the large, plexiglass-covered display case mounted on the wall behind the investigator's desk. It held a wide variety of weapons confiscated over the years, from zip guns to real guns, crude hatchets to spears, clubs to knives. Lots of knives. Cotton had watched the display case grow and evolve during his time there. More than one of the weapons once belonged to him.

The door closed behind the Cuban. Cotton knew the drill. The investigator would plead with, cajole, or threaten each of them, according to his nature, in the hope of getting one or more to turn state's evidence. Turn state's. Rat. Snitch. Stool pigeon. Those traitorous labels. In return, the investigator would promise to transfer the rat away from this hated, wretched maximum-security prison to a sweet, soft joint full of fresh promise. He used to guarantee favorable parole recommendations to the parole commission, until parole was abolished.

Cotton had been through the process countless times, for he had an eerie knack for being in the vicinity of almost every murder that occurred in this hulking prison. It was some kind of weird coincidence, that's all, but even the guards commented on it. Once, on a sleepless night some years before, Cotton got out a piece of paper and tried to recount all the killings he had witnessed over the years. He stopped at around thirty, depressed by the memories and by his difficulty recalling some of them. What did it say about him, he wondered, that he could watch a man be killed and then not be able to remember it? Where did that memory go?

The first one was the most vivid. It always is. A memory still saturated with a surrealistic clarity, a sense of reality so immediate and precise that it defied articulation. The relentless hand moving in and out, the sun glinting on the steel blade, the sense of timelessness, the dull look of puzzlement on the victim's face, followed by recognition that this is it, this is real, that he was dead and helpless to do anything about it. Cotton easily recalled that first one. Also the second one. Perhaps the third. After that they just became statistics.

It isn't easy to kill a man, Cotton reflected. At least not with your hands. It's not at all like in the movies, where you stick a man once and he silently drops like a sack of cornmeal. A gun is one thing, though even then the vitality of the human body could amaze you. A knife or razor, a club or bat, a barbell or padlock in a sock, well, that was wholly different. The primal urge to live, to survive, is powerful, and it takes a lot to overcome that—more than some are willing to give. And when they do die, it is messy, often with bloody reluctance, with thrashing, gasping, begging, imploring, praying, with victims calling to their mothers. Yes, a man will generally fight hard to live, harder than one might think possible. Cotton once saw a man, a small man, stabbed thirty-seven times. The man never stopped moving, never stopped kicking, ducking, bobbing, weaving, fighting, spraying his blood everywhere, burning an indelible vermilion image in Cotton's mind. It was the assailant who finally gave up and fled, hoping the small man would die. They pulled the sheet over his head in the ambulance, but he reached up and snatched it off. His heart stopped twice at the hospital. But he lived. Cotton had seen, and he had learned.

"That Puerto Rican, he'll snitch," declared the thin man. "All that talk about God."

Nobody said anything.

Someone would talk, sooner or later—Cotton knew that.

They always did. As often as not, the testifying inmate had seen little or nothing, but that was not going to stand in the way of his transfer. It was ironic that Cotton, who had seen so many of these killings, consistently refused to rat, while others, who had seen nothing, fabricated convincing stories to sell to the jury. Their colorfully embellished fantasy then became reality, recorded in the law books and newspapers as the gospel truth. Cotton reflected more than once that he seemed to be the only one playing by the rules.

"What is truth?" The words startled Cotton as he realized he had said them out loud. The others looked at him as if noticing him for the first time.

"He had bad nerves," the thin man announced, and Cotton considered this statement. Bad nerves. What did that mean, exactly? Nobody ever proclaimed to have good nerves. And how does one know when nerves are bad, anyway? A man would knowingly state that his nerves were bad, but it seemed impossible to discern the state of his nerves by looking at him. So it was, too, with a man's heart, Cotton reflected. It was like looking at one of those calm, still watering holes frequently shown on nature programs. The placid surface promised safe refuge, yet just beneath lurked the terrible crocodile, infinitely patient, waiting to destroy the illusion.

Cotton considered what he would say to the investigator this time. Usually he just explained that he was sleeping, that he had seen nothing. It was sort of an ongoing joke between Cotton and the investigator now, a tired comedy routine, Cotton always being asleep when someone was killed. It was just easier to say that. The investigator knew, he understood, and he, in his own way, respected Cotton's honoring of the code. He once called Cotton a dinosaur. Someone else would always talk.

This time, though, Cotton really had been asleep. His sixth sense had awakened him to that familiar, awful silence that always signaled something had just happened. Cotton had seen nothing, just the dead body, the blood draining away, pooling beneath Bobby's impossibly white face.

The investigator's door opened abruptly, and the Cuban left the office. Each prisoner silently calculated whether the Cuban was inside long enough to give a substantial statement. Had Cotton's eyesight not been failing, he could have seen the worn outline of the pocket-sized New Testament in the Cuban's back pocket as he shuffled by. But Cotton hated the chunky plastic eyeglasses provided by the state, so now he mostly squinted a lot.

The guard opened the cage door with his big brass key, motioning to Cotton. It was his turn.

Cotton entered the office, leg irons tugging at his ankles with each step, and he sat down without waiting to be asked. In the corner sat a dusty, moth-eaten county fair keepsake: a large stuffed rattlesnake, fangs bared, ready to strike, coiled around a stuffed, ratty, furred mongoose, snarling in response, the two forever frozen in locked mortal combat. As always, Cotton wondered if this was supposed to convey some metaphorical message, or if he was giving the investigator too much credit.

Looking up at the display case, Cotton saw the spear Outlaw had used to kill Ninety-Nine: a long broom handle with a cruel knife lashed to it. Outlaw ran it through Ninety-Nine's belly while the man just stood there in the shower with shampoo in his eyes. Cotton was the only other person in the shower when Ninety-Nine was killed. He remembered how his stomach knotted violently when he saw Outlaw, fully clothed, first step into the shower holding that spear, until he understood that Ninety-Nine was the target. He remembered that after Ninety-Nine fell gasping to the wet floor, Outlaw hesitated, his eyes betraying that he was deciding whether he should kill Cotton too. In such a fleeting moment, one's life can hang in the balance, and Cotton still recalled the strong, coppery taste that had filled his mouth as he locked eyes with Outlaw. That was fifteen years ago. Cotton wondered where he would be now if he had testified against Outlaw, as the investigator and state attorney begged him to. Outlaw was out on the streets now, doing welding work at a shipyard, Cotton had heard.

"Hello, Cotton," the investigator said without looking up. He shuffled some papers and then pushed a tape recorder across the desk. "You know how this goes. I've gotta record this."

The investigator fumbled with a cord. Cotton unconsciously rolled his tongue across his teeth, feeling the worn shards. Not that many years ago, he had beautiful white teeth, almost perfectly straight. Then, for no known reason, he began grinding his teeth in his sleep. He wasn't even aware of it at first. Eventually, the prison dentist gave Cotton a mouthpiece to wear while he slept, but after he chewed through two of them the dentist refused to issue him a third. Now his teeth were ground down to nubs that resembled brown wooden pegs.

The investigator pushed a button and the recorder began its slow spin, hissing faintly. He cleared his throat and covered the microphone with his hand. "I'm sure you were sleeping again, Cotton, but we've gotta put it on tape. For the record, you know? Funny thing, though—so far nobody has made a statement. I know at least ten inmates witnessed this homicide, but nobody wants to talk." The investigator shook his head slowly, as though deeply hurt by rejection. "You reckon I'm losing my touch, Cotton?"

Cotton stared at the sleek computer on the shelf behind the investigator. Desktop computers were not even available when Cotton was last on the streets. All Cotton knew about them was what he saw in magazines. Cotton had never even used a microwave.

The investigator cleared his throat again, removed his hand, and then dutifully spoke into the microphone, loudly pronouncing Cotton's full name, prison number, and the date, along with an assigned case number.

Cotton sighed. He was suddenly weary, tired of memories littered with the compost of life's worst moments, tired of having to explain everything. Why was it, anyway, that some people thought they should know everything? Figuring out life's most difficult questions was hard enough, but when it came to finding the answers—well, even a stupid man knows that many things are simply unknowable. And who's to say that's not the way it should be? Life is bigger than the questions we frame, and a man could go crazy trying to understand everything. Cotton had seen it happen.

He once believed his life could still be a triumph of hope over experience, but now he only knew a certain weary dullness—like a grinding clock inexorably running down, like a looming pressure pushing him off life's narrowest margins. He glanced up at the spear again, Ninety-Nine's dried blood still visible on the linen strips tying the knife to the broom handle. That blood was all that remained of a once-living soul. At this moment, Cotton experienced the same sense of his life hanging in the balance, and again he felt that same coppery taste in his mouth.

"Okay, Cotton, do you have a statement to make at this time, or were you sleeping again?"

"No," Cotton replied. "No, I wasn't sleeping. I saw the whole thing. It was horrible."

ABOUT THE CONTRIBUTORS

ERIC BOYD is a short-story writer living in Pittsburgh. He is an advising editor for *theNewerYork*; his own writing has been featured in several publications. Boyd is a winner of the 2012 PEN Prison Writing Contest, a program for which he is now a mentor. In 2008, he briefly studied at the Maharishi University of Management in Fairfield, Iowa; currently he commutes, via bus, to New York every week to study at the Writer's Foundry MFA in Brooklyn.

KENNETH R. BRYDON'S stories have been included in the anthologies of the San Quentin creative writing program, and can be found at brothersinpen.wordpress.com. He wishes to thank writing instructor Zoe Mullery and the San Quentin Prison University Project for guidance and mentoring. Brydon, incarcerated for thirty-five years, feels that his writing untangles his thoughts, and he is still counting on his faith in Christ.

ZEKE CALIGIURI is a writer/poet from south Minneapolis. He has been incarcerated since 1999 and is the recipient of several awards through the annual PEN Prison Writing Contest. He has recently completed a full-length memoir, and he currently resides at the Minnesota Correctional Facility at Lino Lakes.

B.M. DOLARMAN writes under a pseudonym. He has been behind bars for fifteen of his thirty-five years and is currently serving a federal prison sentence. He is a voracious reader, a writer of fiction, and a creator of pencil-drawn artwork.

STEPHEN GEEZ is the pseudonym of a TV and music producer on prisonly hiatus. He exploits this temporary respite to write and publish novels, essay collections, websites, and writers' how-tos while editing for other authors, teaching prison writing classes, and advocating for the wrongly convicted. A longtime fan of Joyce Carol Oates, he can be contacted at info@StephenGeez.com.

SCOTT GUTCHES was born in 1970 and grew up in and around Paterson, New Jersey. He won first place for fiction in the 2012 PEN Prison Writing Contest and has been nominated for a Pushcart Prize. Gutches currently resides at Fremont Correctional Facility in Cañon City, Colorado, where he continues writing short fiction.

LINDA MICHELLE MARQUARDT is a forty-two-year-old mother of three sons. Each day she tries to live by her father's teachings and be thoughtful, kind, and considerate toward others regardless of her current incarceration at Women's Huron Valley Correctional Facility in Ypsilanti, Michigan. Marquardt is a college graduate with a bachelor's degree in English from Pennsylvania State University. She appreciates the unconditional support of her family and friends.

Charles Gross

JOYCE CAROL OATES is a recipient of the National Medal of Humanities, the National Book Critics Circle Ivan Sandrof Lifetime Achievement Award, and the National Book Award. She has written some of the most enduring fiction of our time, including the national best sellers *We Were the Mulvaneys*, *Blonde*, and *The Falls*. She is the Roger S. Berlind Distinguished Professor of the Humanities at Princeton University, and is the editor of *New Jersey Noir*.

BRYAN K. PALMER grew up in the Detroit area and is currently incarcerated in Jackson, Michigan. He has been published by the University of Michigan's Prison Creative Arts Project, College Guild, and in various publications. His work includes historical fiction, short stories of the noir variety, and poetry. He hopes to pursue writing as a career when he is released in December 2015.

TIMOTHY PAULEY has been in prison since 1980 and is currently at the Washington State Reformatory. Over the years he has seen some very bizarre things in the alternate reality that is prison. His stories bring the reader into that world and show another side to this subculture.

ALI F. SAREINI was born in Kharbit Selim (Valley of Peace), Lebanon. He left the Lebanese Civil War in 1985, was a political prisoner in Berlin, Germany, joined the US Army's 82nd Airborne Division in 1986, and holds a bachelor's degree in business administration from Campbell University and Spring Arbor University. He has just completed his twenty-fifth year of incarceration for second-degree murder.

A. Ahn

SIN SORACCO does not deal well with idiots so she lives far away on the banks of a Northern California river and writes stories. She is the author of the novels *Low Bite, Edge City,* and *Come to Me.*

CHRISTOPHER M. STEPHEN was raised just outside of Chicago (*Westside!*). At the age of twenty-two he left home with no specific destination and no plan except to have a good time. He's been in and out of prison ever since. (Let that be a lesson to you, kids.) He is currently serving time for a bank robbery conviction in the Federal Correctional Institution in Pekin, Illinois, and is due for release in 2014.

WILLIAM VAN POYCK was sentenced to death for his part in the 1987 botched attempt to free his best friend from a prison transport van, during which a guard was killed by Van Poyck's accomplice. A certified paralegal for over thirty years, Van Poyck is the author of an autobiography, *A Checkered Past,* and two novels, *Quietus* and *The Third Pillar of Wisdom.* The State of Florida executed him on June 12, 2013, but his messages of love, hope, and redemption live on in his writings.

Heather Boyes

MARCO VERDONI received a Short Story Award for New Writers honorable mention from *Glimmer Train.* In 2003, as a fifteen-year-old, he was tried as an adult for assault with intent to murder and sentenced to ten years in the Michigan Department of Corrections. He was released on parole in June 2013 and currently lives and writes at home in Saginaw, Michigan.

ANDRE WHITE is originally from Detroit and is currently incarcerated at Central Michigan Correctional Facility. He feels that telling tales and tall tales are as distinguishable as "tell" and "tail"; he's not known for the former, though he prefers to describe and detail the latter.

Also available from Akashic Books

NEW JERSEY NOIR
edited by Joyce Carol Oates
288 pages, trade paperback, $15.95

BRAND-NEW STORIES BY: Joyce Carol Oates, Jonathan Safran Foer, Robert Pinsky, Edmund White & Michael Carroll, Richard Burgin, Paul Muldoon, Sheila Kohler, C.K. Williams, Gerald Stern, Lou Manfredo, S.A. Solomon, Bradford Morrow, Jonathan Santlofer, Jeffrey Ford, S.J. Rozan, Barry N. Malzberg & Bill Pronzini, Hirsh Sawhney, and Robert Arellano.

"It was inevitable that this fine noir series would reach New Jersey. It took longer than some readers might have wanted, but, oh boy, was it worth the wait . . . More than most of the entries in the series, this volume is about mood and atmosphere more than it is about plot and character . . ." —*Booklist* (starred review)

USA NOIR:
BEST OF THE AKASHIC NOIR SERIES
edited by Johnny Temple
548 pages, trade paperback, $16.95
*A 2012 *New York Times* Notable Book of the Year

FEATURING NOIR SERIES STORIES BY: Joyce Carol Oates, Dennis Lehane, Don Winslow, Michael Connelly, George Pelecanos, Susan Straight, Jonathan Safran Foer, Laura Lippman, Pete Hamill, Lee Child, T. Jefferson Parker, Lawrence Block, Terrance Hayes, Jerome Charyn, Jeffery Deaver, Maggie Estep, Bayo Ojikutu, Tim McLoughlin, Barbara DeMarco-Barrett, Reed Farrel Coleman, Megan Abbott, Elyssa East, James W. Hall, J. Malcolm Garcia, Julie Smith, Joseph Bruchac, Pir Rothenberg, Luis Alberto Urrea, Domenic Stansberry, John O'Brien, S.J. Rozan, Asali Solomon, William Kent Krueger, Tim Broderick, Bharti Kirchner, Karen Karbo, and Lisa Sandlin.

"All the heavy hitters . . . came out for *USA Noir* . . . an important anthology of stories shrewdly culled by Johnny Temple."
—*New York Times Book Review*, Editors' Choice

"Readers will be hard put to find a better collection of short stories in any genre." —*Publishers Weekly* (starred review)

DETROIT NOIR
edited by E.J. Olsen and John C. Hocking
192 pages, trade paperback original, $15.95

BRAND-NEW STORIES BY: Joyce Carol Oates, Loren D. Estleman, P.J. Parrish, Nisi Shawl, Craig Holden, Craig Bernier, Desiree Cooper, Melissa Preddy, E.J. Olsen, Joe Boland, Megan Abbott, Dorene O'Brien, Lolita Hernandez, Peter Markus, Roger K. Johnson, and Michael Zadoorian.

BROOKLYN NOIR
edited by Tim McLoughlin
320 pages, trade paperback original, $15.95

THE INAUGURAL TITLE in the Akashic Noir Series, *Brooklyn Noir* features Edgar Award finalist "The Book Signing" by Pete Hamill, MWA Robert L. Fish Memorial Award winner "Can't Catch Me" by Thomas Morrissey, and Shamus Award winner "Hasidic Noir" by Pearl Abraham.

BRAND-NEW STORIES BY: Pete Hamill, Nelson George, Sidney Offit, Arthur Nersesian, Pearl Abraham, Neal Pollack, Ken Bruen, Ellen Miller, Maggie Estep, Kenji Jasper, Adam Mansbach, Nicole Blackman, C.J. Sullivan, Chris Niles, Norman Kelley, Tim McLoughlin, Thomas Morrissey, Lou Manfredo, Luciano Guerriero, and Robert Knightly.

LOS ANGELES NOIR
edited by Denise Hamilton
320 pages, trade paperback original, $15.95

A *LOS ANGELES TIMES* BEST SELLER, featuring Edgar Award winner "The Golden Gopher" by Susan Straight.

BRAND-NEW STORIES BY: Michael Connelly, Janet Fitch, Susan Straight, Héctor Tobar, Patt Morrison, Emory Holmes II, Robert Ferrigno, Neal Pollack, Gary Phillips, Christopher Rice, Naomi Hirahara, Jim Pascoe, Scott Phillips, Diana Wagman, Lienna Silver, Brian Ascalon Roley, and Denise Hamilton.

D.C. NOIR
edited by George Pelecanos
262 pages, trade paperback original, $15.95

BRAND-NEW STORIES BY: George Pelecanos, Laura Lippman, James Grady, Kenji Jasper, Jim Beane, Ruben Castaneda, Jim Patton, Norman Kelley, Jennifer Howard, Richard Currey, Lester Irby, Robert Andrews, Robert Wisdom, Quintin Peterson, David Slater, and Jim Fusilli.

"From the Chevy Chase housewife who commits a shocking act to the watchful bum protecting Georgetown street vendors, the tome offers a startling glimpse into the cityscape's darkest corners." —*Washington Post*